CW01629501

NEW WIFE

An unputdownable psychological thriller
with a breathtaking twist

AMANDA BRITTANY
& KAREN CLARKE

JOFFE BOOKS

Joffe Books, London
www.joffebooks.com

First published in Great Britain in 2022

© Amanda Brittany and Karen Clarke

This book is a work of fiction. Names, characters, businesses, organizations, places and events are either the product of the author's imagination or are used fictitiously. Any resemblance to actual persons, living or dead, events or locales is entirely coincidental. The spelling used is British English except where fidelity to the author's rendering of accent or dialect supersedes this. The right of Amanda Brittany and Karen Clarke to be identified as the authors of this work has been asserted in accordance with the Copyright, Designs and Patents Act 1988.

Cover art by Nick Castle Design

ISBN: 978-1-80405-624-0

To our wonderful readers

CHAPTER 1

Nell

The ringing of the phone grated on my nerves, which felt permanently shredded these days.

'Classic Costume and Props, Nell speaking, how may I help?' It came out without my usual energy and warmth. *Where was Saskia?* It was gone nine, her usual starting time.

'It's Sally North, from Finlay Productions.'

My heart dropped. A regular client, Sally didn't sound happy. 'What's happened?'

'The chairs we ordered have arrived, but they're the wrong ones. We specifically wanted Regency for the ball scene we're shooting today.'

Blood pulsing in my ears, I brought up the details on my computer and went cold as I realised the order had switched from Regency to Victorian on its way from my brain to my fingers. 'I'm so sorry.' No point making excuses. 'I must have typed it in wrong.' Probably distracted, as I seemed to be more often than not at the moment. It was unlike me to make such a basic mistake, but no one else had access to my computer.

'I can get them out to you within the hour,' I promised, wondering how that was going to happen when one of our drivers had the day off, the other had an important delivery later that morning, and Janine, in charge of costumes, had taken a rare day off to go shopping with her daughter, Vikki. Not to mention that I was meeting a prospective client in twenty minutes.

'The velvet chaise-longue isn't here, either.'

'What?'

'We can't afford any hold-ups, Nell.' Frustration bled into Sally's words. 'We're on a tight schedule as it is. We're way behind on filming.'

For a moment, I was frozen by a feeling of helplessness. I wanted to slam down the phone, grab my bag and walk out of the company I'd been so excited to join three years ago. The company where I'd met Oliver, not knowing we would end up married within six months — or that we would need marriage counselling two years later. 'I can't apologise enough, Sally.'

'Look, we can probably manage with the chairs, but we really need the chaise-longue. Preferably before lunchtime.'

Gratitude washed through me. Sally had every right to be furious, but I'd never messed up on this scale before so perhaps she was prepared to be lenient. 'I'll make sure it's there if I have to deliver it myself.'

'Well, it's always nice to see you.' Mollified, Sally's tone warmed. 'I can show you round the set if you like.'

'That's OK.' Finally, I smiled. 'You know I would rather wait until the film hits the screen.' I sat back in my chair and tried to relax as my gaze shifted around the cluttered and shabby office I'd once coveted. Sometimes, it was hard to believe how far I'd come since my first day, when Oliver Cosgrove showed me around the vast showroom he co-owned, radiating charisma as he talked. In truth, I'd been half in love with Oliver by the end of my interview. My confidence had taken a battering that year, after the wedding-planning company I'd worked for folded, followed by my father's death, and a break-up with my then boyfriend. Somehow, it all came pouring out and Oliver had listened, his gaze direct and filled with understanding.

'We used to provide props for weddings,' I told him, returning to the pitch I'd planned and rehearsed in my kitchen the night before. 'I have the skills you're looking for, and I'm keen to learn and progress. I turned thirty last year and want to take charge of my life.' Progression had come quickly after that. *But at what price?*

I ended my call, frowning at my computer. Business was better than ever but my relationship with Oliver had deteriorated. Mainly, I was certain, because of my failure to engage with his grown-up daughters. Ruby, twenty-six, and Poppy, eighteen, had never even pretended to like me; still referred to me as 'the new wife'.

Irritated, I swept my hands through my hair, making a mental note to get my roots done. I almost left my skin when a female voice chimed, 'Hi, hi! So sorry, the trains were running late, and I wanted to bring you a coffee but there was a queue. I promise it won't happen again.'

I looked up with a sigh of relief to see Saskia approaching my desk, silhouetted by the rectangular window behind that looked onto the tree-lined car park. It was unusually cool for late May and the glass was speckled with rain.

She came closer, details emerging like a developing photograph. Brown hair held off a clear-skinned face in a low ponytail; catlike green eyes behind round glasses, crinkled in a smile; full lips, pursed slightly as she held out a cardboard cup of coffee.

'Thanks for this.' I leaned over and removed the lid before placing the cup on my desk. 'You really don't have to buy me coffee when we have a kitchen here.'

'It's nice to have a treat, and that coffee machine's a nightmare.' Saskia's smile widened and I couldn't help smiling back. I'd been resistant to the idea that I needed help but had gone ahead and advertised for an assistant in an attempt to ease my workload. Long hours meant I was struggling to balance my home life, though Oliver worked just as hard these days and was rarely home before seven. After talking to Saskia on the phone — the first person to call about the job, I invited her for an interview, fighting a feeling of intimidation when she turned up, tall, slender, and smart in a dark blazer and trousers, her shiny shoes a contrast to my scuffed ankle boots. Oliver professed to love that I wasn't too bothered about my appearance after the groomed-to-perfection look his ex-wife Fiona had favoured, but I'd felt scruffy with my frizzing sweep of blonde hair, plain blue jeans and oversized shirt, which I realised once Saskia had left had a coffee stain on the hem.

When I asked her where she'd come from, she said, 'Finsbury Park. Only a stone's throw by tube,' which was an oddly old-fashioned phrase that had made me warm to her.

'It's not a very glamorous location, I'm afraid.' I was referring to the North-East London industrial estate where Classic Props — as we tended to call it — was situated. 'We need the space for storage so . . .' I'd trailed off, wondering why I was being apologetic while she glanced around with an interested gleam.

'I actually love it already. I took the online video tour. It's amazing.'

Saskia was twenty-eight, and explained she'd had a career break to take care of her sick grandmother but was keen to get back to work.

I contacted someone she used to work with and, apparently, she's a brilliant organiser, I told Oliver that night. *She's starting on Monday. I've cleared it with Mark.*

Oliver had sold his share in the company a year ago to focus on his family's wine company, and his friend, and former business partner Mark Bradbury, had been forced into retirement six months earlier after a skiing accident left him with a back injury. Mark was still very much involved, albeit from a distance, and had approved Saskia's appointment.

'It's not been a good start to the day,' I told her now, and filled her in on Sally's call.

'Don't worry, I'll arrange to have the chaise-longue delivered,' she said in her unflappable way, shedding her coat as she headed to her desk. She'd only started a week ago, but already it was hard to remember how I'd managed without her. 'It's an easy mistake to make.'

Not for me. 'Thanks, Saskia.' Aware of time ticking down to my meeting, I picked up the coffee and took a sip while grabbing my jacket off the back of my chair. 'Oh, don't forget, I'll need a P45 and your bank details soon, or I won't be able to pay you at the end of the month.'

She looked up. 'I'm so sorry, Nell. There's been such a lot to do since Gran died, clearing out her things, and I've recently switched banks and—'

'It's fine, don't worry.' I remembered with a pinch of grief how much paperwork there had been to deal with after my father died, and how it had at least kept Mum occupied for a while. The sorrow hadn't fully hit home until she'd been left with nothing to do but remember that he was never coming home again.

Watching Saskia's long fingers move deftly across her keyboard, I let my shoulders drop. I needed to stop getting wound up about things and focus on what was important: my marriage. My parents had achieved almost thirty-four years together. I wanted Oliver and I to do the same.

As I turned to pick up my bag, my mobile rang. Seeing the name on the screen my stomach lurched. *Ruby.* She never called my mobile. Had something happened to Oliver?

I moved towards the stairs out of Saskia's earshot to answer the call. 'Hello?'

'Apparently you're meeting my dad this afternoon.'

No niceties, but I'd stopped expecting them.

'That's right.' I wished I didn't sound defensive. 'Is there a problem?

'Not as far as I'm concerned. You're going for marriage counselling.' It wasn't a question. *How had she found out?* 'Really, Nell?' Her tone was droll, mocking. Before I could respond, she continued, 'I'll give you some advice for nothing, shall I? He doesn't want you anymore.' A pause for dramatic effect. 'Your marriage is over.'

CHAPTER 2

Ruby

Ruby dropped her phone into the canvas bag by her feet, her heart thudding, her conscience crying out that she'd gone too far.

Poppy, hunched in a plastic chair opposite, hood pulled up over her long dark hair, threw her sister a twisted smile. 'You rock,' she said, as she poured salt over her uneaten breakfast. 'That told her.'

Ruby had no idea whether her father's marriage to Nell was over — if he was finally moving on from the woman he'd left her mother for — but if she and Poppy had anything to do with it, it would be.

Ruby wasn't mean by nature. In fact, she considered herself a good person overall. She was the best kind of sister and daughter. She'd proved that by giving up her future for them both. She loved animals, especially dogs, gave to charity if she saw someone jiggling a box outside the supermarket, and had a tattoo of a peace sign on her left shoulder. However, where Nell was concerned, her 'good person' image fell away, like a snake shedding its skin, revealing an inner-her, who she didn't like that much. Nell brought out something in Ruby she couldn't seem to control, even now after all this time. Some might say she should accept she had a stepmother. It had been nearly three years, after all. But she couldn't let it go — not while her mum, Fiona, the real Mrs Cosgrove, still hadn't got over her father leaving. Not while Ruby still lay awake at night, the trail of destruction her dad left when he walked out whirring around her head.

'How's Mum?' she asked Poppy now.

Her sister glanced up, and paused from streaming more salt onto her congealed scrambled egg. The damage done to her by the break-up — a then vulnerable fifteen-year-old with issues — had been hard to watch. Ruby worried about her sister constantly. 'Still sober most of the time, if that's what you mean. Still going to AA, following the 12-steps.'

'That's good.'

'Yep.'

'She's getting there.'

'Yep.'

Their mother was nothing like the confident woman she had once been. She had collapsed, deflated, closed in on herself before their eyes when their dad left. It was the shock of how such a strong woman could be destroyed by a man — *their father* — that had dumbfounded the girls. But then Fiona had thought Oliver loved her. They all had.

And Nell had never paid for any of it. Instead she'd thrived. Climbing the ladder at Classic Costumes and Props after Ruby's father sold out to his partner Mark. And when Nell left work at the end of each day, she whizzed down the M25 in her silver hybrid Outlander to their perfect house next to the river in Marlow. Even now, it made Ruby feel sick to think of her dad with that woman. She wasn't even attractive, not in the same way Ruby's mother had been when they were growing up. Fiona had been stunning, wore designer dresses, her hair and make-up immaculate. Now she no longer cared about her appearance.

A tap on the café window beside Ruby made her jump. She turned to see her father waving goodbye, he was dressed in a crisp white shirt and tailored black trousers, his grey hair styled — always styled. When Ruby was in her late teens her friends used to fancy him. *'He looks like Rupert Graves,'* they would say. It made her laugh — he was nothing like the actor as far as she was concerned. He was simply her dad.

The three had had breakfast together. He would often come into London to see clients, and always called to see if his daughters wanted to grab breakfast.

'Love you,' Ruby mouthed. She did. So much. But Nell had stolen him, brainwashed him. Ruby never once blamed her father for the break-up. He would have come home if Nell hadn't stuck her claws in and refused to let go.

'Love you too,' her dad mouthed back. He moved his dark eyes to Poppy, before waving once more and heading away. His coat draped over his arm, despite the coolness of the day and a slight drizzle of rain.

Ruby drained the last of her coffee, her mind drifting back to ten minutes before when she'd seen the alert pop up on her father's phone. He'd left his mobile on the table when he'd nipped to the loo, and a reminder had flashed on the screen *2.30 p.m. First session with Carla — Marriage Counsellor with Nell.* The sight of those words had made Ruby's heart thud, to the point she'd had to take deep breaths when her father sauntered back to the table, in an attempt to control the sudden joy — the hope — the burst of happiness. Would Nell soon be out of the picture? Would her parents get back together?

Poppy, slouched down in the chair, slammed down the now empty salt pot. 'Are we done here?'

'Yep.' Ruby rose, picked up her bag, and looped it over her shoulder. 'Let's go.'

For now, Ruby worked for a catering company owned by her friend Benita. They served takeaways, and delivered sandwiches to companies in the area. She'd snapped up the route that included the unit that housed Classic Costume and Props. It was a chance to spy on Nell. She wasn't proud of the fact.

Ruby had recently moved out of her childhood home, back to Finsbury Park. She desperately wanted to perform in the West End, a dream that had slipped through her fingers when her parents broke up. At first, when Fiona and Oliver's marriage fell apart, Ruby had buried her head to the pain swirling within the walls of her beautiful childhood home in Richmond-on-Thames, but eventually she'd put her acting career on hold and moved back in, cared for her sister; propped up her fragile mother.

It had been a difficult time. On top of her parents' break-up, her toxic relationship with Sean — a delivery driver and mechanic at Classic Props — had ended badly.

Ruby pushed open the door of the café and stepped onto the busy London street, Poppy right behind her. A glance at her watch told her she was running late for work.

'Can I come with you?' Poppy's hood was still up, hands wedged in the pockets of her black jeans.

'OK.' Ruby took her umbrella from her bag, and shot it up, moving in closer to her sister so it covered both their heads. She would often take Poppy with her on the job, trying to keep her occupied while she looked for employment. She'd been through three jobs in the last two months — two in cafés and one in a factory — walking out without explanation. 'But we're not listening to your crap music in the van, and we need to get a move on.'

* * *

'You're late.' Benita barely looked up, her face flushed, a trilby hat with a netting snood covering her shiny black hair, a white catering jacket hanging loose over her slim body. She owned the catering company: a small business that had been passed down the generations. She'd worked there since she was sixteen, taking over from her parents when her father became ill, and her mother had given up work to care for him. She was thirty, single, strong, and fiercely independent. 'I love you Ruby, you know that.' She looked up, brown eyes narrowing. 'But you need to improve your timekeeping, or you're out.'

'Sorry.'

'You will be.' Her tone was sharp, and Ruby felt chastised. She picked up a crate of sandwiches, Poppy grabbed another, and they headed out the back to a van with the words "Sharma's Sandwiches" on the side and unlocked the back doors.

'She can be a right cow, at times.' Poppy turned up her nose and shoved a crate inside with force.

'She's stressed. I was late.'

'Five minutes, is all. I don't know how you put up with her. I'd walk out.'

'I know you would. And that's why I've got a job and you haven't.'

'Whatever.' Poppy made her way round to the passenger side and let herself in, as Ruby climbed into the driver's side.

They had barely turned out of the back entrance, when Poppy turned on the radio, and started searching the channels.

'I said no heavy metal.' Ruby changed gear, and indicated at the end of the road, the windscreen wipers thrashing the screen as the heavens opened.

'Fine.' Poppy switched off the radio, and folded her arms. Sometimes it was hard to believe she was no longer a child.

After several deliveries they pulled up next to the tall trees that fringed the car park outside Classic Costume and Props, the rain now a fine drizzle. There were no deliveries there today, only a crate of sandwiches for the unit next door. Ruby cut the engine and was about to get out of the van, when she spotted Nell.

'Look at her.' Poppy spat out the words, as her eyes followed the woman across the car park, her hands balling into fists. 'She really thinks she's something special.'

Ruby stared. Nell didn't seem to have her usual confidence. Her head was bowed, her shoulders rounded, her strides short and quick. 'I don't know—'

'What?'

'Well, she looks pretty stressed to me, that's all I'm saying.' Ruby's tone was hopeful.

'Christ!'

Ruby turned to see Poppy was looking up at the row of office windows above the warehouse unit that housed the props. She shuddered, and slipped down in the seat.

'What?' Ruby scanned the building. 'What's wrong?'

'Nothing—'

'It doesn't look like nothing, you're shaking.'

'It was Sean, is all,' she said. 'He was staring out of the window at Nell, then down at us. He still creeps me out.'

Ruby looked up at the windows, her eyes moving along the long panels of glass, the thought of him making her uneasy. 'I can't see him.'

'He was there a second ago.'

'Well, he does work there, Poppy,' Ruby said, trying not to read anything into it.

'Yep. You're right.' She nibbled the skin around her thumbnail. 'As I say, he gives me the creeps, is all. I reckon he still has a thing for you —'

'That was over a long time ago.' Her mind drifted to how he stalked her for months after their break-up, the way her father threatened him, told him he would lose his job if he didn't leave Ruby alone. 'Last I heard he'd started seeing Janine's daughter. He really has moved on.'

'If you say so.'

Ruby moved her eyes across the windows to Nell's office. A woman was sitting at a desk in front of a computer screen. 'Who's that?' She turned to her sister.

But Poppy's eyes were back on Nell climbing into her car. She lined up her finger like a gun, her black hair falling about her face as she took aim. 'Bang — bang — bang,' she whispered, and burst into laughter.

CHAPTER 3

Nell

'I'm sure he'll be here in a minute.' I perched on the edge of a grey fabric sofa in the artfully cosy counselling room and placed my bag at my feet.

'No problem.' Carla gave a bland smile as she crossed her long, slim legs and folded her hands over her notepad. She was somewhere in her mid-thirties with sleek blonde hair pulled back in a low bun, and pale skin stretched across high cheekbones. According to her website, she'd been a couples' counsellor for eight years and several testimonials had credited her with saving marriages.

I was fighting a feeling of deep embarrassment but told myself she must have heard it all. By comparison, mine and Oliver's problems didn't amount to much. No violence, no affairs, no bad behaviour — not really. It was hard to describe exactly, but it felt as if Oliver's feelings for me lately had been turned down, like lights on a dimmer switch. And there was the question of children. Both his, and the ones I hoped to have.

Feeling twitchy as I shrugged off my jacket, unable to forget the abrupt call from Ruby earlier — *did she know something I didn't?* — I tried to relax my features and reached for the glass of water on the table in front of me. My hand shook slightly as I took a quick sip and put the glass down. *Why was everyone late today?* At least Saskia had been apologetic and more than made up for it by taking control of the phones while I met my client, and calling in a driver to deliver the chaise-longue to the film production company, assuring me she would be fine as I left for my 'dental appointment'. I couldn't bring myself to divulge the real reason I had to go out. Unusually, I'd had no qualms about leaving her in charge — with strict instructions to ring me if any problems arose — but maybe that was down to Ruby's call, which had unsettled me more than I was willing to admit. It remained a daily sadness that after all this time, Oliver's daughters still couldn't bear the fact that I was married to their father. Worse, longed for our marriage to be over.

The first time we went out for dinner, it had been Oliver's turn to open up to me. He explained — haltingly, as though loathe to paint his wife in a bad light — that during their long marriage, Fiona had always put her job first, and that she drank a lot, blowing hot and cold with him and their daughters to the point where he'd gradually fallen out of love with her. He told me how he'd tried his best to make things work for Ruby and Poppy's sake, until he couldn't take it any more and moved in with his mother. That was a month before he interviewed me for the job at Classic Props. He told me the separation from Fiona was permanent, and the chemistry between us had been so strong, I hadn't thought too deeply about how she must have felt. When Fiona phoned his mother's a few weeks later begging Oliver to come home, and he told her he'd met someone else, she fell apart.

Maybe you should give things another try, I'd said, a little scared, though I already couldn't bear the thought of losing him.

He pulled me into his arms and buried his face in my hair. *I can't go back, Nell. I couldn't be happy, and that wouldn't be good for the girls. And besides, I'm falling in love with you.*

Fiona still hadn't moved on, creating tension with Ruby and Poppy as she demanded to know Oliver's every move whenever they spent time with him. I'd suggested to Oliver that I could perhaps meet her, naïvely thinking that, face-to-face, I'd be able to reassure her I only wanted to be a friend to her daughters, not replace her, but he said it wasn't about the girls — she didn't want him to be with anyone else. Meeting me would make her angrier and that would create more problems for Ruby and Poppy, who couldn't have made their dislike for me clearer when we were finally introduced. I'd tried to understand while secretly hoping that, one day, they would accept me, but it was getting harder to think that way. Did they really still believe that Oliver would go back to Fiona, and they could be a happy family, or would it be enough that he was no longer with me? The *man-stealer* Ruby once called me, her expression tight with contempt. I felt terrible for them that their mother hadn't been well since the divorce, which she hadn't wanted. *Destroyed* Poppy had dramatically put it, but I wondered sometimes whether Fiona fed off their hatred of me, encouraged it even. I desperately wanted the girls to give me a chance, but how could that happen when they saw me as the cause of their mother's terrible unhappiness?

Maybe I should have suggested we *all* have counselling. Poppy, in particular, would benefit from talking to someone, but as she and Ruby tended to rein in their feelings about me around their father, it looked as though I was being over-sensitive if I mentioned anything. No way would they have agreed to family therapy.

As Carla glanced discreetly at the wall clock behind me, I rose and crossed to the window. An ancient oak tree dripped rain outside, splashing the puddles beneath. The room was on the second floor of a Georgian house, an eight-minute drive from Finsbury Park, on a quiet residential street. I'd picked it primarily because of its proximity to work, which Oliver had twitched his eyebrows at, commenting that it was ironic, considering work was part of the problem. Still, he'd agreed to make the effort to drive from our home in Marlow where he ran Cosgrove Wines.

As I peered at the street, I noticed the tail lights of a van on the corner, indicating to turn right. It looked like the one that Ruby drove, reminding me that I'd seen it as I left the office and had to stop myself hurrying over and confronting her about the phone call. Ruby worked in catering and had recently started delivering lunches to some of the businesses on the industrial estate. She was obviously keeping an eye on me, perhaps trying to catch me doing something I shouldn't be. She knew the staff at Classic Props from when Oliver had been in charge and she and Poppy used to sometimes drop in. The fact I was now running the business and doing well no doubt fuelled their suspicion of me, despite the fact that Oliver was happier in charge of Cosgrove Wines.

Where was he?

I was about to apologise to Carla again before texting Oliver, when I heard footsteps on the stairs. Seconds later, the door flew open, and Oliver came in with a flurry of apologies — 'an appointment with a client ran over' — rubbing a hand over the silver-white hair that made him stand out in a crowd. That and his height, his intelligent dark eyes, and the mouth that always looked on the verge of smiling.

The effect on Carla was briefly electrifying. She got to her feet and stared for a moment, the notepad dropping to the soft, grey carpet, her pale lips forming a silent 'oh'. Oliver paused, eyes widening slightly, and I suppressed an inner sigh. I should be used to the effect my husband had on women — something indefinable that I could hardly deny when I'd fallen for it myself — but I'd somehow assumed a marriage counsellor would be immune to his magnetic gaze.

To her credit, she recovered quickly, bending to pick up the notepad, and to perhaps disguise the flush blazing across her cheeks. When she straightened, she inclined her head and said evenly, 'I'm glad you could make it.'

'Me too,' I chimed in, trying not to mind that Oliver had put his client meeting before our session.

'Better late than never,' he said smoothly.

Carla sat back down, running a hand over her hair as Oliver whipped off his coat before dropping beside me. He loosened his tie as he pressed cool lips to my cheek, his two-day stubble grazing my skin. He smelt of expensive shampoo and the inside of his car — a vintage Saab that had belonged to his father and wasn't remotely economical or environmentally friendly — and something vaguely alcoholic. Oliver didn't drink much but regularly tasted wine which tended to linger on his breath. 'Sorry, Nell.'

'It's OK,' I murmured, squeezing his hand, his wedding ring — a platinum band that matched mine — pressing into the flesh of my fingers.

His eyes briefly searched my face before he turned to Carla. 'What have I missed?'

'We haven't started, yet.' Composed once more, Carla's eyes flicked between us and I wondered what she made of our dynamic, our body language; whether she secretly thought him too good for me. 'When you booked the appointment,' she continued, then cleared her throat. 'Nell . . . you mentioned in your email that there was a distance between you and Oliver that you were worried might get worse, and you were struggling to communicate as a couple.'

'We work long hours and I suppose it's getting in the way,' he said with a hint of impatience. I felt it was costing him to be here, baring his soul to a stranger; that maybe it didn't fit with his idea of himself — Oxford educated, from a good background, popular and successful. *I* was the problem, his demeanour seemed to say, an attitude I'd picked up on recently. Only a few months earlier, he'd booked a spa day for my mum as a special treat for her birthday and when I thanked him he'd brought his forehead to mine and murmured, *If it makes you happy too, it's worth every penny.*

He wouldn't be here if he wasn't willing to work on our marriage, I reassured myself. He was out of his comfort zone, that was all.

Carla switched her gaze to him. I couldn't tell whether her eyes were grey or green, or somewhere in between.

'I took over my family's wine-importing business quite recently,' he continued, and I detected pride in his voice, mixed with something I could never quite decipher. His father had started Cosgrove Wines from his bedroom as a young man and worked up to being one of the best in the country, but although Oliver had been expected to join the company, he'd wanted to make his own way in the world, eventually doing so with Mark, his friend and fellow philosophy and economics student at Oxford, whose father worked in theatre production and would pay his son to source props during the holidays. 'I'd had itchy feet for a while at Classic Props,' he went on, more talkative now. Carla scribbled something on her notepad with a gold pen. 'I enjoy my work, and know Nell loves her job too,' — he flashed me an admiring look that warmed my heart — 'but sometimes we're like ships that pass in the night.'

That was a bit strong. 'I make an effort to get home in time for dinner most evenings,' I protested. If anything, Oliver was the one working harder; sometimes out of the country, leaving me alone in our silent house. 'One of the main issues is that his daughters haven't accepted me.' I hadn't intended to say it so bluntly, but Ruby's call was still at the front of my mind.

Oliver leaned back with a sigh, combing a hand through his hair. He rested one foot on the opposite knee, his brown suede shoe bobbing. 'They're doing their best, Nell, but you know that their loyalty lies with their mother.'

'It's been almost three years.' I addressed my words to Carla, wondering what it would take to disturb her expression, which looked determinedly serene. 'Ruby called me today to tell me Oliver doesn't want me anymore and that our marriage is over.'

'What?' He jerked forward, shoulders stiffening. 'She doesn't even know about . . .' he waved his hand between us and Carla, who was writing in her notepad again, eyes averted. 'About any of this.'

'Well, she must have found out.' I bent to dig my phone from my bag, hating that we were doing this at all, let alone in front of a virtual stranger. 'Look.' Face burning, I showed him the call to my phone from Ruby's number. Before I could react, Oliver had plucked it from my hand and was ringing her.

'Hey, Rubes,' he said, and even as I felt a prickle of sweat on my upper lip — the room was far too warm — I couldn't help picturing his eldest daughter's surprise at hearing her father's voice on my phone. 'What's this about you calling Nell?' He was using the indulgent tone he reserved for his daughters, as though they were younger than their years — something I'd pointed out once and knew I wouldn't again, flooded with guilt and shame when he looked at me with hurt eyes. *They'll always be my little girls, Nell. Remember, they're innocent in all this.*

I caught Carla's eye as Oliver listened to Ruby's response and she quickly looked away. My muscles clenched as Oliver said soothingly, 'That's OK, don't worry. I'll talk to her.' He ended the call and handed the phone back, a groove between his eyebrows. 'She saw a reminder on my phone about our appointment.' He flicked Carla an apologetic wince, before looking back at me. 'It was wrong of her to phone you, but she was worried. She said all she did was ask you whether our marriage was over.'

'That's not true,' I began, knowing it was pointless to say more. Ruby and Poppy had their father wrapped around their little fingers. By bad-mouthing them, I was putting myself in the wrong.

'You must have misunderstood.'

'Sorry,' I murmured, hand closing around my phone as it vibrated with a notification. I resisted the urge to look, suddenly wishing I was back at work, that I'd never suggested counselling in the first place. Now Ruby and Poppy knew we were having problems, it gave them an advantage over me. No doubt they would take great pleasure in telling their mother.

'What was the other issue?' Carla's voice broke in as I blinked away tears, only partly reassured when Oliver's warm hand cupped my knee in a gesture of solidarity.

'Sorry?'

'You said, *one* of the issues was your stepdaughters.' She leaned forward, her gaze holding mine with sudden intent. 'What was the other?'

'I want a baby, but Oliver has changed his mind.' Another fact I hadn't intended to blurt out, but what was the point of being there if I didn't get to the point? 'He knew I wanted us to have children one day and I thought he did too.' I turned as he made to speak. 'I know you say you can't remember, but you said it, Oliver.' I looked at Carla. 'Now, he doesn't.'

'I don't want to go through those early years again.' He massaged my knee with strong fingers, his eyes finding mine. Expecting to see frustration — we'd had this conversation several times already — I saw his eyebrows pull into a V of concern. 'We have the freedom to do whatever we want. A young family is a massive responsibility.'

'I want children, Oliver.' I'd never been this vocal about it before. *Did I want a baby that badly, or was I digging my heels in because he was saying no?*

Oliver's mouth dropped open, but before he could reply, my phone vibrated again. I wondered whether Saskia was having an emergency at work.

'Sorry,' I turned the phone over as Oliver sighed and moved his hand away. He exchanged a look with Carla, who was fiddling with the silver chain around her neck.

I looked at my phone screen where two texts leapt out. They didn't make sense, so I read them again, aware Oliver was leaning over to read them too.

Hey, thanks for the chat the other night. Let's do it again soon XX

Is it too soon to say I'm madly in 'L' with you?

'What is it?' Carla's question broke the awful tension spreading through the room. 'I usually advise my clients to turn off their phones during our sessions, so there are no—'

She stopped as Oliver jumped to his feet and stared at me with something approaching horror. 'Who was that?'

'I . . .' My phone slipped through my fingers and thudded onto the carpet. 'It must be a mistake. I've no idea who sent those messages, but they weren't intended for me.'

'What's going on?' Carla's tone grew urgent. 'What messages?'

Oliver's eyes didn't leave my face. 'Nell, are you having an affair?'

CHAPTER 4

Ruby

'Do you think Nell saw us?' Ruby had slipped down low in her seat, wondering what possessed her to go along with Poppy's idea to follow their stepmother. 'Oh God, what if she did?'

'I couldn't give a crap.' Poppy turned her phone over after glancing at the screen. 'And neither should you.'

Ruby stared at the phone in her sister's hands. 'Who were you texting?'

'When?'

'Just then.'

'Some bloke who follows my Twitch, nobody you know. Not that it's any of your business.'

Ruby's mind began working overtime. Had her sister got a boyfriend? It would be a first. She'd never allowed anyone close before. 'Just be careful, Poppy. There are lot of weirdos out there. Promise me you won't go meeting up anywhere lonely.'

'Jeez, Ruby. I'm not a kid.' Poppy shoved her phone into her hoodie pocket. 'And I'm not about to arrange any meet-ups any time soon.'

Ruby glanced back up at the window, and fired the engine. 'We need to go before Dad sees us.'

'Can you drop me off home?' Poppy slumped down lower in the seat, and pulled up her hood. 'I can't be arsed to get the tube.'

'It's hardly dropping you off.' Ruby was agitated, her neck still tingling from when Nell looked out at them. 'It would take me an hour to get to Richmond and back. Benita needs the van. Not to mention she'd wonder why I'd used so much petrol.'

'Then let's drop the van off and pick up your car.' Poppy narrowed her eyes, her face morphing into the sullen sister Ruby knew so well. 'Oh go on, Mum hasn't seen you for ages.' Emotional blackmail was one of Poppy's specialities.

'I was only there at the weekend.' Admittedly, it had only been to pick up some stuff she'd left behind when she moved out. But she'd stayed awhile, had coffee with her mum, who had made the conversation all about her dad. He'd taken to dropping in over the last few weeks. *Checking in on her*, he called it. Fixing the guttering, trimming the tall trees that fringed the property. Something he hadn't done in all the years they'd been separated, and, if Ruby's memory served her right, hadn't done much of when they were together.

'I keep wondering when he's going to realise he should never have married that woman,' her mum had said. And Ruby had wanted to add *and realise he still loves you.* But she hadn't voiced those words, however much she wanted them to be true. After all, her dad must have loved her mum once, and he'd never given a clear reason why he left, simply saying that he'd tried his best, but couldn't stay. And now her dad and Nell were going to counselling. Maybe there was a chance for her parents, especially if she and Poppy helped the process along — gave things a nudge in the right direction.

After chatting with her mum, Ruby had made her way upstairs to Poppy's room: a dimly lit space with posters of horror films pinned to black walls. Her sister was sitting at her desk, streaming herself playing 'The Evil Within 2' on Twitch.

'That looks creepy.' Ruby shuddered as her sister's online character moved around an old house, and someone crept up on her with a knife.

'I'm just pausing the session for a moment, guys,' Poppy said to the screen. 'Back in two, and we can kick butt some more.' She turned on her swivel chair to face Ruby. 'I've got two hundred followers, and sixty subscribers. Pretty good, right?'

Ruby nodded. She wasn't into gaming — never had been — or Twitch. In fact, she barely used social media, had closed her Facebook profile down after Sean posted a stream of lovesick messages on her newsfeed three months ago, saying they were meant to be together, and he would never give up.

After a brief chat, Poppy had spun her chair back towards the screen, and continued the session. A few minutes of watching her sister was enough. Ruby left the room, and headed into her childhood bedroom. It was packed up with the final things she needed for her flat in Finsbury Park. Tears filled her eyes. Her childhood had been a happy one. Her friends were envious that her parents seemed like the perfect couple. They had been tactile, affectionate. Ruby, as a young teen, would tell them to get a room if she caught them kissing. Though, thinking back, it was always her mum who initiated the affection.

'You could stay for dinner. I could cook.' Poppy's voice brought Ruby back to the moment. She turned to look at her sister in the passenger seat, who had clapped her hands together as though praying. 'Please.'

'Since when did you learn to cook?'

Poppy screwed up her face. 'OK, you got me. I could order a takeaway. Or you could order a takeaway. I'm broke.'

'Sorry. No can do, sadly.' She put the van into gear, and released the handbrake. 'And I can't stay anyway. I have an audition this evening.'

'Yeah, you bragged about it to Dad. Flutter Theatre. It sounds made up.'

'Hey! You know how much getting back on the stage means to me. Give me a break.'

'Sorry.' She didn't sound it.

'I'll come round tomorrow, I promise. In the meantime I'll drop you off at the underground.' She glanced once more up at the counsellor's window where a woman stood, arms folded across her slim body, blonde hair pulled back in a neat bun.

Had Nell seen them down here, spying on her? Had her dad seen them? She shouldn't have come. She was twenty-six, not a kid. But then she needed to know what was going on between Nell and her father. She needed to know if there was hope for her mum.

She dropped a moody Poppy off at the tube station, and made her way back to Sharma's Sandwiches, manoeuvring the van into the small area at the back of the shop. Once out of the van, she leaned in through the back door, and hung the keys on the rack. 'I'm done for the day,' she called through to a harassed looking Benita.

'Cheers, Ruby. Good luck with the audition. I hope your heart isn't fluttering too much — did you see what I did there?'

'I did!' She smiled. 'And thanks.'

* * *

Ruby's flat was round the corner from Sharma's Sandwiches. A bit of a dive, but all she could afford to rent right now. She'd needed to get out from under her mum's roof, as much for Poppy's sake as her own. Her sister had become reliant on her, which was fair enough at first. But Poppy was eighteen now — needed to find her own way. Ruby would always be there for her sister, but she wanted to start living her own life again — could no longer be her constant support.

'Hey, Rubes.' It was the bloke from the top floor, heading down the stairs towards her, humming 'Red, Red Wine' under his breath. The lift hadn't worked since she arrived, despite the landlord promising it would be fixed soon when she signed the lease. 'How you doing, girl?'

'All good,' she said. 'You?'

'Always good — sun is shining — and I've got a nice piece of haddock and a bottle of Stella for me dinner — life is a blessing sent from God.' He smiled, showing a gap in his white teeth. 'I see you got an admirer, girl,' he went on as he passed.

'Sorry?' She turned to watch him disappear onto the next flight of stairs.

'The chocolates on your doorstep,' he called, not looking back. 'I hope you'll save me one.'

Ruby raced up the remaining stairs, and along the corridor towards her flat. A gift hamper from Hotel Chocolat — her favourites — was on the doorstep, a card attached. She crouched down, scanned the words on the card.

I hope one day we'll be together again, Ruby. I'll never stop loving you. Sean x

Her heart sank. *Sean.* He must have heard she'd moved out. Now lived alone. How the hell did he know where her flat was? She rose, looked about her. Shuddered at the idea of him watching her. She'd thought he was out of her life. That he was seeing Janine's daughter. But it looked as though Sean hadn't moved on at all.

CHAPTER 5

Nell

It was good to be back in my car, driving to work. My heart raced as I turned the corner, Carla's parting words a sympathetic echo in my head. '*If you want to come on your own, you can. Marriage counselling isn't only for couples.* Oliver had left by then, saying he needed time to clear his head, leaving me in a state of frustrated disbelief that he'd thought for a minute those texts were meant for me.

'Would I be here, trying to fix our marriage, if I had a secret lover?' I'd said, heart thumping with shock. 'They were probably intended for someone with a number similar to mine.' I held the phone under his nose. 'No mention of my name.'

As he took my phone and scoured the messages he'd seemed to deflate, his features twisting with remorse. 'I'm sorry, Nell. I don't know . . . it's odd, that's all. I mean, how likely is it that someone got the number wrong when they're obviously this keen?'

I shook my head, baffled at the unwelcome intrusion. 'How likely is it that anyone would send *me* a message like this?' I took the phone back and quickly typed *Who is this?*

before turning to Carla, mortified that she was caught up in this unlikely scenario, but her eyes were fixed on Oliver's face. 'I would never cheat on my husband,' I said, as if appealing to a jury. 'I take my marriage vows very seriously.'

When Carla didn't respond Oliver subsided. 'I believe you,' he said. 'Let's pretend this never happened.'

'Actually, Oliver,' Carla had said, head cocked. 'I'd like to explore why you thought Nell might have been seeing someone else.'

'Those texts?' Oliver raised a hand before she could comment. 'Look, can we do this another time?' He swung a sad look between us. 'I'm sorry, Nell, I need some air.'

'You can't go now.' Stunned, I reached for his hand. 'We've hardly started.'

'Please, Nell.' He seemed to struggle with himself, before getting to his feet and reaching for his jacket. 'I'll see you at home.' He pressed a kiss on my forehead and then he was gone, leaving me to apologise to Carla, who couldn't quite maintain her impartial expression as I blinked away tears and gathered my things, checking my phone for a reply. There wasn't one, which had made me wonder whether it hadn't been a mistake after all. *Could Ruby have sent the text to stir up trouble?*

That was when Carla suggested I come back to see her on my own, obviously believing our marriage was in real trouble and that it was somehow my fault.

Heading back to Classic Props, I trembled. I hadn't even got on to the subject of my stepdaughters, or their mother. I knew Oliver had been going round to see Fiona at their former family home in Richmond lately, to help out with this and that. I thought I knew why. He was hoping she would put their large house on the market and wanted it to be in a good state — she hadn't bothered much with it since he left — but didn't want his daughters to know yet, worried they'd be upset about losing their family home. I was certain that he still worried Fiona might try to harm herself, and the impact that would have on Ruby and Poppy and, deep down,

I was too. She'd taken an overdose when she heard we were getting married — it turned out she hadn't taken anywhere near enough tablets to end her life but it had been a shock all the same when we found out later — and I knew that in spite of everything, Oliver felt guilty.

If I'd known the day I met him that Oliver hadn't long been separated from his wife, and of the effect our relationship would have on her and his daughters, would I have stepped away? I knew I wouldn't, my attraction to him too strong. I recalled how we'd talked for hours in the corner booth of that warmly-lit restaurant where Oliver had told me about his marriage and his strained relationship with his daughters and how, later, his eyes hadn't left my face as we moved on to other topics; how he'd made me laugh properly for the first time in ages and the ache of missing my father began to ease. We'd spent the night together at my flat, kissing for what felt like hours, and the next morning he abandoned making breakfast to help my neighbour put out her bins in the rain.

I'd liked being with a man who was older, a grown-up who wore a tie and drove a vintage car and was as comfortable discussing the plot of a romantic film as he was the characteristics of a good wine. He wasn't old enough to be a father figure, despite my mother's concerns, but mature, and comfortable in his own skin. I could tell he liked who he was in my eyes, and in turn that made me feel confident, more certain that he was someone I could be happy with for a long time.

Are you sure you're doing the right thing? my mother had asked a couple of days before the wedding. *Maybe you should give it a bit longer.* She liked Oliver but hated that his daughters wouldn't accept me and worried about the age gap. *Being married is about more than the wedding day.*

I'd known that of course and squashed any doubts Mum's words had raised, convincing myself that everything would work out. Neither Oliver nor I had wanted an extravagant wedding — especially as Ruby and Poppy had declined to attend — settling for a register office ceremony on a sunny day in June, with two witnesses — my mother and his, a pairing neither enjoyed — before flying to Denmark on our honeymoon where we'd explored the canals of Copenhagen and the ancient Viking territory of the Faroe Islands, feasting our eyes on cascading waterfalls and fairy-tale castles. Happiness had replaced the sadness of the past year, my mind and heart filled with bright, new memories. But apart from a romantic weekend in Venice on our first anniversary, we hadn't been away since. Maybe, instead of counselling, we should have gone on holiday. Even as I thought it, the idea slipped away. We had too many commitments between us, and I had a feeling that far from leaving our worries behind, they would simply follow us, lingering like a bad smell. Better to get to the root of the problems with Carla's help and work them out. If only those weird texts hadn't turned up. Mistake or not, they'd ruined our first session.

Fresh apprehension surged as I parked in my usual spot outside the warehouse. Despite my earlier confidence, Saskia hadn't been at the company long and it was the first time I'd left her in charge. What if something had gone wrong and she hadn't wanted to tell me? Heart tripping, I got out of the car and hurried towards the building, almost bumping into Sean coming out.

'Hi.' I fixed a smile in place, never quite myself around him. 'Did the delivery go OK?'

He nodded, and a strand of dark-blond hair fell across his forehead. 'All done, delivery form signed and in the office.'

'Great. Thank you.'

'No problem.' He released a flicker of a smile that didn't reach his pale green eyes. He was friendly enough on the surface, but I sensed a seam of dislike running underneath. I knew he'd had a relationship with Ruby, but it had been over for a while. I was surprised he'd stayed on once Oliver left the company, had assumed his job at Classic Props was a stepping stone — we'd had several young staff who had come and gone — but I'd overheard Ruby telling Oliver he wasn't ambitious and as long as he had money coming in, didn't much care what he did. It was one of the reasons they'd gone their separate ways, apparently. He was seeing Janine's daughter, Vikki, now. I'd seen them going into a nearby pub after work one evening, her arm wrapped around his skinny waist, but he occasionally asked about 'the family' with a hungry gleam in his eyes, as if he couldn't help himself, and I had the impression he was fishing for information about Ruby.

'You can go home now if you like,' I said.

'I told Sally I'd drop over a bunch of those chairs she ordered and do a swap.' He rubbed the back of his neck, where I'd seen some words tattooed in faded black ink, though I couldn't make out what they said. 'She explained about the mix-up.'

'Oh well, that would be good, if you don't mind.' That was the thing about Sean. He might have issues in his personal life, but I couldn't deny he was a good worker — a former mechanic he'd even fixed his van when it broke down — as well as reliable. 'Thanks again.'

He nodded curtly and headed to his vehicle, which had *Classic Costumes and Props* emblazoned on the side in red and gold, where he slid the doors open. He was slight but with a wiry strength that showed in the swell of muscles on his upper arms.

Turning away, I hurried inside, nodding a hello to Janine who was shaking out a crinoline dress, and ran upstairs to the office, to find Saskia at her desk where I'd left her.

'Everything OK?' I was out of breath and clammy-faced. I should probably start exercising. Oliver tried to fit in a game of squash with a friend twice a week, while I relied on 'running around at work' to keep fit. 'Sorry I've been so long.'

'No worries.' Saskia smiled brightly, nudging her glasses up the bridge of her nose. 'How was it?'

Remembering my fictitious dental appointment, I feigned a wince. 'Not too bad, but I'll probably have to go back.' Heat shot to my cheeks. I hated lying, but I didn't know Saskia well and couldn't face her pity. 'Any phone calls?'

'Just a reminder that the chest of drawers and shop signs you supplied to Criterion TV need picking up.' She glanced at a scribbled note by her keyboard, eyebrows raised. 'It was supposed to be this morning, but I noticed it's in the diary for tomorrow. Anyway, they were fine with that.'

'Oh . . .' Flustered, I tried to think. The pick-up hadn't been on today's schedule, I would have remembered. The mix-up must have been on Criterion's side. 'Well, thank you for dealing with that,' I said. 'Why don't you take a late lunch?'

'I brought food in with me, thanks. I've already eaten.'

'Of course.' My gaze moved to the bouquet of flowers, partly blocking her computer: a spray of pink roses and greenery, and delicate little white flowers. 'Those are lovely,' I said, trying to push everything else from my mind. I wriggled out of my jacket and crossed to my desk. 'You have an admirer?'

'Actually they're for you.'

'Me?' A frown formed. 'Unlikely.'

'From your husband, maybe?'

'Only if it was a special occasion.' I dropped my jacket and bag on my desk and returned to pick up the bouquet. 'I prefer seeing them in a garden.' Even so, I felt a small burst of pleasure as I sniffed the silky petals, their fragrance reminding me of the soap my grandmother used to use. Maybe Oliver had sent them as a way of apologising for believing — even briefly — that I might have been having an affair.

'He's not feeling guilty, is he?' Saskia watched as I drew out a small envelope with my name printed on the front. 'The last time my boyfriend bought me flowers, it was because he'd forgotten my birthday.'

'You forgave him?'

'Yes, because he'd tucked a ring inside the flowers, and asked me to marry him.' Saskia's voice radiated happiness, and a dreamy smile illuminated her face.

I glanced at the rose-gold diamond ring on her left hand. 'That's nice,' I said, thinking it sounded a bit unimaginative

— but what did I know? Oliver hadn't proposed as such but had looked into my eyes across the table in my kitchen one evening — we'd been seeing each other for about three months and he'd practically moved in, desperate to escape his mother's house — and said, 'I can't wait to marry you, Nell.' To me, it had been perfect.

'There must be lots of vases in the warehouse,' Saskia was saying as I took out the card inside the envelope. 'I can go and find one if you like.'

I didn't answer, as I read the simple message printed in black font inside the card.

I love you XX

'Hang on, don't tell me it's someone's birthday?'

I spun round as Oliver materialised, his hair ruffled by the wind outside. He was smiling, ridiculously handsome in the shabby office.

'Thanks so much for these.' I waved the card, hoping he'd come to tell me he knew I hadn't been the intended recipient of those silly texts. 'It was thoughtful of you.'

'I thought it was about time I met your new recruit.' His smile had dimmed as he took in the flowers dangling from my hand. 'I didn't send you those.'

'What?' Mindful of how he'd reacted to the phone messages, I shook my head. 'Are you sure?' I said, stupidly. 'Nobody else would send me flowers.'

'Maybe they *are* from my boyfriend,' Saskia butted in, as if sensing a change in the atmosphere. 'He's romantic like that, always leaving little gifts for me, and of course he knows I work here.'

I looked at her doubtfully. 'Do you think?'

Seeming to pick up on my desperation, Saskia nodded. 'They'll be from Alex,' she said with conviction. 'They're my favourite roses.'

'Lucky you.' Oliver seemed to take her words at face value. 'Maybe you should go and put them in water.'

'I'll do that.' She stood up, seeming suddenly shy as she glanced at him through her lashes. *The Oliver effect.* I felt a bit sorry for her. *He's only human,* I wanted to say. *Flawed, like the rest of us.* 'Nice to finally meet you, Mr Cosgrove.'

'Please, call me Oliver.' He strode forward to shake her hand. Her smile was small and cool, and she didn't meet his eyes. 'How is it going so far?'

'Early days, but fine.' She glanced at me with an expression I interpreted as *help.* Taking her cue, I stepped forward and handed her the flowers. 'Would you put them in the sink in the kitchen, please?'

She took them and nodded, rushing away without a backward glance, seeming less assured than she had before Oliver turned up.

For a second, I thought he was going to challenge me about the flowers, link them with the texts, but then he shook his head. 'Sorry I disappeared like that.' He reached for my hands. 'I'm not exactly covering myself in glory at the moment.'

'I'm glad you're here.' I let him kiss me, trying not to think about whether the bouquet really had been intended for me. 'And I'm pleased you've met Saskia. She's been a godsend. It will make such a difference to my workload. I'll be able to come home earlier and things will get better, I know they will.'

'Great.' His enthusiasm sounded forced. *Didn't he want me home earlier?* 'I'll make more of an effort too.'

'Listen,' I said, impulsively. 'Why don't you invite the girls round for dinner tomorrow evening.'

He gave me a narrow look. 'Are you sure?'

'It'll be good,' I said brightly. 'I'll cook my special curry, let them see another side to me.' A side that would look like I was competing with their mother, no doubt. Even so, it was about time. 'Will you invite them for me?'

After a brief hesitation, he nodded and switched on a smile. 'Thanks, Nell.' He leaned in and pressed a kiss on my cheek. 'I'll text Ruby now. She'll persuade Poppy, she listens to her sister.'

'OK.'

He turned to leave, and I watched him go, already regretting the invitation. Oliver's daughters hated me, and I had a feeling that no amount of chicken curry was going to change that.

CHAPTER 6

Ruby

> *Hi Ruby. I'm afraid we've found someone in this afternoon's auditions for the part. Letting you know, as we didn't want to waste your time. Best wishes, Sarah, Flutter Theatre Company.*

Ruby slumped down on her bed, flopped her head against the pillow, and closed her eyes. It was only a small role with a tiny theatre company on a London back street, and yet she couldn't even get as far as the auditioning process.

Tears stung her eyes. Was she even capable of getting back on the stage? Despite sticking to a strict exercising regime over the past few years, Ruby knew she was no longer as flexible and fit as she once was. Did she need to rethink her future? Abandon her dream.

A tear escaped. Rolled, cold against her skin, and into her hair. Memories swirled. She'd worked so hard since she was a child, her parents always so proud of her. At first, from the age of seven, she'd attended a weekend performing arts academy, joining full-time when she left school. It had been gruelling, but she'd loved every moment, getting a BA with honours in musical theatre by the time she was twenty-one.

When she then moved out of her childhood home, she'd landed some minor parts in big productions and things had looked promising. By the time she was twenty-three she'd had call-backs for big parts. It was only a matter of time before one of those roles would be hers. But then everything had gone so wrong, and she'd returned home.

She dragged herself up and swung her legs round the bed, wiped away the tears. It was old news that this was Nell's fault — but it was. Nell hadn't only stolen Ruby's dad, she'd stolen her dream — her future. And not only that, she'd messed up Poppy's head, and turned Fiona into a faded, crumpled version of the mother they once knew.

Her phone pinged. A WhatsApp message from her dad to the group 'Us' appeared on the screen. Poppy had set up the group a while back, for her, Oliver and Ruby.

She was about to open the message, when the phone rang.

'Have you seen it?' Poppy yelled down the phone. 'The message from Dad.'

'I was about to—'

'Nell wants us to go to Marlow for a meal.'

'What? You're joking.'

'No. It's for real. We're to go tomorrow. She's cooking a curry. What the hell is she thinking? Does she really believe we'd want to go to her house and play happy families?'

Ruby took a deep breath. 'But they're having counselling. Which means their relationship is on the rocks. She'll be out of the picture soon. Why would she—?'

'Maybe she thinks if she can get in with us, Dad won't leave her?' Poppy let out a cruel laugh.

Ruby closed her eyes. The thought of spending an evening with Nell and her dad was the stuff of nightmares.

'I think we should go,' Poppy said, slyness in her tone.

'Really? But—'

'We can mess with her, Ruby. Don't you see? We can make things so much worse.' Poppy laughed again. 'Dad doesn't need to know what we're up to. We can be all like super-nice to her face when Dad's about, and then, bam!'

Despite Ruby's moral compass telling her to keep away, to not encourage her troubled sister, she couldn't help being tempted. Surely making things difficult for her wouldn't be so bad. Nothing too serious: just a few games to tip the marriage fully into the danger zone. She wouldn't go too far. Wouldn't let Poppy get out of hand. 'OK.'

'Great. Let's tell Dad we'll be there. Shall I message him?'

'OK.'

'Brilliant! So are you heading to your audition now?'

'It got cancelled. To be honest, I'm gutted.'

'Oh, I'm so sorry, Rubes. There will be others though, right?'

'I hope so. I love Benita, but delivering sandwiches isn't exactly my dream job.' She looked across at the chocolate hamper she'd put on her dresser earlier. 'And there's something else. It's Sean.'

'Sean? What about him?'

'He's left me a chocolate hamper.'

'Hotel Chocolat?'

'Yep.'

'Oh God, that's what he used to buy you all the time.'

'I know, and it's unnerved me a bit, if I'm honest.'

'I'm not surprised. But I thought he was over you, was dating Janine's daughter, Vikki.'

'I thought so too. It doesn't make sense. He hasn't done anything like this for ages.'

Ruby had met Sean at Classic Props when her dad still owned the place. He'd taken a liking to her, but things soon became claustrophobic. When she ended things, he hung about the house, leaving gifts, typically her favourite chocolates, with notes saying he would always love her. When her father stepped in, he'd backed off.

'Maybe it's because you've left home.'

Her sister had voiced her worst fear, and a chill ran down Ruby's spine, a lump rising in her throat at the thought of Sean starting up his old tricks again.

'Are you OK?' Poppy's voice had taken on a serious tone.

'Yeah, yeah, of course.' But she felt far from it. The whole thing was unsettling her.

Once they'd signed off their call, Ruby slipped on her jacket. She needed to put a stop to Sean's ridiculous game before it got out of hand. It was only 6.30 p.m. He would still be at work. She would catch him in the warehouse. Have it out with him.

* * *

Once at Classic Props, Ruby climbed from her car, and approached the building. She knew the door code — it hadn't changed since her dad was there — so pressed the numbers into the keypad, and let herself in. Reception was in darkness, dim spotlights lighting the curved staircase leading to the offices. Nell would be at home by now.

Ruby made her way through the double doors into the warehouse, where the lights were on. Sean should be about somewhere.

The place had fascinated her when she was younger: the maze of musty rooms, the historical costumes, jewellery and wigs, the elaborate furniture, light fittings and ornaments, were almost magical. Though it had a creepy vibe too, particularly when nobody was about. She pushed down a doubt that perhaps she shouldn't be here alone. But Sean wasn't dangerous. He was just a nuisance, *wasn't he?*

She made her way through the rooms. Should she call out? Someone must be there if the lights were on.

She continued, passing a suit of armour, a box of colourful feather boas.

Suddenly quick footsteps approached from behind. She swung round to see an unfamiliar face.

'Can I help you?' The woman in front of her was wearing black trousers and a grey silky top, her light-brown hair tied up. It was hard to judge her age, perhaps a few years older than Ruby.

Ruby's heart pounded, she could feel it throbbing under her fingers as she gripped her chest. 'I'm Ruby,' she said, slightly breathless.

The woman's eyes widened behind her glasses, 'Ruby,' she said, as if she'd heard the name before. 'Oliver Cosgrove's daughter?'

'Yes. My dad used to jointly own the place. I'm looking for Sean.'

'Oh. Well, he went home a while back. Had a date with his girlfriend, I believe.' She held out a slim hand. 'I'm Saskia French. I've just started as Nell's assistant.'

'Oh, OK.' Ruby took her hand. Why would perfect Nell need an assistant? She was the type who liked doing things herself. 'Nice to meet you,' she said, though it was just a line. This woman meant nothing to her.

Saskia released Ruby's hand. 'Nice to meet you too.'

'Is Nell still here?'

'No, I said I would stay on and lock up.' She lifted a bunch of keys, and smiled. Things must be slipping if Nell was letting a stranger lock up.

'Right.' Ruby felt suddenly awkward. The woman seemed to be drinking her in, wouldn't avert her stare. 'Well, I'll leave you to it then.'

As Ruby headed for the exit, she knew she would still have to face Sean sooner or later. But why if he was out with his girlfriend, would he be sending Ruby chocolates?

* * *

Ruby picked up Poppy at seven the following evening. Her sister had barely made an effort, wearing her usual black jeans and hoodie, a flash of black eyeliner around her eyes.

'Have you told Mum where we're going?' Ruby asked as she pulled away, seeing her mother's outline in the downstairs window, and trying not to feel guilty. They weren't going to Marlow to try to bond with Nell, like their father seemed to want, but rather to damage their relationship further if possible. But she didn't want to tell her mother that. It would only get her hopes up.

'I thought it best she didn't know.' Poppy sniffed. 'You know what she's like.'

'Agreed.' The memory flashed up of how her mum was the last time she saw her — obsessed with their father, still refusing to meet up with her friends. In fact, most of her friends had disappeared. Tired of her talking non-stop about Oliver, tired of her refusal to go out, move on. A few had stayed around, saying they were there if needed, though Fiona hadn't called them. And the sociable set, her parents were once part of, were getting on with their lives without her.

'Dad and Nell will be history soon, and things will be as they should be,' Poppy went on. 'Dad will move back, and . . .'

Ruby glanced at her sister. 'And what?'

'Nothing. Just things will be good again. You know. Like they once were.'

Ruby placed a hand on her sister's arm, not sure she could fully remember how things had been between her parents after she'd left home. 'I really hope so.'

It was a forty-five minute drive from Richmond-on-Thames to Marlow, and they spent most of the journey listening to George Ezra, barely speaking until they pulled up outside Nell and Oliver's house, overlooking the river.

'Here we are then.' Ruby pulled on the handbrake, and stared out at the bay-fronted window ablaze with amber light. She'd seen the house before. Drove down to look where her father had set up home with his new wife. The sisters had found excuses not to visit in the past, and their dad had never pushed the issue, perhaps worried how they would react in Nell's company. It seemed strange he was inviting them now — now the couple were having counselling. Did he really think inviting her and Poppy round for dinner would help? Perhaps he hoped they would like Nell if they got to know her, and that part of his world would become easier.

But the thought of her dad inside laying the table or opening a bottle of wine, as Nell cooked, made Ruby's heart race with anxiety. Made her feel sick. He should be at home with their mother, making plans the way they used to.

'Showtime!' Poppy threw open the door, and climbed out of the car.

Ruby reached over to the backseat and grabbed the bottle of red wine Poppy had taken from their mum's cellar. She smiled, knowing their dad had let it slip a while back that Nell was allergic to red wine, that her sister had picked it out to annoy her.

She took a deep breath, and got out of the car, her eyes flicking over the house, over her father's vintage Saab on the cobbled drive.

Let the games begin.

CHAPTER 7

Nell

It was almost 7.45 p.m., and my nerves were jumping. Oliver was upstairs in the shower, happy both girls had accepted his invitation to dinner.

'It's going to be fine,' he'd said that morning in bed, waggling his phone at me. 'They wouldn't make the effort if they didn't like you, would they?'

It was frustrating that he didn't see how things really were. All the excuses they'd made for not visiting before, not even attending the housewarming Oliver insisted on throwing after we moved in, inviting our neighbours to a BBQ in the garden. *Too busy, sorry*. Or *Mum's not well.* I'd tried to put myself in their shoes — imagine how I would have felt if Dad had left Mum and married a younger woman, causing Mum to fall apart with me stuck in the middle — but it was difficult. My parents had had such a great marriage and I was certain that if they *had* split up and met new people, I wouldn't have behaved in a way that would hurt them. But I reminded myself constantly that we didn't always know how we would react until something happened, so I mostly kept quiet and told myself to give Ruby and Poppy time. *How much time*? Mum wanted to know when I confided in her, but seeing how worried she was, how hard she was trying to move on after Dad's death, I'd brushed her concerns aside and kept my worries buried.

'Something smells delicious,' Oliver called from the landing, as if he didn't know exactly what I was cooking.

'Hope it tastes as good,' I called back, grabbing a wooden spoon. I didn't really enjoy cooking. My chicken curry had been perfected only because I'd made it so many times — my go-to dish. My food loving Dad had taught me to make it one rainy afternoon, when I was stuck at home recovering from flu, and I'd liked the feeling of us doing something together.

I sipped from my glass of white wine as I stirred the sauce, gazing at the pan of simmering rice. It would become a sticky mess if I didn't keep an eye on it. I was glad I'd showered and changed as soon as I got home from work, making an effort — but not too much — with my hair and outfit and smoothing on some make-up, though it felt as if it was already sliding off.

'Keep on being nice,' Saskia had said earlier that day, as if it was the most obvious thing in the world. 'It's hard for people to carry on being rude if you don't react.'

'I'm trying. I've even got their favourite beers in, but I doubt it'll help. I can almost cope when they're rude. It's when they act as if I'm not there, it's hard. They won't let me in, let me get to know them as people.' I'd been surprised to find myself confiding in Saskia — even confessing about the marriage counselling the day before — but there had been something liberating about explaining to someone who wasn't invested, who didn't know the players. Saskia had asked if I was OK after noticing me staring blankly at my computer as I tried to decide on the best way to deal with Ruby and Poppy that evening, unable to ignore the uneasiness I'd felt since Oliver confirmed they were coming. 'I know stepfamilies sometimes struggle to get on,' I'd said, trying to play fair, 'but it does cast a shadow, and I'm sure it's partly why Oliver is reluctant for us to have a baby, even if he won't admit it.'

'You want a baby?' She'd sounded surprised.

'I know he's a lot older than me, and his daughters are grown-up so he's done the "fatherly" thing, but I always thought we would have children of our own. He's made it clear now that he doesn't want any more.' To my horror, tears had sprung to my eyes. 'God, listen to me. What must you think? I'm sorry.' I flapped a hand in front of my eyes. 'I promise I'm not usually this unprofessional.'

'No, no. It's fine. I understand.' Saskia's face had flushed pink. 'I'm . . . we're trying for a baby, so I get it.' I looked at the way her hand automatically moved to her midriff and, seeming suddenly awkward, she moved it away. 'Sorry, that was insensitive of me.'

'Not at all.' I made an effort to pull myself together after that, reminding myself I was her boss, that she was my new assistant — not a friend — but she tilted her head, and with a small frown, said, 'I know it's none of my business, but . . . you're not thinking of getting pregnant to keep him, are you? I mean, without him knowing?'

My laugh was more a cry of shock. 'God, no! I would never do that,' I assured her, wondering what impression I must be making. 'That sort of deception would be . . . well, it's unacceptable. I wouldn't want my husband to stay with me because I was pregnant, and it would hardly be fair on a baby.'

'No, of course not.' Saskia adjusted her glasses, flashing me an unreadable look. 'I had a friend do that once and it was the end of them, that's all.'

'Well, nothing like that is going to happen. We're going through a rough patch, that's all, and I'm certain we'll be fine.'

Saskia opened her mouth as if to comment, then closed it again. She was probably thinking that if a couple had reached the counselling stage after less than three years of marriage, they were doomed. The thought had crossed my mind too, but I wouldn't let it settle, recalling instead my wedding day and the light in Oliver's eyes as he held my hands outside the registry office and told me I'd made him the happiest man in the world. My mum had snapped a photo at that point, which we'd had enlarged and framed. I briefly wondered now whether I should take it off the living room wall in case it upset Ruby and Poppy.

'Don't be ridiculous,' I muttered to myself, almost leaping out of my skin when the doorbell pealed through the house. It was too late now, anyway.

Oliver tripped lightly downstairs to answer the door, flinging me a smile as he passed the kitchen. My heart thundered as though his daughters were police officers about to arrest me.

'Hey, gorgeous girls!' he greeted them, his voice warm with affection.

I realised I'd been hoping they wouldn't turn up and, chiding myself, reached for my half-empty wine glass then put it down. I'd already drunk more than usual for Dutch courage. I couldn't afford to make a fool of myself. It was a good sign his daughters were here, that they hadn't cried off at the last minute. Despite my misgivings, I was going to make the most of it; turn things around. Not let them get to me as Saskia had suggested.

Funny how neither of us had mentioned the flowers turning up at the office. Perhaps she hadn't wanted to risk upsetting me. They were still in the sink when I'd turned up for work that morning, already wilting, so I knew they couldn't have been from her fiancé or she would have taken them home, and I didn't want to think about what that meant, so I'd dropped them in the wheelie bin outside and pushed them from my mind.

As the girls murmured something I couldn't hear that made Oliver laugh, I took a deep breath and turned down the heat under the pans. I wished my hands would stop trembling. I was a grown woman for God's sake.

About to leave the kitchen, I paused, catching a movement to the side of the double doors that opened onto the patio, as if someone had slipped out of sight. But that was silly. To get round the back of the house, they would need to come round the side and through the tall wooden gate we kept locked from the inside. Either that or sneak up the long garden that led from the river or climb over our neighbour's wall. Surely I would have noticed?

I gasped as something slid into sight. A pair of startled green eyes looked in at me, surrounded by shiny black fur. *A cat.* I'd seen it before, stalking birds in the garden, but didn't know who it belonged to. I let out a long breath, shaking my head.

'Would you like a drink?' Oliver was saying, his voice coming closer. In a nervous rush, I hurried to the fridge and flung open the door, reaching for the pack of beers he'd put there for the girls. *They love this stuff*, he'd said with a trace of disapproval. He only ever drank wine or whisky, which they weren't fans of. Neither was I. Oliver had been disappointed to discover I was allergic to the tannins in red wine and never touched the stuff.

The beer wasn't in the fridge. I turned to see Oliver entering the kitchen, adopting what I hoped was a look of friendly expectancy in case Ruby and Poppy had followed, but he was alone. 'I thought we had some beers.'

'We did.' He came closer and peered past me, his aftershave competing with the cooking smells in the kitchen. 'That's weird.' He scanned the empty shelf, smile melting into a frown. 'Did you move them?'

'Why would I do that?'

'Well . . . I don't know.'

It wasn't the first time something in the house had disappeared or been moved recently. Nothing serious; rearranged books on the shelf, a photo turned backwards, a jumper I liked, that Oliver had bought me, missing from the bedroom cupboard — it still hadn't turned up. He thought I'd put it somewhere and forgotten. *You might be super-organised at work, but you're absent-minded at home* he'd reminded me, referring to the time I searched the house for my phone, only to find it was in my bag all along.

'Everything OK?' It was Ruby, calling through from the hallway. A trained actress, she knew how to project her voice which was lovely and clear, like a musical note.

My shoulders stiffened. Not having her favourite drink in the house immediately put me at a disadvantage, especially if Oliver started joking about my forgetfulness. To my relief, he winked at me and called back, 'No beer. You'll have to make do with wine or water.'

'Very biblical.' Suddenly she was there, all wide dark eyes and flowing, chestnut hair, a glint of hooped earrings, and smelling of fresh air. Like her father, she was tall and lithe, and beautiful, especially when a smile lit up her face which was flawless, even without make-up. She never normally smiled at me, but now she was. It was like being bathed in sunlight. I blinked, trying to rearrange my expression. How did she manage to look so good in simple black leggings and a long T-shirt with a heart on the front, a big khaki jacket thrown over the top, and her feet bare? Oliver must have asked her and Poppy to take off the boots they favoured at the door. 'What about some of this?' She held out the bottle of wine she'd had tucked under her arm. *Red*, I saw with a sinking heart. 'Poppy grabbed it from the cellar at home. Thought it deserved an airing.'

'That's so thoughtful.' Oliver cast me a wary look before taking it from her outstretched hand and studying the bottle. '*Bordeaux*.' He gave an approving nod. Sylvia, his mother, still spent part of the year at the house they owned there. 'Vintage,' he added, narrowing his eyes. 'Still, wine is made for drinking. I'll get the corkscrew.'

Had he forgotten my allergy? Even if I explained, I knew refusing a glass would make me look petty in the eyes of his daughters, as it was hardly life-threatening, just that the tannins brought me out in itchy blotches. Another black mark against me.

'I love the house,' Ruby switched her gaze to me. I felt skewered, like a butterfly under a pin. 'You're so lucky to live here.'

My cheeks burned. *Was it a dig?* I knew how lucky I was. Growing up in a nice but ordinary street in Aylesbury, Marlow had been somewhere we visited during school holidays, feeding the ducks on the river and eating ice-cream while my parents admired the period properties on the opposite side of the Thames. *Imagine living there, with your own boathouse. All that space.* That was Mum, who I knew was perfectly happy where we lived.

And now I lived in one of those homes: The Coach House; eighteenth century, double-fronted, beams and cornices and a remodelled kitchen — a world away from the quirky, small London flat I'd shared with my ordinary, trainee accountant ex-boyfriend. If I was honest, The Coach House felt too grown-up sometimes, its value overwhelming. Not that I'd told Oliver. It made me sound naïve and unappreciative.

'Make yourselves at home,' I said now with a smile, hoping Ruby would take the hint. I needed a moment to regroup — and to stir the rice. 'I'll finish preparing dinner and bring it through to the dining room.' *Where was Poppy?* As if on cue, she wandered in, her narrow face untroubled by a smile. 'I'm starving,' she announced, catching a warning glance from her sister. 'Smells . . . nice,' she added, glaring at the bubbling pan of rice as though it had annoyed her. Poppy was striking, with a mane of long, black hair. Neither girl was blonde like their mother, though Poppy had inherited Fiona's delicate features and arched eyebrows — I'd seen a photo of her online — giving her a vaguely surprised air. She tended to slouch around in black — jeans and hoodies, mainly — sleeves pulled over her hands, perhaps to hide her bitten nails. 'I'm so glad you could come,' I added warmly, encompassing them both as I spoke. Neither replied. 'I hope you like curry.'

'Da-*ad*.' Poppy stretched it to two syllables, like the young child I often pictured her as. 'Can I sit next to you?' As she wound a strand of hair around her finger, I felt a flush of guilt, remembering Oliver explaining that she'd been diagnosed with depression before his break-up with Fiona, and had started self-harming since. Knowing I was partly responsible for her mental health issues was like a knife in my ribs.

'You can sit where you like,' I said gently, turning back to the stove, but not before catching the heavy-lidded look she slid my way, chin jutting forward like a snake about to strike.

'Of course you can sit next to me.' Oliver opened the traditionally corked wine bottle. It made a hollow *pop*. I felt eyes on my back and tried not to squirm with nerves.

'Can we go out on the river sometime, in a boat?' Poppy was asking now.

'Of course,' Oliver said, always eager to do what would make her happy, though I knew that while he liked looking at the water, he didn't much like being on it.

Catching the sunset glow of the river in the distance as they left the kitchen, I wished I was out there right now, but instead I made myself get the plates out of the oven where they were warming, along with a couple of serving dishes. I felt slightly disconnected — as though I wasn't really myself, only playing a part — and tried to think of a topic I could raise at the table that wouldn't offend anyone. At the very least, I could ask how Ruby's auditions were going. Oliver had mentioned she was trying to get back into acting.

As I tipped the rice into a bowl — perfectly light and fluffy — wondering what they were talking about while I wasn't there, Oliver came into the kitchen.

'Poppy found this.' Seeing the set of his jaw, the dark look on his face, I felt a sense of foreboding. 'It was on the floor, half under the mat.'

Panic started beating at my temples when I saw what it was: a small card, like the type you send someone to thank them for a gift, the words inside:

> *My darling Nell, I can't wait to be with you forever. You make me so happy. I love you XX*

CHAPTER 8

Ruby

Ruby and Poppy had followed their dad into the kitchen, and now stood either side of him like bodyguards.

'I found it in the hallway.' Poppy's voice was low; her eyes pinned on Nell. 'Are you having—'

'It's not what it looks like.' Nell held the card in trembling hands, her eyes wide as Ruby glanced over her shoulder and read the words:

> *My darling Nell, I can't wait to be with you forever. You make me so happy. I love you XX*

Poppy had taken a while to come into the kitchen when they'd arrived. She'd hovered near the front door scanning a heavy oak unit, picking up Nell's keys, looking at the mail, lifting up ornaments, inspecting them. Ruby had seen her slip something into her pocket. But she hadn't noticed her picking up the card.

Now, Poppy's arms were folded tightly across her chest, face pale, jaw set tense.

The sudden chime of the doorbell sent Nell scurrying from the kitchen, head down like a scolded puppy.

'What's going on, Dad?' Ruby turned to face Oliver. 'Is Nell—?'

'No,' he said, as if he'd known exactly what Ruby was going to ask. He shook his head several times, as though this was all too much. 'She wouldn't,' he continued, but Ruby heard the doubt in his voice, the way he gazed at the door Nell had left through. Ruby couldn't help a burst of hope. She hated the thought of her dad unhappy, but if he broke up with Nell he might come back to her mother.

'Do you want us to go?' Ruby touched his arm, and his eyes sprang open.

'Maybe it's for the best.' He rubbed his hand across his chin. 'Nell and I will need to talk, that much is obvious.'

A noise in the hallway made the three of them turn in unison. Ruby recognised the woman standing next to Nell. Saskia. Nell's assistant.

'Something smells good,' Saskia said with a smile. She was wearing a black jacket, double-breasted with gold buttons and dark trousers. 'I've clearly caught you when you're about to eat, so I won't keep you.' She turned to Nell. 'I thought you might miss your phone.'

'I would have, thank you.' Nell turned her work iPhone over in her hands. There was no longer any sign of the ominous card. It was as though she'd done a magic trick, and made it disappear. 'I seem to be super forgetful at the moment, I don't know why.'

'Overworked,' Oliver said, his tone blunt.

Nell turned to Saskia. 'How did you know where I lived?'

'I asked Janine.' She smiled. 'The fountain of all knowledge.'

Janine was that. She'd worked for Classic Props since it first opened, and there wasn't much she didn't know about the business, and all the employees. She hadn't hidden her disapproval when Oliver left Ruby's mother, and things became awkward in the months leading up to Oliver selling his share of the company. Janine couldn't bear men who walked out on their wives. Her husband had left her and their daughter Vikki for a younger woman, and she couldn't believe Oliver had done the same thing to his family. The two never got on the same after that, and Janine even talked about leaving the company. But when Oliver sold up, Janine stayed, seeming to accept Nell as more a victim of a philandering man than a deliberate marriage-wrecker.

There was an awkward silence for a few moments, before Saskia shrugged. 'Well, I'd better head off, leave you guys in peace.'

'No, stay, have a glass of wine.' Nell rushed to get the bottle of red that the girls had brought with them, and splashed it into a glass, sploshing some over the worktop.

'Hey, careful,' Poppy said. 'That's expensive stuff.'

Hand still shaking, Nell pushed the glass towards Saskia, who took it, her eyes widening. Did Nell really think bringing Saskia into the house, forcing her to stay, was going to defuse things?

'So,' Nell went on, high-pitched, slightly manic. 'You've already met my husband, Oliver, and these two beautiful girls are Ruby and Poppy, my stepdaughters.'

Saskia took a sip of her drink, and undid a couple of buttons on her jacket. 'Nice to meet you, Poppy.'

Poppy didn't respond, simply narrowed her eyes and grunted.

'And I've already met Ruby,' Saskia said.

Oliver and Nell darted Ruby a look.

'Only briefly,' Saskia added.

Ruby's heart hammered against her chest. 'I was on my sandwich rounds,' she said, hoping this woman would realise she shouldn't have been inside the Classic Props warehouse and take pity on her.

Saskia stared at her for a few moments. 'Yes, that's right.' She threw Nell a smile.

'Listen, why not go through to the lounge, while I serve up?' Beads of perspiration appeared on Nell's upper lip. The kitchen was far too hot. 'There's plenty here to feed an army. You really must stay, Saskia.'

Oliver looked at Nell, then Saskia. 'Yes, why not?' He sounded resigned, shrugged. 'The more the merrier.'

Ruby furrowed her forehead. Did he want to put off the moment when he had to confront Nell? He'd sounded so sure that they should leave, a moment ago.

'Well, if you're sure,' Saskia said with a smile. 'It does smell good.'

'Of course I'm sure. Ruby would you mind taking Saskia's jacket, please?'

The lounge was a large, comfortable room with oak floorboards, tasteful sofas, and artwork on the walls that Ruby instinctively knew her father had chosen. There wasn't much sign of Nell's influence, except in the soft-focus wedding photo over the fireplace Ruby couldn't bear to look at. Saskia shuffled out of her jacket and handed it to Ruby, who wanted to throw it in a heap in the corner. *Was she Nell's butler now?*

'Your secret's safe with me,' Saskia whispered, as Ruby folded the coat over her arm. It smelled oddly musty, as if it had sat in an antique wardrobe for years.

'Thanks. I appreciate it.' Ruby knew she meant her trespassing. And although she knew Mark probably wouldn't have minded her being on the premises — he always made a fuss of her and Poppy, not having children of his own — she didn't want her dad to know Sean was up to his old tricks. Oliver had made it clear last time, that Sean would lose his job if he didn't leave Ruby alone, and with Nell still working at Classic Props, and Mark a good friend of his, he wouldn't hesitate to follow through with his threat, and that might make Sean worse. No, Ruby wanted to deal with it herself, in her own way, and at least confront Sean first. *I'm not afraid of him*, she told herself, but she knew, deep down, a small part of her was.

· ·

'How are you settling in at Classic Props?' Oliver said, as they served themselves from white dishes in the oak-panelled dining room which had intricate parquet flooring, and a long, shiny table Ruby suspected never hosted more than her dad and Nell. Her father had never been keen on the dinner parties their mother used to enjoy hosting. 'I hope my wife isn't being too much of a tyrant.' He laughed, but his eyes were full of angst.

'Nell's amazing.' Saskia smiled at Nell. 'She's made me feel so welcome. And the job has come at just the right time as my partner and I are trying for a baby.'

'So you're going to go straight onto maternity leave?' Poppy said, shovelling curry onto her fork. 'Bet you didn't know that, Nell.'

'Poppy,' Oliver said, his eyes on Saskia. 'I'm so sorry. My daughter—'

'Don't apologise for me, Dad. I'm only saying it like it is.'

'She has every right to start a family, Poppy,' Nell said.

Saskia turned to Ruby. 'So Nell tells me you're an actress.'

'I let it slip how talented you are.' Nell's tone is defensive, as though afraid she'd said the wrong thing. 'That you almost got a role in *Chicago*.'

'Yes, well, things were going well, until . . .' Ruby couldn't help the glare she threw at Nell.

'So you're hoping to get back to it?' Saskia lowers her cutlery, looks genuinely interested.

'I am yes. I had to give it up.' Ruby stared again at Nell. 'My mum and Poppy needed me after Dad left.'

A silence descended, as though nobody knew how to follow Ruby's revelation, the sound of cutlery clanging against china too loud.

'This is delicious, by the way.' Saskia said eventually. 'Thanks so much, Nell, for inviting me.'

Nell half-smiled. She hadn't touched her food.

Saskia turned to Ruby. 'I have a friend who owns his own theatre company. They're auditioning at the moment. If you're interested, I could introduce you.'

A rush of hope filled Ruby's body. 'That would be brilliant. Thanks.'

'Great. Are you free tomorrow? We could grab a coffee with him perhaps?'

'Amazing.'

'Thanks,' Oliver said, meeting Saskia's eye. He'd been quiet until then, seeming to merely observe the conversation. 'That's very kind of you.'

'No, not at all, Stefan is always looking out for new talent. His company isn't huge. Just a backstreet theatre, but it would be a foot in the door.'

'Is that really what you want, Ruby?' Poppy stabbed a piece of chicken with her fork. 'Surely it's a bit of a come down.'

Ruby's joy was punctured. 'It would be a start. Be happy for me. Please.'

'I am. I think you deserve more, is all.'

'So what do you do?' Saskia asked, turning her gaze to Poppy.

'She's making a living on Twitch, aren't you, darling?' Oliver laughed.

'I've got loads of followers, Dad,' she said. 'Don't take the piss.'

'Of course you have, sweetheart.' He smiled, and turned to Saskia. 'My daughter the influencer.'

Saskia smiled. 'I'm impressed. I couldn't do it, I'm far too self-conscious.'

Ruby placed her hand over her sister's and was about to say something encouraging when she noticed Nell had left the table, her plate untouched. She smiled. It wouldn't be long before she wasn't only gone from the table, but from their lives. She and Poppy just needed to keep nudging until she tipped over the edge.

CHAPTER 9

Nell

'I felt as if I'd walked in on something last night.' Saskia placed a mug of milky coffee on my desk, having finally got to grips with the temperamental machine in the kitchen. She took a step back as though she'd thrown a grenade at me. 'I hope you don't mind me mentioning it.'

'It's fine.' My eyes were gritty with tiredness and a headache was brewing, making it difficult to look at her. 'Poppy found a card I think had been pushed through the letterbox.' It felt good to get it off my chest. 'I didn't know what to say, especially as Ruby and Poppy were there. I'm not sure Oliver believed that I didn't know who it was from, but it's obvious that someone's trying to make trouble between us.'

'What did it say?' Saskia wore a deep frown that made my unease feel justified.

'Whoever sent it apparently can't wait for us to be together.'

'That's so weird.' Saskia shook her head. 'Could it be Oliver's ex, do you think? Maybe she's hoping he'll think you're cheating and go back to her.'

I hadn't considered that Fiona would go to those lengths, but then again, I didn't know her personally. I didn't know exactly what she was capable of. 'But why now?' I said. 'If she was going to do something like that, wouldn't she have done it before now?'

The meal last night had been torturous, knowing Oliver was waiting for everyone to leave so he could confront me, not wanting to do it while his daughters were there and give them something to report back to their mother — though it had been obvious to me that was exactly what would happen. Ruby had barely been able to disguise her glee, and she and Poppy had taken their time with the food, acting as though they loved it, stretching things out while they enjoyed my discomfort. I wasn't that good an actress and could barely force down a mouthful. I'd left the room at one point, certain I was going to be sick, feeling the burn of Oliver's eyes on my back. *Who had sent the card, and how hadn't I seen it sooner?* Poppy must have been thrilled to find it, and I could hardly tell her off for opening it, considering what the envelope had contained. Like the card with the flowers, it was impossible from the writing to guess who had sent it.

Saskia had held things together in the end, making small talk, offering Ruby the chance of an audition through a friend of hers, though Poppy's eyes had darkened further at that. She was deeply attached to her sister, who seemed able to keep her anchored, and didn't like her attention being elsewhere.

Once they'd all left, Saskia squeezing my arm at the door as Poppy hugged her father — throwing me a knifelike stare over his shoulder — Ruby jittering her keys in her hand, Oliver had announced he was tired and was going to bed.

'I honestly don't know who that card is from,' I told him, following him up to our bedroom. 'I don't know what's going on, but I promise I'm not seeing someone else.'

'I want to believe you, of course I do.' He bent to take off his socks. 'I know you're not a deceitful person.'

He was right about that. I was a terrible liar, which made the whole thing all the more ridiculous. As I reached for him, he leaned back, his brow pinched. 'Does the age gap bother you?'

'What?' I stared. 'Oliver, how can you think that? I'm not—'

'You might want a younger man.'

It wasn't the first time he'd referenced our age difference, but in the past it had been a joke, said with a smile that meant he knew it wasn't an issue. Insecurity wasn't one of Oliver's traits. 'I can't believe you're serious.'

'What would you think if it was the other way round and someone was messaging me and sending cards declaring their love?'

'I would think there had to be another explanation.' A week or so ago, someone had called Oliver's mobile while he was in the shower — a name I hadn't recognised.

'Who's Birdie?' I'd asked when he came out, a towel looped around his waist, his body taut and toned from years of playing squash.

For a split second, a look had crossed his face that I hadn't been able to read and a chill passed through me. 'John Bird. He's an old contact of my father's, a wine producer in Italy.' He grimaced as he ruffled his hair with his hands. 'He wants to know when I'm flying out to sample their new range, but I've been putting it off.'

The look had made sense. He hated talking about his father, who had given Oliver a hard time growing up, always finding fault. 'Sorry,' I'd said, banishing a fleeting image of a young blonde woman secretly calling my husband.

I hadn't questioned him further; hadn't doubted for a second that he was being truthful, and I didn't want him doubting me. *My darling Nell, I can't wait to be with you forever.* I supposed it was a miracle that he wasn't tearing the house down, demanding to know who this person was.

'I think someone's trying to make trouble,' I told him once his socks were off and he was unbuttoning his shirt.

He gave me a puzzled look. 'Who would do that?'

I longed to say I could think of three people — *your daughters and ex-wife* — but couldn't bring myself to voice it. He desperately wanted to believe that Fiona was getting close to accepting he was never going back, and that his daughters wanted him to be happy, even if they didn't do a very good job of showing it.

For a second, I'd thought of Sean and the look on his face when I bumped into him outside the warehouse. What if he thought that driving a wedge between Oliver and me — even breaking us up — would win him brownie points with Ruby, perhaps win her back? But again, saying it aloud would make me sound paranoid, and Sean had moved on with Janine's daughter. 'I don't know,' I said, lamely.

'I believe you, Nell, of course I do.' Oliver held out a hand, but let it fall before I could react. 'Let's sleep on it,' he said, turning his back once I'd climbed into bed, his breath deepening into sleep while I stared at the outline of our bedroom furniture, too upset to close my eyes.

I'd drifted off as daylight crept round the curtains and when I woke and rolled over, Oliver's side of the bed was empty, a trace of his scent on the pillow.

'Why don't I call the florist's and find out who sent those flowers?' Saskia's voice — touchingly eager to help — landed me back in the moment.

I shook my head. 'Thanks for offering, but I doubt they'll have given a name, or that the florist's will give out any information.' I dredged up a smile, realising I'd forgotten to brush my teeth before leaving home. 'Oh, and thanks again for returning my phone last night. I can't believe I didn't realise it was missing.'

'No worries.' The sympathy in Saskia's soft green eyes was hard to look at. 'You've obviously got a lot on your plate at the moment.'

'Do you think I'm having an affair?' I wasn't sure why it mattered what Saskia thought, but it was too late to take back the question.

'No.' Her instant response was so genuine I felt the fizz of tears. If only Oliver was as certain. Despite his reassurances that he believed me, I wasn't sure he meant it. 'I mean, you don't seem the type, and it's obvious you love your husband.' She lowered her gaze. 'I think you have an admirer, that's all, though it is a bit creepy, if I'm honest. Declaring feelings like that when you don't even know who it is.'

'More like a stalker, you mean?' Goosebumps flashed up my arms. 'I hadn't thought of that.' Instinctively, I glanced around, as if whoever it was might reveal themselves, mentally scrolling again through all the men I knew. It would be a man, I was certain. Men generally tended to think all women appreciated flowers. Maybe it was someone I'd spoken to in passing, a client even, that I'd been nice to, and they'd taken it to mean something more. But they would have to be unstable to read anything into a friendly conversation . . . which meant whoever it was could be dangerous.

I suddenly longed to call my mum and tell her what was happening, let her reassure me and talk me down, tell me I was being silly — and if I wasn't, that she would protect me, as she'd always tried to do. But Mum was still getting her life back on track, reconnecting with friends, starting to go out again. I couldn't bear to worry her. 'I'm sorry I dragged you into this,' I said to Saskia, who shook her head, a tendril of hair drifting around her face. She was wearing another smart outfit, a cream shirt buttoned up to her throat.

'No need to apologise.'

'Thank you for being kind to Ruby,' I added, recalling the offer Saskia had made. 'She's desperate to get back to acting.'

'No problem. She and her sister seem . . .' she nudged her glasses with her forefinger, appearing to struggle to find the right words. '. . . a bit troubled,' she finished, frown deepening. 'I'd have thought they would have a strong bond, but they don't even seem to like each other much.'

'Ruby's more the protector,' I said, feeling an urge to defend her. 'It's a lot of responsibility.' Saskia nodded as though she understood. 'But you can see what I mean now about them not liking me being married to their dad,' I added wryly. 'Last night was the first time they'd been round for dinner, and of course it had to go wrong.'

'They obviously enjoyed the food, and I'm sure the more they see you and their father as a unit, they'll grow to accept it.'

I wished I had her confidence. 'How long have you and Alex been together?'

Unfazed by the change of topic, she said, 'Four years,' a smile tilting her lips as she moved back to her desk. 'Don't forget the Mary Queen of Scots-style dress for the Bankside Theatre has to be delivered tomorrow.' Saskia was looking at her computer now, and I was embarrassed and grateful at her attempt to put things back on a businesslike footing. 'Couldn't they pick it up if it's only the one outfit?'

'It's our responsibility. We're the ones with insurance if anything happens to it on the way.' Despite the tightening tension in my stomach, I was determined to concentrate on work, at least for now. Oliver was meeting a customer in Dorset and wouldn't be home until late. There was nothing I could do but carry on as normal — if I could only untangle my thoughts and forget that he'd left for work without a word.

'Oh, and a woman called.' Saskia's head was bent low to read a note, hair gleaming with a hint of gold as sunlight streamed through the window. The recent rainfall had given way to a burst of summery weather. 'Fiona,' Saskia continued, seeming not to notice me freeze in my seat. 'She wanted to speak to you. I said you'd call her back when you got in.'

'Fiona?' I echoed, aware of my uneven breathing. Why was Oliver's ex-wife calling me at work? *Why was she calling me at all?*

'She didn't give her surname, only a number.' Saskia held out the slip of paper, obviously waiting for a response.

I got to my feet, feeling unsteady. 'The only Fiona I know is Oliver's ex-wife,' I admitted, gratified when Saskia's eyes grew wide with horror. 'I'd better make the call outside.'

'Of course,' she said, becoming brisk. 'I'll hold the fort here, don't worry.' The phone was ringing and as she reached to answer it, I picked up my bag and ran downstairs.

Outside, I moved round the side of the building and, under the shade of a plane tree, punched in the number on the paper, wishing I'd at least drunk my coffee first. My mouth was so dry, I struggled to swallow. I blew out a breath to steady myself and jumped when a voice in my ear said, 'Hello?' It was soft and hesitant, as if she was unused to getting calls. 'Is that you, Poppy? Don't tell me you've got another new phone.'

'It's Nell.' I cleared my throat, a pulse beating in my temple. 'You wanted to talk to me.'

'Nell?' She said my name as though it left a bad taste. 'Why on earth would I want to talk to you?'

Surprised by the venom that had entered her voice, I said truthfully, 'I don't know.'

'Isn't it enough that you have my family?' Oh God, she sounded as though she was about to cry. 'I suppose you're not happy about Olly coming around here, doing little jobs, but he offered,' her vowels were clipped. 'I didn't ask him.'

'You called my office.' I wondered whether she'd been drinking. Oliver told me once that she had a habit of adding whisky to her coffee. No point taking issue with her comment about Oliver doing odd jobs for her. *Olly*. He hated his name being shortened. 'What did you want to say to me, Fiona?' Maybe we could have it out, once and for all. Maybe I should have insisted on meeting her three years ago.

'I've nothing to say to you at all,' she snapped. 'I'm working this morning and you dragged me away from a client.' She was an interior designer, or had been before her breakdown. I hadn't been able to resist looking her up, curious to see what she looked like, but didn't glean much from the photo on her website. Straight blonde shoulder-length hair, high-arched brows, good bone structure, and a bland smile that barely crinkled her light blue eyes. A well-preserved forty-seven — two years younger than Oliver. She was the daughter of a friend of his father's, and they'd known each other since their teens. Married too young, according to Oliver. *I didn't know what love was, not really, but our daughters filled the void between us for years*. 'I don't know what game you're playing—'

'I don't play games.' Tiredness stripped away good manners. 'You left a message, I'm calling you back, that's all there is to it. I'm not interested in making life difficult for you or your daughters and would appreciate—'

'Leave my girls out of this,' she practically snarled. 'You have no idea of the damage you've done, have you?'

'Your marriage was over when I met Oliver, but I am sorry for everything you've been through.' I desperately didn't want to be having this conversation, especially now, when my own marriage felt fragile. 'Wouldn't it be better for you and your daughters to try to move on with your life?'

'Our marriage was over, was it?' She huffed out a high-pitched laugh. 'It wouldn't have been if you hadn't turned up. He would have come back to me, I would have forgiven him.'

Tears pushed behind my eyes. 'Look, Fiona, if you called me for a reason, tell me what it is. I'm working too.'

'Of course you are. I bet Olly loves that you're doing so well there,' she said. '*Your* office.' She sniffed. 'That's my husband's office, at the company he helped create and probably regrets leaving. You must know how competitive he is, or haven't you figured it out yet?' She paused, but I had no idea what I was supposed to say. 'Cosgrove Wines was only ever a hobby, but I suppose you persuaded him to take the reins full-time.' Before I could react, she continued in a brighter tone, 'Still, I gather you're having relationship counselling, which doesn't bode well for your future.'

So Ruby had told her. 'Look, whatever you've heard, our marriage—' The line had gone dead. Fiona had hung up. All I could hear was the uneven thump of my heart in my ears.

What was that all about?

I shook my head, as if to dislodge the conversation. Why had she denied calling me? My stomach twisted as I imagined her telling Ruby, who would no doubt tell Oliver. *Why did Nell call Mum this morning? It really upset her.*' Should I tell him first? I tried his number, but it went to voicemail, and I didn't want to leave a message.

About to head back inside, I paused, spotting a Twitter notification on my phone screen. Sometimes companies credited us, linking to our account after a successful show or production to thank us for the props. It was good publicity.

Still shaky, a sourness in my throat, I opened the app and felt my colour drain.

The post at the top of our Twitter page read DO NOT USE THIS COMPANY @ClassicProps @NellCosgrove. The poster was named @*wellwisher123* — no profile photo or followers — and above two images captioned, *what we ordered, what we got* displaying the mix-up with the Regency chairs, were the words *Lost a day's shooting, thanks to these losers. #badservice.*

A quick check of our Facebook page showed they'd posted there too.

Just when I'd thought the day couldn't get any worse.

CHAPTER 10

Ruby

Ruby had arranged to meet Saskia and Stefan at 3 p.m. at a coffee shop just off Leicester Square.

As she headed through the throng of Londoners, past the bronze statue of Mary Poppins, her mind drifted to the night before. The sisters and Saskia had spilled out of the house after the embarrassing evening, and into the cool air. Their father had kissed each of his daughters' cheeks before closing the door, a troubled look on his face. Saskia hadn't wasted a moment chatting to Ruby about her hopes of getting back on the stage, as a bored-looking Poppy had fiddled with her phone.

Once in the car, and heading back to Richmond, Ruby's head had spun with excitement.

'If we can find out who sent those flowers to Nell, and that card,' Poppy said, her fingers dancing on her phone screen, 'we would know who Nell is having an affair with, and then we can break her and Dad up once and for all.'

Ruby had come down with a thump. 'You really think she's having an affair?'

'Don't you?'

Ruby pulled up at a red light, and looked at her sister. 'What did you take?'

'What are you talking about?' Her eyes were dark, heavy as though she hadn't been sleeping, her shoulders hunched into her hoodie.

'I saw you, Poppy. You took something from the cabinet in Dad's hallway.'

'OK. A key, if you must know.' She pulled it from her pocket, laid it on her outstretched palm.

A horn from a car behind made Ruby jump. The lights had turned green. She pulled away with a roar of the engine.

Poppy shoved the key back into her pocket. 'It's to the back door of their house. You never know when it might come in handy.'

'You need to take it back,' Ruby said, indicating and turning a corner.

'No can do, I'm afraid.' She paused for a moment. 'Ruby, if you want Dad to come back to Mum we have to do what it takes. No holds barred. You do get that, right? We've waited long enough.'

'I don't know, Poppy.' Ruby sighed. Her sister was volatile, and she was beginning to fear things were getting out of hand.

'Dad's been coming round to see Mum, lately. Nell's clearly having an affair, and they're going to marriage guidance. We just have to give them that extra push, is all.'

'I guess so,' Ruby had said, but she wasn't sure she meant it.

* * *

Now Ruby headed down Lisle Street, a strange sense of unease washing over her. She stopped, turned quickly to see a face in the crowd she recognised. Sean. What was he doing there? Was he following her? She blinked and he was gone, disappearing into the throng. Had it really been him? Maybe she was mistaken. Why would he be in Leicester Square?

She picked up speed. It was almost three o'clock, and her stomach fluttered with nerves. Reaching the coffee shop, she peered in, spotting Saskia in a window seat looking at a menu.

Ruby pushed the door open, and was greeted by the aroma of coffee and pastries. 'Hey!'

Saskia looked up and threw her a wide smile. 'Great, you made it.'

'Of course.' She slipped off her jacket, hung it on the back of the chair, and sat down opposite Saskia. 'I wouldn't miss this for the world.'

In front of Saskia was a tall thin glass with a slice of lemon and ice cubes bobbing in the top. 'Can I get you a drink? I've only got water, but—'

'An Americano would be great.'

Saskia rose and ordered from the barista, returning to the table with Ruby's drink.

'So what time will Stefan be here?' Ruby asked, glancing out of the window, unsure what to expect from this man.

'I told him quarter past.' Saskia glanced at her watch. 'I thought we could have a quick chat first.'

'Sure. So how do you know Stefan?'

'I think I said last night that we went to university together. He was known as Stephen when we first met, but when he got involved in the amateur dramatics he started calling himself Stefan. We all had stage names back then, that we didn't use again after university.' She laughed, took a sip of her water. 'But he kept his. I knew even then he would do something in the theatre.'

'So you used to act?'

'Yes, for a while at uni. Stefan put on some fairly big productions back then.'

'But you didn't carry on.'

She shook her head. 'You know yourself how hard it is, and I didn't have that burning ambition you have.' She took another sip of her drink. 'You'll love Stefan. He's extrovert and flamboyant. You know the type?'

Ruby nodded. 'So what's the name of his theatre company?'

'Stefan Andrew's Theatre Company.' She smiled, eyes shining behind her glasses. 'I know, not very original. It's in Islington, a lovely little theatre. I've been a couple of times, and the productions are amazing. I believe they're auditioning at the moment for an interpretation of an Agatha Christie novel. Is that something you'd be interested in?'

'God yes.' Truth was, Ruby would have taken anything — anything to get her foot back on the London stage. She took a large gulp of her coffee, lubricating her dry throat.

'I left Nell in a bit of a state,' Saskia said, her voice reduced to a whisper. 'If I hadn't been meeting you, I would have stayed. I felt quite sorry for her. She was almost in tears.'

Ruby widened her eyes. 'About last night?'

Saskia shook her head. 'No, someone's put some awful reviews on social media.'

'About Classic Props?'

Saskia nodded. 'She was so upset, I really felt for her, as the jibes seemed to imply she'd got something wrong.'

'Don't feel sorry for her, Saskia.' Ruby sometimes shocked herself how cruel she sounded. But this was Nell — Nell who'd ruined everything. 'She's brought it all on herself.'

'I can tell you and Nell have a long way to go before you call a truce. But I think she'd love to make things work with you and . . .' Saskia's eyes drifted to the window, her forehead furrowing. 'Is that Sean from Classics?'

Ruby spun round in her chair, to see Sean approaching the restaurant with long confident strides, his legs encased in narrow jeans, ripped at the knee. He lifted his hand in a wave. 'Crap. What's he doing here?'

Saskia moved her eyes from the window, focused them on Ruby. 'What's wrong? Are you OK?'

Ruby shuddered as the door was flung open. 'Sean's my ex,' she whispered. 'Things didn't end well between us.'

Suddenly he was by the table, pressing his body up against it. His close proximity, the familiar scent of his aftershave, sent a chill down Ruby's back. 'So, what's this about?' he said, looking at Saskia.

'Sorry?'

He moved his gaze to Ruby, who had slipped down in her seat, as though the action would make her invisible. 'Hey, Ruby, how are things?'

Her mind drifted to the chocolates left outside her flat. She opened her mouth and closed it again. Now wasn't the time.

Sean's eyes returned to Saskia. 'Reception said you wanted to see me. Something about an urgent delivery?' He sounded so plausible, so friendly.

Saskia shook her head. 'I don't know anything about that. Someone must have made a mistake.'

He looked back at Ruby, then to Saskia. 'Reception said you'd called, that you needed me to take a tiara to Bransfield Productions urgently for filming late afternoon. To collect it from here.'

'I know nothing about it, Sean.' Saskia sounded irritated. 'As I say, there must be some sort of mistake.'

Sean's pale green eyes fixed on Ruby for some moments — eyes she'd once found attractive, but now felt invasive.

'I could murder a coffee,' he said.

'I would invite you to join us, but we're about to meet someone,' Saskia said.

Sean's kept his eyes on Ruby. 'Well, maybe another time, aye?' He finally turned, left the coffee shop, the door slamming closed behind him.

'That was weird.' Saskia looked relieved he'd gone. 'He's a bit odd isn't he?'

Ruby watched as he dragged his fingers through his fair hair as he walked away, disappearing into the crowd. He still made her uneasy, and her heart thudded against her ribs. How had she thought she loved him once? 'Sean's always been a bit . . .' She pulled her gaze from the window, her eyes meeting Saskia's. 'Unnerving.'

Saskia placed her hand on Ruby's. 'Do you fancy a muffin or something? Another coffee? Stefan often runs late, but I'm sure he won't be long.'

Ruby ordered coffee and cake, and as she returned to the table the door opened and a tall, slim man in his twenties with a mass of curly dark hair flounced in wearing a red and black checked suit. 'Sassy, love,' he cried, air-kissing Saskia's cheeks. 'It's so good to see you.'

The next twenty minutes went by in a whirlwind. Stefan, not eating or drinking, but talking fast and furiously — his hand gestures so dramatic Ruby had to duck a couple of times — told her everything she needed to know about his theatre company, suggesting she swung by for an audition.

'Well, I should go,' he said, finally. 'It was great to meet you, Ruby.'

He smiled at Saskia, put his hand on her arm, before glancing down at the engagement ring on her finger. 'You will call me if you need me, darling, won't you?' he said. 'In fact, I'll pop round one evening for a catch-up. Are you still at 2 Devlin Court?'

'I am indeed.' She touched his cheek. 'I know you're always there for me, darling, and I'm grateful for that.'

'And that was Stefan,' Saskia said with a smile, once he'd risen and leapt through the door and away, yelling, 'Toodles, lovelies.'

'Well, he isn't stereotypical at all.' Ruby watched him disappear into the London throng. He'd left her with a time and date for an audition, promising to give her his full attention. 'He's great,' she added, turning to Saskia. 'Thanks so much for introducing me, I really appreciate it.'

'You're welcome. I hope it pays dividends. He's a good bloke. And if you're as amazing on stage as your father said you are, I'm sure he'll snap you up.'

'And Dad isn't biased at all,' Ruby said with a laugh.

Once they'd finished their drinks, Saskia rose, 'I'd better get back, Nell will wonder where I've got to.'

'You like her, don't you?' Ruby said, rising too, and holding open the door.

'I do, yes. I know you've got issues with her and I understand why, but she's been nothing but nice to me.'

They headed down the road towards the tube station, pushing through the crowds. 'You saw the flowers, didn't you? Have you any idea who sent them?' Ruby asked.

Saskia shook her head. 'There was no name on the card.'

'It's just Poppy and I are so worried about Dad. We love him so much, and we don't want to see him hurt. I know this is a big ask, but can you let me know if you see anything suspicious, any signs Nell is seeing someone else?'

'Of course, but I think you're worrying over nothing. Nell seemed genuinely shocked by the flowers, and she seems so fond of your father.'

Ruby followed Saskia through the underground barriers. It was true, Nell did seem to love her father, and, even though she didn't like the woman, if she was honest with herself, she didn't seem the sort to cheat — but something was going on, and Ruby needed to find out what.

CHAPTER 11

Nell

'How did it go?' I asked Saskia as she settled at her desk, half-wishing it had been me meeting Ruby, offering her the chance of an audition. In the past, Oliver — and even Mark — had used their theatre contacts to get her seen for roles, but by the time I started at Classic Props, Ruby was working for the catering company and taking care of her sister and their mother. Even if I'd offered my help when she decided to resurrect her career, I knew she wouldn't have accepted it.

'It went well.' Saskia nodded decisively. 'Stefan seemed impressed with her.'

'That's good.' I squashed a pang of envy. Ruby would never go out of her way to impress me. Not that I wanted her to. A friendly word would have done.

'Thanks again for letting me take a late lunch.' Saskia's smile was replaced by a worried frown. 'Stefan's hours are a bit erratic, but I wanted to be there to introduce them.'

'You did explain, and it's absolutely fine. Don't give it another thought. I'm glad things might be looking up for Ruby.' In truth, once Saskia had rushed out, I'd been too busy with damage limitation to think about their meeting.

I'd called Sally at Finlay Productions to apologise once more for the mix-up with the Regency chairs, but she'd seemed bemused when I mentioned the Twitter post.

'No one here would do something like that,' she said. 'I told you at the time that I understood you'd made a mistake, and your delivery guy, Sean, swapped the chairs in the end.' Her tone had been sharp, as though I'd accused her personally.

Pressing my fingers to my forehead, I said, 'I know, I'm sorry, it's . . . posts like that can be very damaging.'

'I get it, Nell, but I'm telling you, I can't think of a single person here who would bother posting something mean like that. Apart from anything else, we're too busy to be trolling people online.'

It just seemed odd that *@wellwisher123* knew about the mix-up with the chairs. 'Anyone new there, passing through?' I said. 'Someone who might stir up trouble?'

'We're a tight team here, Nell. You know that.'

'I do know that, but—'

'For what it's worth, I would look closer to home if I were you.'

'Sorry?'

'There's been a rumour going around that standards there are slipping since Oliver left and Mark retired after his accident.'

The shock of her words felt like a slap. 'Where did you hear that?'

'I can't recall who told me. Who knows how these things start?' Impatience leached into her voice. 'Look, I don't pay attention to that sort of thing. You've never let us down before, at least . . .'

. . . not until the other day. The words had hovered, all the more powerful for remaining unsaid. Glancing through the window, I'd watched Sean push something in the back pocket of his jeans before leaping into his van.

'So, you think that whoever started the rumour might have put up the posts?' Ruby's face slid into my mind. She was harder to read than Poppy, whose attitude was as subtle as a brick, but she clearly wanted me out of their lives for good. Was this a way of showing me in a bad light? An attempt to make Oliver see he'd misjudged me — that without Mark at the helm of Classic Props, I was in danger of ruining the company they'd built together? He might no longer work here, but Oliver still saw it as his and Mark's brainchild.

The only silver lining I could find was that Oliver didn't know about the social media posts and I intended to keep it that way.

After apologising to Sally once more, wishing I hadn't called in the first place, worried they might not use us any more, I called a quick meeting to tell the staff what had happened, reassured by their shock and outrage — apart from Sean, who was presumably out on a job, though I couldn't think what it was.

'We've got your back, Nell, don't worry,' Janine had said, still clutching a pair of silky knickerbockers she'd been repairing, her heartfelt response eliciting nods of agreement from the others 'We'll keep our ear to the ground and let you know if we hear anything.'

I'd sometimes wondered where Janine's loyalties lay — she'd clearly disapproved of Oliver leaving his family and, by association, I'd assumed she disliked me, despite her friendly veneer — but it struck me then that her loyalty was to the company, and to Mark, who had employed her in the first place.

I looked at Saskia and wondered how I was supposed to take a step back from work with all this going on. As if reading my mind, she said, 'I'll try and get those posts taken down.'

'I don't think it's possible. It's the first thing I thought of.'

'Of course.' Her cheeks glowed red. 'I wasn't insinuating—'

'It's fine,' I cut in. 'I'm sorry. It's just . . . this is the last thing I need.'

She nodded briskly, fingers tapping her keyboard as she logged into her computer. 'It's probably best to ignore it all and hope not too many . . . oh.' Saskia's face slackened.

'What is it?'

She swallowed hard.

'Tell me.'

She hesitated, absently picking up a pen. 'A few people have piled in with comments, that's all, and they sound quite personal. Someone's mentioned that you used to work for . . .' Saskia leaned closer to the screen, the brightness blanking her eyes. 'Indigo Weddings?' Her eyebrows formed a question. 'It says here, they went bust after a wedding day disaster. They've tagged you and the owner — the previous owner, I should say. Indigo Weekes?'

Uneasiness slid through my stomach. 'It didn't go bust after a disaster.' My throat strained around the words as bad memories resurfaced. 'Indigo was pregnant with severe morning sickness at the time. The sort where you end up in hospital. I took over that day for her and everything was fine, but the bride didn't understand. She was a bit of a diva, if I'm honest, said it was unprofessional. She wanted Indigo in charge, not me. Anyway, Indigo lost confidence after that and decided to fold the company.' It had been a wrench, losing a job I'd loved. Indigo and I had been friends as well as co-workers, but although we stayed in touch, it had been awkward. She felt bad I was out of work 'because of her' as she put it. Soon, she was wrapped up in motherhood while I was dealing with my father's death and break-up with my then boyfriend. Then I applied for the job at Classic Props and met and married Oliver, who I still hadn't introduced to Indigo. It all felt like a lifetime ago. 'Who even knows all that?' I said, bringing up Twitter on my own computer and glancing at the comments. My queasiness intensified. I instantly recognised the bride who was insisting her day had been spoilt — her profile showed her cheek-to-tanned-cheek with her serious banker husband, her false eyelashes like spider's legs, her lips plumped and pouting — and guessed she'd been alerted by the tag to Indigo, which must have appeared on her feed.

Fortunately, someone called Magdalena had posted underneath:

@IndigoWeekes is a true professional. We were so grateful to find you at the 11th hour and that you pulled together a blissful day we will never, ever forget XX

I remembered that wedding too; the weeping bride-to-be, let down by a wedding planner who vanished with her deposit, and the hours we'd put in to give her a day to remember. She hadn't mentioned me, but it didn't matter — Indigo's name was being dragged through the mud here too, and I was glad someone was defending her.

My heart skipped a beat when I saw that Indigo had 'liked' Magdalena's post. For some reason, I hadn't imagined her being on social media much, but when I clicked on her profile there were plenty of updates featuring baby Arthur's milestones and her joy at being his 'mummy'. A twist of regret that I'd missed out turned to anxiety when I saw I'd had a private notification. I clicked on the message, relief swooping in that it was from Indigo, asking whether I was OK and urging me to get in touch if I wanted to talk.

Miss you, Nell xx

Thanks.

I typed quickly, feeling the tendrils of Saskia's curiosity.

Things are a bit weird at this end. Sorry you've got involved.
I'll try to close it down. Hope you're all well xx

'Indigo reached out to me,' I told Saskia, resisting an urge to defend myself to the Twitterati, knowing it would only make things worse. 'She seems fine.'

'That's good. I've contacted Facebook and they've promised to take down the post there.'

'That's brilliant, thank you,' Saskia's words brought another flood of relief. 'Let's hope that's the end of it.'

'You have that local newspaper interview coming up the day after tomorrow.' Saskia glanced at her screen once more. 'It'll be a chance to show how good you are.'

I'd almost forgotten about it; arranged months ago, a piece about women in business, specifically unusual industries. It would appear online as well as in the paper, and a photographer would be coming to take pictures. Saskia was right. It was an opportunity to show the company in a great light, and when I emailed Mark, he'd been childishly enthusiastic, requesting I mention the company's origins, though the information had been out there for years already. 'Thanks for reminding me,' I said, half-wondering whether to make an appointment to have my roots done.

'So, you were a wedding planner before?' Seeming grateful she'd been of help, Saskia gave a tentative smile, twirling the pen she was holding. 'Your wedding day must have been spectacular.'

'It was small.' I switched screens to check the diary myself, keen to move on. 'But perfect,' I added quickly, guessing she'd hoped to hear more. 'Neither of us wanted a big fuss, it being Oliver's second marriage.'

'I want the full works.' Saskia rested her chin on her palm, her dreamy demeanour at odds with her previous, businesslike persona. 'I know it's old-fashioned these days, but I only intend to marry once, and I want it to be a magical day.'

'I'm sure everyone only intends to marry once.' It came out so sharply that Saskia flinched. 'Sorry, but a marriage is about more than the wedding day.' I tried to soften the words with a smile. When Oliver had said it should just be the two of us, no fuss, no worry, no stress, I'd joked *That's what wedding planners are for. I could plan a special day for us in my sleep, with all the trimmings. It wouldn't have to be stressful.*

I want our focus to be on us and our future, not on whether someone's aunty is going to be furious at being left out, or whether the bridesmaids are happy with their dresses. You and me, Nell. We don't need anyone else.

I knew it was really because his daughters refused to be there, a fact I was upset but not surprised by, considering their opinion of me, though I'd hoped they would make the effort for Oliver's sake.

'It suited me anyway because my father couldn't walk me down the aisle.' I paused, the grief I'd felt pulling at my chest as I remembered Mum's bittersweet tears and the absence of Dad at her side. 'It's only a piece of paper at the end of the day.'

'I suppose.' Saskia sounded oddly disapproving and I stifled a twinge of guilt.

'Did Ruby say anything about me this afternoon?' I hated myself for asking.

'I didn't tell her about the phone call you got from her mother,' Saskia said quickly. So she'd guessed it was *that* Fiona, probably from the look on my face when I returned to the office afterwards, though apart from offering a sympathetic wince, she hadn't probed for details. I'd decided not to mention it to Oliver and deal with the fallout when Fiona told him herself, which she undoubtedly would. 'And no, Ruby didn't say anything.' It was clear from her tone that Saskia was lying. 'I mean . . .' she pursed her lips and shook her head. 'No, it's nothing.'

'Just say it, Saskia.'

She blinked a couple of times at my tone. 'Look, it's obvious that Ruby doesn't trust you, especially after your husband found that card. She . . . well, she asked me to keep an eye out for, you know.' She lowered her voice, her gaze miserable. 'For signs you're having an affair.'

'Oh no.' My chest felt tight. 'I'm going to have to speak to Oliver.'

Saskia shook her head, strands floating from the clip holding her hair back. 'I've no intention of spying on you and reporting back, Nell. I don't think you should say anything to your husband. That's what she wants, don't you see? To cause trouble.'

I had to admit she was right. By bringing up Ruby's request to spy on me, I would be playing into her hands.

Even if Saskia backed me up, Oliver might take Ruby's side if she denied it — which she would. What with the flowers and the texts, the card, and the marriage counselling, and now the sense that even at work things were getting away from me . . . I let out a groan and slumped in my chair. It felt as if my life was collapsing in on itself.

'If it will help, I'll tell her that nothing's going on.' Saskia's voice was gentle. 'In fact, I'm going to do my best to get her on side, to see you for the lovely person you are.'

'You don't have to do that,' I said. 'I appreciate it, believe me, but that's not what you're here for.'

'I'm here to help, aren't I?'

'Yes, and I'm lucky to have you.' I was overwhelmed with gratitude that here, at least, people were on my side. *But how had it come to this?* 'Oh, by the way, do you know what Sean's up to? I saw him going out earlier, but he didn't say where.'

'Actually, he turned up at the restaurant.' Frowning slightly, Saskia smoothed a strand of hair off her face. 'He said reception called, told him I needed to speak to him about a job.'

'Really?' That didn't make sense. I rose to my feet, peered outside and saw that the van was back. 'I'll have a word with him. I need to sort out that costume for the theatre drop anyway.'

Grateful to have something to do, I made my way down to the warehouse, past stands of period furniture, old fireplaces and lamps, Persian rugs, and shelves of old books, to where the period costumes were kept in boxes, wrapped in acid-free tissue paper, only a couple — a velvet royal-blue waistcoat and tuxedo and a ruffled, dusky pink ball gown — displayed on tailor's dummies. I never tired of walking around the place, of the slightly musty smell, of seeing the displays — bygones from a former age — waiting to be used once more, be brought to life. At first, I used to accompany Oliver when he scoured antique shops for finds, learning what to look for and how much to pay, and spent long evenings searching eBay too. Lately, I hadn't had as much enthusiasm for it, concerned that the time it took was time not spent on my marriage, or with Oliver, worried that now it was no longer a pastime we shared it was driving us apart.

I should train Saskia — if Mark agreed — yet the thought made me itchy and somehow resentful; like a child forced to give up its favourite toy. *I'm happy the company is in good hands*, Oliver had said when he left, but sometimes I caught his expression when I came home filled with enthusiasm about a new contact, or an antique fair I'd heard about and couldn't wait to visit — as though he missed that side of things, yet when I'd suggested he come with me, he always declined. The wine business needed him full-time.

'Have you come for the Mary Queen of Scots dress?' Janine materialised from behind her antique desk. As well as looking after the costumes, sometimes altering them to a specific fit on her sewing machine, she manned the old-fashioned till for passing trade hiring outfits for upscale fancy-dress parties and events. 'It's good to go, and I've got the shoes ready too.' She nodded at a pair of dainty black satin shoes with a diamond buckle I'd found in a charity shop in Marlow. 'The dress is here.'

She lifted the box carefully, as respectful as if it was a living thing. Remembering she suffered from lower back pain — though the box wasn't heavy — I took it from her. 'Have you seen Sean, by the way?'

Her slim face puckered with worry. 'He came back in a foul mood from wherever he'd been and said he was going home.'

I nodded, careful not to engage in gossip, mindful that he was dating Janine's daughter. 'I wish he'd told me first.'

'I said he should, but he's a bit of a law unto himself,' she frowned. I wondered whether she felt as uneasy around him as I did and worried about him seeing Vikki. Then again, maybe he was different around her.

'Not to worry.' I lifted the box lid to check it was the right garment inside — though Janine would never get it wrong — and felt my legs weaken.

'What is it?' Janine's voice seemed to come from a distant corner, then her grey-haired head bobbed into view. 'Oh my God!' She reeled back, crashing into the desk. 'Is it blood?'

I couldn't find my voice. My arms felt nerveless, and the box slid to the ground, spilling its contents. Not blood but rusty-red paint, mixed with scraps of ruined fabric.

The dress had been shredded.

CHAPTER 12

Ruby

'I'm so pleased for you, Rubes,' Poppy said, as they climbed the concrete steps towards Ruby's apartment, passing the man from the floor above, who tapped his forehead with two fingers in a salute, and smiled, showing the gap in his teeth.

Poppy had been waiting for Ruby when she got home from having coffee with Saskia. She was sitting on the concrete floor, leaning against the front door, hood up, legs sprawled out in front of her, claiming she was desperate to hear how it had gone with Stefan. They'd talked for a while, before Poppy insisted she was starving, so they'd headed out to the fish and chip shop.

Now Ruby pushed her key in the front door, aware her sister's tone had changed since the night before at their dad's house, from grumpy to upbeat supportive sister.

Picking up a parcel addressed to her that was propped against the brickwork, Ruby opened the door, and stepped inside. She still wasn't used to the cramped flat, after living in her mum's spacious house, or the slight aroma she couldn't quite put her finger on. The hallway was a small square area with doors leading off to her bedroom, the kitchen, and a lounge-diner where there was barely room to swing a tiny kitten. But it was her independence. Her step in the right direction. Her escape from the claustrophobic years spent with her mum and sister. And it felt good to do be doing it alone after saving up while living at home. She knew her mum would have helped out, but she was glad she didn't have to ask. She was equally aware that her father wouldn't have offered financial support — always believing his daughters should fend for themselves.

'I want a front row seat to your first performance.' Poppy followed her in, unzipping her hoodie.

'Thanks.' Ruby clasped the wrapped fish and chips against her chest like a hot water bottle, the parcel dangling in her free hand. 'But, as I said earlier, nothing's definite yet.'

'Yes, but, you're amazing. You'll get the part. What is the role, by the way?'

Surprised by Poppy's keen interest, she turned and stared at her sister, who was taking off her hoodie and hanging it up by the door. 'So what's with all the praise?' She narrowed her eyes. 'What are you after?'

'Nothing. Honestly.' Poppy smiled, touched Ruby's arm. 'I guess I feel bad for being an arse last night, so gave myself a talking to and I'm now a super lovely sister.'

'That's very grown-up of you.' *And quite out of character.*

'I am a grown-up, in case you hadn't noticed.' Poppy laughed, scooping her hair behind her ears. 'Most of the time.'

As Ruby turned, her eyes glanced over a dark stain on the cuff of Poppy's sweatshirt.

'I'm bloody starving,' Poppy said, not seeming to register where Ruby's eyes had landed, and pushing past her into the kitchen.

Ruby followed, unwrapped the fish and chips, and took cutlery from a drawer, two plates from the cupboard. She wanted to mention the stain, but held back.

'God, this smells good.' Poppy sprinkled on salt and vinegar, popping a chip into her mouth. 'Got any ketchup?'

She unscrewed the lid of a litre bottle of cola, and splashed the dark, fizzy liquid into two glasses she'd upturned from the drainer. 'I can't wait to tuck in.'

Once they'd eaten, they flopped on the sofa. It had been there when Ruby arrived. In fact, the whole place came fully furnished. Though most of the stuff was dated and worn. The only thing she had invested in was a new mattress, and she was still paying for it monthly.

'I've been thinking about the key you took.'

Poppy shuffled up in her seat, and darted Ruby a quick look, her eyes bright. 'Yeah. Me too.'

'The thing is, I'm still not sure you should have it. Dad would be gutted if he knew. Maybe we should take it back. We don't have to say anything, just return it to where you found it.'

Poppy screwed up her nose. 'God-sake, Ruby, you're such a chicken. If we can go through Nell's things while she's out, we might prove to Dad she's having an affair.'

Ruby stared at her sister for several moments. Her pupils were dilated, her eyebrows red, and patchy. It was obvious she'd been tugging at them, something she did when she was stressed or anxious. 'It's not about courage. I'm quite capable of going into the house while Dad and Nell are at work, it's not like Dad would report us to the police if he found us.'

'Exactly.'

'But that's just it. It's like I said, I worry more that Dad would be upset if he caught us in there, may even get angry.'

On cue, Poppy tugged at her eyebrows. Gripped a single hair. Ripped it out. 'You do know Mum's upset because that bitch phoned her?'

'I know. But didn't Nell say Mum left a message asking her to call?'

'Christ, Ruby, whose side are you on? She accused Mum of refusing to accept Dad doesn't want her anymore. Told her to move on.'

Ruby shook her head. 'That's out of order,' she muttered, but however much she loved her mum, she couldn't imagine Nell being so unkind.

'Too right it is,' Poppy said. 'Just give it some thought, because I'm going in that house, with or without you.' She drew her legs up, cradled her knees.

Ruby stared at her sister for a long moment, her battered eyebrows, her pale complexion, and the dark stain on her cuff. Poppy had drifted off the rails even before Dad left. She'd got in with the wrong crowd at fourteen, and they'd broken into an off-licence. Got drunk on their spoils. She was admitted to hospital. Had to have her stomach pumped. Later that same year, she was suspended from school for supposedly bullying a teacher — though she insisted she hadn't known what the group she hung out with were going to do. Dad called her his live wire when she was small, but in later years those wires had crossed, tangling further when their father walked out.

'Are you going to open the parcel?' Poppy asked after a silence, moving to reach for her glass. Knocking back the last of her cola.

Ruby furrowed her forehead. 'I guess so. I'm not sure what it can be, I'm not expecting anything.' She rose, grabbed the parcel from the table, and ripped it open. Pulled out a clear plastic bag with a red jumper inside.

'Who's it from?' Poppy said, looking over her shoulder.

Ruby peered inside the outer bag. There didn't seem to be any clue to who it was from. 'Not sure,' she said, pulling open the inner bag, and removing the cashmere sweater. 'Weird.'

Poppy screwed up her nose. 'It looks like something Nell would wear.' Her eyes widened. 'Do you think it's from Sean?'

As Poppy said the words, Ruby's heart thudded. 'Surely not. Why would he send me a jumper?'

'Well, he sent you those, didn't he?' She nodded towards the hamper of untouched chocolates.

Ruby shuddered. She needed to bin them. 'There was a label on the chocolates. It was clear they were from Sean.' She examined the jumper, running her hand over the soft fabric, pressing it against her nose, picking up on a floral scent that seemed somehow familiar. 'But there's no label on this.' She dropped it on the table, recalling how Sean turned up at the coffee shop when she was with Saskia. Had he done that deliberately? She took a deep breath.

'I'm going into Classics tomorrow,' she said. 'I'm going to have it out with Sean.'

'That's my girl,' Poppy said with a smile. 'Hang on.' Her eyes were focused on a small white envelope on the carpet. She picked it up, handed it to Ruby. 'It must have fallen out.'

Ruby ripped it open:

To Ruby, Love Dad x

'It's from Dad,' she said, running her hand once more over the jumper. 'It's not like him to send me gifts — especially clothes.'

'He better not send me a frumpy jumper,' Poppy said with a laugh.

Back on the sofa, Poppy flicked on the TV. 'Haven't you got Netflix?' she asked, rolling her eyes.

'What part of 'minimum wage' don't you understand?'

'I know nothing about minimum wage. I make my living as an influencer.' She laughed, in no doubt that she was small fry in Twitch world.

Ruby put the jumper down on the table. 'Be careful, Poppy. There are some odd people out there.'

Poppy shook her head. 'It's not the strangers I worry about, it's those closest to us. You should know that from experience.' She rose to her feet. 'Are you sure you won't come with me to Dad and Nell's house? I just want to look around. See if I can find anything that will prove Nell's lying. Dad will come back to Mum if she is, can't you see that?'

Ruby wished she could be as sure of that outcome as her sister was. She rose too, noticing tears shining in Poppy's eyes, the break in her voice. Her sister needed this. And what harm could it really do? 'OK,' she said, and hugged Poppy close. Perhaps they would find something in The Coach House that could change everything.

CHAPTER 13

Nell

'I just don't know why you would call Fiona.'

'I told you, she left a message for me to ring her.' I stared at Oliver from across the kitchen. 'Why on earth would I call your ex-wife for no reason?'

'She said you accused her of causing problems between us.'

Great interpretation, Fiona. 'Only because she was making assumptions about our relationship, based on information fed back to her by your daughters.' Oliver's eyes thinned. 'I know you don't like hearing it, but Ruby and Poppy would love it if we broke up.'

He turned his head, locking me out of his thoughts. 'Now you're being silly.'

'Don't call me silly, Oliver.'

Something in my voice made him look at me more closely. Staying where he was, he softened his tone. 'Fiona swore on Ruby's life that she didn't leave a message. She said you called her out of the blue.'

'So, you're telling me Saskia lied?' It was an effort to press down the anger surging through me. 'Why would she tell me there was a message from Fiona if it wasn't true? And how would she have got Fiona's mobile number?'

Seeming stumped, Oliver combed his fingers through his hair and blew out a long sigh. 'I . . . don't know,' he admitted. 'I suppose I didn't want to believe Fiona would swear on Ruby's life if she was lying.'

'You believed Fiona over me.' Tears threatened. I swallowed, determined not to show how upset I was. 'What reason would *I* have to lie?'

'I don't know, but Nell . . . you would be well within your rights to have a go at her.'

'I *didn't* have a go at her!'

He held up a hand and continued, 'But I'm telling you, Fiona and the girls are trying to get on with their lives and accept you and I are together, although . . .' his words trailed off. He dug one hand in his trouser pocket, the other smoothing the marble surface of the worktop.

'Although?' Suddenly, my heart was racing, my mouth dry. 'What are you trying to say?'

'The way things are between us at the moment, it doesn't feel as though we're *together*.' He emphasised the word, crossing two fingers as if to demonstrate.

'Why do you think that is?' The wobble in my voice betrayed my seesawing emotions. I hadn't even got round to telling him about the ruined costume at work.

After finding the dress in tatters, Janine and I had run back up to the office where she, Saskia and I studied the footage from the CCTV we kept trained inside the warehouse. Classic Props had never yet been broken into, despite some of the pieces being worth a lot of money.

'I can't see anything,' Saskia had said, running through the footage for a second time, but I'd glimpsed a movement, noting the time: a few minutes after midnight the previous night. Nothing specific, more of a shadow, maybe a sleeve — a hood? *Poppy,* I'd thought, but hadn't said it aloud, ashamed she was the first person to come to mind.

'I can't tell,' Janine had said tearfully when I rewound and pointed out the shadow. 'Wouldn't the alarm have gone off if someone had broken in?' *Not if they knew the code.* 'You can't think it was one of us.' Her normally healthy complexion was devoid of colour. 'We wouldn't do something so awful, you know that, Nell.'

'Of course I don't think it was you.' Janine treated the costumes with the utmost respect, as though she'd designed them herself. 'But someone did this, and they chose that outfit knowing it was due out today.'

'Mark will be so upset.'

I looked at Janine. 'There's no point bringing him into this. It's my responsibility.' I thought for a moment. 'What about Sean? He went out earlier and seemed in a strange mood.'

'Sean?' echoed Janine.

'I'll talk to him,' I said. 'Though he's hardly likely to own up.'

As Janine's face crumpled into bewilderment, I remembered again that Sean was a potential son-in-law, if his relationship with her daughter worked out. 'I don't think he'd damage property like this and risk getting fired,' she said. 'And why would he?'

I could hardly tell her the thought that sprang into my head. *Because he's not over Ruby.* Though destroying a costume and risking being seen on camera was hardly the way back into the Cosgrove family. 'I don't know,' I admitted.

'Somebody's got it in for Nell,' Saskia pointed out.

Janine's eyes swivelled towards her, glassy as marbles. 'Like a vendetta?'

I nodded. 'To discredit either me, or the business. Or both.'

'There was no trace of any paint, or anything else,' Janine said. We'd looked for clues like third-rate detectives, my stomach churning with nausea. 'Whoever it was must have done the damage off the premises and slipped it back in last night.'

'So there's not a lot to go on,' Saskia said.

'We should still report it to the police.' Janine's face had resumed some colour. 'It's criminal damage.'

'Good idea.' But even as I said it, my heart dropped. Calling the police made it real. Someone was out to get me — or get *at* me.

'Could it be . . . ?' Saskia paused again, glancing at Janine. I guessed she didn't want to say whatever was on her mind.

'Janine, could you have a quick look to see if we've a similar costume we can send before I call the theatre?' My heart plunged further at the thought of phoning them with the news.

'I doubt we have, but I'll look.' She bustled away, muttering softly and shaking her head.

When she'd gone, Saskia took a deep breath. 'I know it sounds awful and it's not really any of my business, but could it have something to do with your stepdaughters?'

Even though I'd wondered the same thing myself, I was reluctant to lay the blame at their feet. 'They know how much the company means to their dad, and to Mark. I don't think they would go this far to spite me.'

'Of course not, I'm sorry,' Saskia backpedalled. 'I shouldn't have said that, only, from what you've told me . . . it was only a thought.'

'No, you're right.' As she removed her glasses and brushed a hand over her eyes, I laid a hand on her shoulder. 'I'd be lying if I said the same thing hadn't popped into my head, but my money's on . . .' I glanced round, checking Janine was out of earshot. 'Sean.'

Saskia nodded, as though it made sense. 'I wondered about him too. I don't know him that well, it's just a feeling.' With a half-smile, she replaced her glasses and tightened her ponytail. 'Would it be worth getting . . . Mark, is it? . . . to have a word with him?'

'Like I said to Janine, I would rather this didn't get back to Mark.' I went hot at the thought of his reaction. Mark trusted me, and that meant dealing with problems as they arose. Even problems I would never have anticipated.

After calling the Bankside Theatre and absorbing a five-minute rant about incompetency that only ended when I promised to source an extortionately expensive replacement costume from another hire company and deliver it myself, I'd set out, leaving Saskia in charge, and a still-shocked Janine riffling through the rest of the dresses *just in case.* I'd then driven home from the theatre on autopilot, the director's cold-eyed annoyance at the forefront of my mind. Despite a show of sympathy when I explained what had happened, I had a feeling she wouldn't be using Classic Props in future.

Back at The Coach House, I barely had time to remove my jacket before Oliver started his line of questioning. I wasn't in the mood, and the thought of relaying what had happened at work brought a wave of anxiety so strong, my knees went weak.

'It's been a difficult day,' I said now, when he didn't move to comfort me, or kiss me like he used to back when we would chat about our day while preparing dinner. I wished we hadn't got so heated about Fiona. 'I'm going to have a shower and an early night.'

I expected him to reach for me, to apologise even — to wonder why my day had been difficult, knowing I would tell him if he asked. But he didn't. His gaze was distant as though he hadn't heard, and I went upstairs, wondering how we were supposed to rescue our marriage when I was the only one trying.

* * *

The following morning, Oliver was gone when I woke, and I couldn't recall him coming to bed. He'd left a note on the dressing table in his cramped writing, saying he had a supplier meeting, and that a crate of sample wine might turn up before I left for work.

I remembered him saying once that he was good at compartmentalising — *it makes life a lot easier* — and hadn't thought much of it at the time, but guessed it was why he was able to carry on as though nothing was wrong. I wondered which compartment I was in. The one labelled *annoying wife*? I supposed, like most people, I hadn't believed his ability to close off from issues he didn't want to deal with would apply to me.

I'd slept heavily but still felt tired as my head filled with yesterday's events. I decided I would speak to Sean — hopefully while Janine was busy elsewhere — to put my mind at rest, and then call the police. I still baulked at the thought. What if it had been Ruby or Poppy? If the police investigated and found proof, Oliver might never forgive me. *They were acting out, that's all,* I imagined him saying. And while I didn't doubt he would never return to Fiona, she was bound to be there for him, gloating, waiting to console him. His family would be united against me.

'It shouldn't be like that,' Mum said when I called her on the way to work, partly to apologise for not visiting the previous weekend, but mostly because I wanted to hear her voice. 'I thought the ex-wife situation had been dealt with by the time you two got together.'

'So did I,' I said, realising it was an assumption I'd made based on my fairy-tale belief that I was Oliver's fresh start, the woman he'd been waiting for all along, his ex and his daughters storybook figures I couldn't quite bring to life. 'Look it'll be fine, Mum.' I felt guilty for worrying her. 'We've hit a bit of a rough patch, that's all.'

'I'd like to meet those daughters of his and give them a piece of my mind.'

I pictured Mum, in our old house in Aylesbury, surrounded by happy memories, and wondered whether that would ever be Oliver and me. 'How are you?' Her unflappable optimism, badly shaken by Dad's death, had recently started to return and she'd talked about volunteering at the local library — *keeping busy* as she put it. She needed to feel as though she was living and not merely existing. *Your dad wouldn't have wanted that.*

'I'm good,' she said, in a new, upbeat tone. 'I start at the library next Monday, part-time, and Judy's asked me to go on holiday with her later this year, to Mallorca.' Judy was her oldest friend, single and child-free. 'I'm thinking about it.'

'Mum, that's great.' My throat tightened. She and Dad had planned to buy a camper van and travel around the country before they got too old. It was hard to accept it would never happen now. 'You should definitely go.'

'He was so proud of you, you know.'

'I know, Mum.'

She'd said the same thing once before on a rare visit to The Coach House, not long after we moved in, and Oliver's mouth had tightened in a way I hadn't seen before, reminding me that he'd had a troubled relationship with his own father.

I'd tried to get him to talk about it after I'd driven Mum home, remembering how he'd opened up about his marriage, but he told me the past was the past, and there was no point dwelling on it. *Be grateful you had a father who loved you,* he said, in a way that had made me feel guilty.

'He would have been so interested in your job,' Mum continued. 'At least you have that.'

'I have Oliver too,' I said, but there wasn't much strength in the words. 'We'll get through this, I know we will. Though it would be easier if I got on with his daughters.'

Mum diplomatically changed the subject and by the time I arrived at work, I felt marginally better until I saw Sean jump out of his van.

'Can I have a quick word?' I locked my car. Glancing up, I saw Saskia near the window, talking to someone.

Sean strode over with a belligerent swagger, his heavy brows drawn together. 'What's up?'

Striving for a confident tone, I said, 'One of the costumes due out on hire yesterday was ruined. It had been cut up and covered in red paint and I wondered—'

'Whether I had something to do with it?' His eyes blazed with dislike. With his hands bunched in the pockets of his leather jacket and his shoulders hunched, he looked like a sullen teenager. I wondered whether Janine had seen this side of him.

'I was going to say, I wondered whether you might have seen something. Anyone behaving suspiciously.' It wasn't what I'd been going to say, and he knew it.

'No.' The word was almost a growl. 'I didn't see anything, and it wasn't me.' His attention flicked up to the office windows and his whole expression changed.

Turning, glad to escape the burn of his gaze, I spotted a familiar flow of dark hair and realised the person Saskia was talking to was Ruby. *What was she doing here?*

'Sounds like you're suffering from the Cosgrove Curse.' Sean's gaze returned to me, a new wariness in their depths. 'You're not the first.'

'What are you talking about?' *Cosgrove Curse.* The words lodged in my mind like splinters. 'Sean?'

He shifted his feet, squinting as the clouds parted and bright sunlight hit his eyes. 'I didn't mean anything.' He glanced at his van as though longing to drive away. 'Look, I'd better get to work.' His jaw tightened. 'That's if I still have a job.'

'Yes, I . . . of course.' Knowing I'd handled him badly, I hurried inside and ran upstairs, dreading whatever it was that Ruby had come to say.

'Everything OK?' I hoped Saskia hadn't mentioned yesterday's disaster with the shredded costume. Ruby would love another reason to bad-mouth me to Oliver.

'Fine,' Saskia said, but her smile seemed fixed and her usually pale cheeks were flushed. 'I just opened up and was about to go through today's itinerary when Ruby arrived.'

'Is it about your audition?' I said to Ruby. Saskia flashed me a grateful smile and crossed to her desk, shedding her coat on the way. 'I heard your meeting with Stefan went well.' Determined not to show how rattled I was, I tried to smile and put Sean's words to the back of my mind. *Cosgrove Curse.* It was the sort of belief he was bound to have, considering his history with Ruby.

'It's not about that,' she said.

'Oh.' Thrown by her tone, I glanced at her outfit — specifically the jumper she was wearing under her leather jacket. It looked oddly familiar. 'What?' She glanced down as if tracking my gaze.

'Your sweater,' I said. 'It's like one of mine.'

'Oh?' Chin down, she plucked at the woollen hem. 'It's not my usual thing, to be honest. Dad bought it for me.'

I wondered when that was. He hadn't mentioned it. Not that we needed to share our purchases with each other, but I'd thought it might be something he would bring up. 'Oliver bought you a jumper?' I wondered whether he'd bought Poppy one too. 'It's exactly like one of mine that went missing.' The remark was meant to be light and jokey but came out like an accusation. Crossing the floor, boots clumping, Ruby thrust her chin at me. 'What's that supposed to mean?'

'Nothing, I only meant—' I looked closer, zoning in on a tiny discoloration in the dye around the neckline, barely noticeable unless you knew it was there. 'It *is* mine.' I reached out to touch the soft cashmere. 'Did you take it?'

'What?' Ruby jerked away as though I'd slapped her. 'I told you, it was a gift. Why would I steal a jumper from *you?'*

The emphasis stung. 'But it's identical.' I pointed at the neckline, my eyes skimming down. 'It's too small for you.' I shook my head, disbelieving. 'There's no way this was a gift, Ruby. Be honest with me.'

Ruby's outraged gaze met mine. 'Poppy was there when I picked up the parcel and I have the gift tag if you don't believe . . .' She paused. 'I mean, it was printed, not handwritten, but why would Dad . . . ?' Now Ruby was shaking her head, hair swinging. 'Weird; it smelt faintly of perfume when I put it on.' She was almost talking to herself now, anger deflating, her gaze turned inward. 'It's not the kind of thing I would normally wear, no offence.'

'So, you took it to wind me up, and now you're . . . what?' I stared, trying to hold onto my conviction, because what other possibility could there be? 'Pretending it was a present from your father? And how did you get into our house?'

'Hang on, I—'

'What's the end game, Ruby?' I was genuinely curious. 'You go running to Oliver to tell him I accused you of something you supposedly didn't do?'

'I didn't steal your bloody jumper.'

The strength of belief in her voice did nothing to douse my certainty. 'You would say that though, wouldn't you?'

She gave a contemptuous snort. 'Listen to yourself.' Her eyes iced over, and before I could stop her she'd whipped off her jacket, tossed it onto the floor and was tugging the jumper over her head. She had a vest-top on underneath that rode up, revealing her pale, flat stomach. 'Have the stupid thing, I don't want it.' She was breathing heavily as she flung the jumper onto my desk and pushed her hair off her face. 'What does my dad even see in you?'

Saskia cleared her throat, breaking a tension thick enough to slice. 'Ruby came to have a word with Sean, but I told her he wasn't in yet.'

I looked at Ruby who was pulling her jacket back on, lips pressed into a hard line. 'Wait,' I said, reaching for the jumper. The sleeve was dangling over my computer, as if deliberately obscuring the screen-saver image: a snap of Oliver and me on our honeymoon. I recognised a tiny loose thread by the cuff. *Definitely mine.* What were the Cosgroves playing at? 'I don't understand.'

'Join the club.' Ruby's scowl gathered strength. 'Don't worry, I'll see myself out.'

'Ruby!'

She paused in a half-turn at the top of the stairs.

'Where was Poppy the other night?'

'What?' Her brow cleared. 'What has my sister got to do with anything?'

Deciding I'd gone too far, brain still reeling from the shock of seeing Ruby in my missing jumper, I shook my head. 'Nothing. Forget it.'

She gave me a hard look before thundering down the stairs.

For a moment I could only stare at the spot where she'd been, nerve-ends tingling with a feeling of dread I couldn't pin down. Then I sank into my chair and met Saskia's dumbfounded stare. 'What the hell was that all about?'

CHAPTER 14

Ruby

Ruby reached the bottom of the stairs, and paused, her breathing ragged, her chest tight. She closed her eyes for a moment. She hated confrontation; had always shied away from conflict. That's how she'd ended up staying with Sean for too long, allowing him to control her. But she wasn't about to let Nell talk to her like that. Her dad had sent her the jumper, hadn't he?

She opened her eyes, took another deep breath. But then why had the jumper smelt of Nell's perfume? And how had Nell known about the discoloration on the neckline? Nell had said the jumper had gone missing. Was someone playing games? Her mind jumped to Sean. Could he have got into The Coach House to take it?

Maybe she should leave challenging Sean for today, she wasn't in the right place mentally to handle him right now.

'Morning, Ruby.'

She turned to see Janine, tall, confident and caring, her arms folded across her slim body, her short dark hair speckled with grey. Ruby liked Janine, who was in her fifties. She'd always made a fuss of her and Poppy when they visited the company as children. Would have sweets or cakes to offer them. And when their father was busy, she would take them on magical journeys around the warehouse showing them all the beautiful clothes and props, telling them stories about the shows and films the clothes had been used for. Sometimes she would bring her daughter into work, and they would all play together. Vikki had been a quiet, shy girl, younger than Ruby, but they'd got on OK. Ruby hadn't seen Vikki in a long time; though Janine constantly updated her, mentioning recently that Vikki was seeing Sean. She talked of her daughter with such pride: '*She's bought her own one-bed flat.*' '*She's just passed her teaching degree.*' Always bringing up how she'd been a father and mother to her all her life. Never missing an opportunity to mention how her husband walked out when Vikki was a baby, that they'd never heard from him again. Not that she'd have let her daughter see him anyway.

'Hey,' Ruby said now, as Janine inched closer and took her in her arms. 'It's so good to see you.'

After a brief hug, Janine released her, and stepped back. 'We don't see you around these parts very often these days.'

Ruby looked up the stairs towards the closed door that led to Nell's office. 'No, well, you can guess why.'

'Mmm.' She touched Ruby's cheek. 'It must be hard for you girls.'

Ruby closed her eyes, biting back a flood of emotion, desperate to change the subject. 'I don't suppose you've seen Sean recently?'

'He just arrived.' Janine pursed her lips and took a deep breath. Ruby knew she'd witnessed how difficult it had been for her when she tried to break things off with him. 'I know you don't like him, and I understand that, with your history. But he's always more than polite to me, and he seems to make Vikki happy.'

'I'd like to think he's moved on,' was all Ruby could think to say.

'I'm sure he has. Vikki seems to be a good influence on him.'

'Good. Well, I'd better head off.' Ruby didn't want to prolong the conversation. Janine was clearly happy her daughter was seeing Sean. She smiled, raised her hand, and whisked by Janine, leaving the woman standing in her wake, feeling her eyes on her back as she hurried past an Edwardian display cabinet and into the warrens of the warehouse.

Out the back, Sean was loading his van with crates. Her plan to talk to him, to ask him why he'd sent her the chocolates, had evaporated. She couldn't face him. She turned quickly, started making her way towards her car.

'Ruby?' She heard his footsteps heading briskly towards her. She stopped, turned.

'Sean.' He was practically on top of her, towering over her. Her blood chilled, memories of his intensity flooding back, the way he didn't like her going out with friends, how he slowly revealed his hatred for her performing on stage, '*where other men could ogle her*'.

'Twice in as many days.' She assumed he was talking about the coffee shop. 'What are you doing here at Classics?'

She thought about the jumper, but wasn't about to mention it. 'I came to see Nell.'

He laughed. 'Did she tell you how she's making a right mess of things here? I thought that would amuse you.'

She took a deep breath, needing to mention the chocolates, at least. 'I got the hamper you sent.'

He smiled, pushed his fingers through his hair, almost coy. 'Do you like them?'

'You shouldn't have sent them.'

His eyes widened, as though hurt. 'But they're Hotel Chocolat, your favourite.'

'That's not the point. You're with Vikki now.'

He shook his head. 'God, Ruby, you've got it so wrong. It was a flat-warming gift. No big deal.'

'But . . .' The words on the card flashed through her head. *I hope one day we'll be together again, Ruby. I'll never stop loving you.*

'What's your problem, Ruby?' He stared deep into her eyes, making her uncomfortable. She turned from his intense gaze. 'Christ, you're so ungrateful at times, Ruby — always were. All I did for you—'

'I have to go, Sean.' She fumbled in her bag for her car keys, dropping them to the ground.

'Sometimes you act like you're afraid of me. What's that about?'

'I'm not afraid of you.' She reached down for her keys, pointed the fob at her car, unlocking it. But the truth was he still made her feel uneasy.

'You know, I hate the way things ended between us — how misjudged I was,' he said, as she opened her car door, and went to climb in. He was suddenly beside her. 'I'm with Vikki now. I've moved on, Ruby. It's serious, and I'm happy. She appreciates me for who I am.'

'So why send me chocolates?'

His pale green eyes looked so cold. He grabbed her arm. 'Because I thought we were friends.'

She snatched her arm away. 'You don't tell friends that you'll never stop loving them.'

'Aren't you supposed to be loading up, Sean?' It was Nell, some distance away, hands on her hips.

Sean looked over at her, narrowed his eyes, before heading back to his van.

'And you should be off the premises, Ruby.' She glared at her. 'Please leave. Now.'

* * *

Ruby finished her sandwich deliveries around two o'clock, and dropped off the van behind Sharma's Sandwiches. She poked her head into the back door to yell goodbye to Benita, who looked rushed off her feet as always, before making her way towards the underground. She'd wanted to go home before her audition — to shower and change — but there really wasn't time now.

A packed train, where she stood far too close to a sweaty man with a shiny forehead, who kept staring at her, didn't help her feelings of anxiety.

It was half an hour later, as she made her way up Shillingford Street, a quiet, narrow road ten minutes from the underground, that a sudden feeling of being watched made the hairs on her neck stand up. She stopped, turned quickly, feeling sure she saw someone crouching behind a car. She picked up speed, relieved when she reached the theatre: a modern building with a large sign advertising 'Stefan Andrew's Theatre Company'. It was set in a quiet courtyard area, away from the hustle and bustle of central Islington. She passed through the arched doorway and stepped inside, the door creaking closed behind her. Her eyes flicked over a small reception area, a ticket booth, a small bar. Posters of past and present productions were pinned to the walls, and long cushioned benches filled the area.

'Hello?' A chill tickled her neck when there was no reply. What was wrong with her? 'Hello?' She opened a door and peered in at the dimly lit, silent auditorium. It felt somehow creepy with its rows of empty seats, heavy velvet curtains across the stage. 'Hello?'

She let the door swing shut, and returned to the foyer. After a few moments she sat down on one of the benches, butterflies erupting in her stomach — what if she messed this up, after Saskia had gone to so much trouble?

The main door creaked open. And as though she'd conjured her up, Saskia peered round the door.

'Hey,' Ruby said, rising, relieved to see her. 'What are you doing here?'

'I thought I'd come for moral support.' She smiled. Pushed her glasses up the bridge of her nose. 'I know what Stefan's like — he'll probably be late — and I had visions of you leaving and missing your chance.'

'Wow, thanks. That's so kind, but shouldn't you be at work?'

'I'm going to make up the time later. Nell agreed I should come. She felt bad about this morning. Said things got completely out of hand, and wanted me to come and support you.' She touched Ruby's arm, tilted her head. 'I don't know

Nell that well, but from what I've seen, I think she's a good person, most of the time.'

Ruby stiffened. 'Good people don't get involved with other people's husbands. Dad was still married to my mum even if they weren't living together.'

'Love does funny things to people.'

'Ruby! Sassy!' The women turned to see Stefan, flamboyant as ever, appearing through a door that Ruby hadn't noticed. It looked like part of the wall.

'You're on time.' Saskia laughed, moving towards him, kissing him on both cheeks. 'That's got to be a first.'

He laughed. Fake. Loud. 'Right, let's get this show on the road, shall we?' He led the way into the auditorium, thrusting a script at Ruby.

* * *

'You were absolutely fantastic.' Saskia looped her arm through Ruby's elbow, as they headed away from the theatre, and along Shillingford Street towards the underground.

'Thanks.' Ruby couldn't stop smiling, her heart dancing a jig, Stefan's words as he offered her the part repeating on a loop in her head. It was a fairly big role too, one that would be enough to kick-start her career — give her back her confidence. She was elated. 'Thanks so much for introducing me to Stefan, I really appreciate it.'

'No problem, I'm just thrilled you got the part.' Their eyes met. Saskia had a lovely smile, and although not much older than Ruby, she seemed more mature. Ruby was glad of her support. It felt good — like the beginning of a friendship. 'So, about Nell.'

Way to ruin a moment. 'What about her?'

'She's got a local newspaper reporter coming to interview her tomorrow morning. Why don't you and Poppy come along?'

'Why would we do that?' Ruby pulled away from Saskia, bumping into a young man approaching from the opposite direction.

'Hey, watch where you're going,' he said, gone before she could apologise.

'Hear me out, Ruby, please,' Saskia said, her tone serious.

'I'm not sure I want to even see her. It was bad enough going round their house for dinner.'

'The thing is Nell comes alive at work,' Saskia continued as though Ruby hadn't spoken. 'I just want you to see that, Ruby. Get to know the real Nell. See what I see.'

'No offence, but you haven't known her that long.'

'First impressions are often the right ones.'

'Well I know Poppy won't come.' Ruby shook her head. 'Even if I agreed . . .' Why was she weakening? There was no way she wanted to get to know the real Nell, whoever she was. As far as she was concerned, she was still the woman standing in the way of her parents being together. And after the jumper incident things were bound to be even worse between them. 'Poppy hates her.'

'Hate is a strong emotion, Ruby.' Saskia sounded more like a mother than someone in her late twenties. 'Your sister is young, rebellious.'

'You've got that right.'

'It was the same with my sister and me when we were young. Except I was the rebellious one.'

'Really?' Ruby smiled. 'You don't look the rebellious type.'

'Oh, I can be at times.' She laughed, and took Ruby's arm once more as they entered the underground. 'Think about it, please. It's not healthy to hold on to so much anger.'

* * *

'Are you sure this is a good idea, Poppy?' Ruby said, as they headed towards Marlow that evening.

'Totally.' Poppy sounded more cheerful than usual, as she fiddled with her phone. 'We're not doing anything wrong.'

'I'd hate to hear your version of wrong.'

'It's fine. Dad's at a conference in Bedford, and Nell is working late.'

'And you know that, how?'

'I texted Dad.' She sounded proud of herself.

'And he didn't wonder why you were asking?'

'I said I wanted to see them both, and asked when would be a good time, and he said *not tonight because . . .*'

'Ah, OK.' Ruby slowed at a roundabout, looked to her right for oncoming traffic.

'So, did you talk to Sean about the chocolates?'

'Yeah, he admitted he left them, said it was a flat-warming gift, that he thought we were friends. Which is ridiculous. I've no idea what he's playing at.' She pulled onto the roundabout, glancing at her sister who was nibbling at the skin around her thumbnail, making it bleed. 'You really hate Nell don't you?'

Poppy turned fast, stared at Ruby. 'Don't you then?'

Ruby moved her gaze back to the road in front. 'I would give anything for her to be out of Dad's life, and things be as they once were.' Her mind drifted to how things had been growing up: Her father had worked long hours, her mum always trying to keep him home. *The girls never see you, Oliver.*

'But you don't hate her?' The surprise in Poppy's voice was tangible.

Saskia's words flew into her head. *Hate is a strong emotion.* Did she really want to feel that much painful emotion for someone? Was it healthy to carry it around every day?

'Ruby?'

'Yes, yes, I guess so. Yes.'

'Good, because I thought for a minute you were softening.'

Ruby wasn't softening. She would never like Nell. But feeling so angry all the time was taking its toll. 'Nell's got an interview with the local newspaper tomorrow,' she said.

'Bully for her.'

'Saskia suggested we go into Classics and watch her be interviewed. Get to know the real Nell.'

'Christ's sake.'

Ruby shrugged. 'I know it's a bit odd. But perhaps she has a point. We don't really know her, and perhaps if we did—'

'You've got to be kidding me.' Poppy banged her phone against her forehead. 'Jesus, Ruby.'

Ruby shook her head. 'Yeah, ridiculous, right?'

Poppy was silent for some time before she said, 'OK.'

'OK?'

'Yeah.' Poppy gave a careless shrug. 'Whatever. Let's do it.'

* * *

They arrived outside The Coach House just after 7 p.m. Dusk had settled. Ducks slept in pairs on the riverbank, the water gently rippling in the light breeze. A willow tree swayed. The whole area was quiet, peaceful.

'We need to park round the corner,' Poppy whispered, as though someone could hear them in the confines of the car.

'Why?'

'In case Dad or Nell come home, they might recognise your car.'

'Oh God. Should we really be doing this?' Ruby pulled the car into a side road, cutting the engine.

'Ready?' Poppy dragged up her hood, and they climbed from the car and made their way towards the house.

'Wait!' Ruby took hold of Poppy's arm. 'Look. The neighbours have CCTV.'

'Thought of that,' Poppy said with a grin. 'Firstly, they'll have no reason to check it. And secondly, even if they do, we'll say we popped round hoping to find Dad in.' She pulled from Ruby's grip, and headed onwards. 'Relax, everything will be OK.'

Once they were at the back door, Poppy turned the key.

'Let's go home, Pops.' Ruby's eyes swept the area. 'We probably won't find anything anyway. What's the likelihood of Nell leaving evidence about her affair?' *If she was having an affair.* Ruby couldn't help recalling Nell's confusion about the jumper — how she didn't seem any good at hiding her feelings.

'We're in.' Poppy pushed the door open.

'Oh God, am I really doing this?' Ruby sighed, looked about her one last time, before stepping in after her sister. 'What are we hoping to find?'

'Receipts maybe. A diary?'

'A diary? You think Nell would be daft enough to keep a diary about her lover?'

'Let's try upstairs first.'

They made their way up to the spacious landing, and entered their father's bedroom. Poppy wasted no time rummaging in drawers, lifting out Nell's black underwear and making crass comments. Ruby stepped back, her heart thudding. This wasn't the right way to do things.

'I'm thinking of following her.' Poppy slammed a drawer closed, heading for the bedside cabinet. 'Are you up for that?'

'Shh!'

'What?'

'I thought I heard the front door.'

Ruby crept onto the landing, floorboards creaking. *Oh God,* someone was downstairs.

'I'll have a quick shower, and meet you at seven-thirty.' It was their father, talking in a low whisper. A pause followed by a laugh. 'Oh, and get a bottle ordered, Birdie.'

Ruby's head swam as a memory flashed up. She'd heard her father talking in the same way once before, a long time ago. Her parents had argued a lot around that time, her mother spending days sobbing in her room.

'I thought he was at a conference,' Ruby whispered, her voice frantic, as she moved back into the bedroom.

'That's what he said.' Poppy looked horrified, as she shoved things back into the bedside cabinet. 'What the hell are we going to do?'

'You got us into this—'

'But I'm just a kid.' Her tone was satirical, but there was a wobble in her voice.

Ruby looked about her. Would her dad use the main bathroom or the en suite? They couldn't afford to be in there.

He would need a change of clothes. 'Follow me,' she said, and they tiptoed to the guest room and crouched behind the bed.

'We could confront him about the call?' Poppy said, fidgeting.

'No, he'll never forgive us for being here.'

They could hear him downstairs: a chair being dragged across quarry tiles in the kitchen, the shuttered blinds being closed.

Finally, he ascended the stairs, humming. Ruby's heart continued to hammer against her ribs, as he made his way into his bedroom and rummaged in his wardrobe. Finally the sound of the shower cascading triggered them to rise from their crouched position and make their escape.

* * *

'Never again will I listen to you,' Ruby muttered, once they'd clambered into the car, their breathing raspy after their run from the house.

Poppy pushed down her hood. 'Sorry, but I thought if we could find something out.'

But all Ruby had found out was that her father was meeting up with someone called Birdie, and they were about to share a bottle.

Was it possible her father was the one having the affair?

CHAPTER 15

Nell

I called Carla on my way to work the following morning, relieved when she picked up straight away. 'It's Nell Cosgrove. Could I make an appointment to see you on my own?'

'Of course.' Her measured voice soothed away some of my tension. 'I could fit you in this evening if that would be convenient. Six-thirty?'

I hadn't expected to see her today, but I was desperate to talk to somebody away from everyone I knew. Plus it was outside work hours. With everything that was happening, I wasn't confident about leaving Saskia alone for too long, however capable she seemed. 'That would be great, thank you.'

'I'll see you then, Nell.' Carla sounded accepting, as though she got calls from distressed wives and stepmothers all the time. *Maybe she did.* She hadn't asked why Oliver wouldn't be coming, but maybe she'd guessed after our last meeting that he wasn't particularly receptive — to anything, it was starting to appear. When he arrived home around ten the night before, after a client dinner, I'd launched into telling him about Ruby turning up at the office wearing my sweater, claiming it had been a gift from him — which even she had seemed unnerved about — but after listening with a quizzical expression, he simply said he hadn't a clue what I was talking about, that he hadn't sent her a gift.

'I could have sworn there was someone in the house earlier,' he'd gone on, swinging around as though checking we were alone. 'I was on the phone when I came home, so wouldn't have noticed anything wrong, but when I was having a shower I thought I heard the front door close.'

'Are you sure?' My heart had leapt painfully in my chest.

'By the time I got out and looked through the window there was no one there.'

'I'm telling you Oliver, something strange is going on. Those texts, that card, and now my sweater—'

'I should get some proper security cameras installed,' he'd cut in, crossing to his laptop on the coffee table in the living room. 'It's ridiculous we haven't got them already.'

'You don't think . . . it wouldn't have been one of the girls, would it?' I wasn't even sure what prompted me to ask, but I kept seeing Ruby's expression as she threw my sweater onto my desk, her eyes loaded with dislike. 'Do either of them have a key to our house?'

Oliver's brow lowered, though his eyes stayed on his screen. 'No they don't, and why would they sneak in?' He shook his head, as though I'd said something silly, which I supposed I had. If either of them had been in the house, they would hardly have left without speaking to their dad.

Oliver had refused to discuss it further, pouring himself a glass of red wine he was sampling for a potential customer. When I went up to bed, my feet felt like lead, my mind churning with unspoken thoughts, he stayed up to do some 'paperwork' though I heard the television blaring as I drifted off to sleep.

Now, the knowledge that I could unburden myself to Carla later allowed me to narrow my focus to the newspaper interview that lay ahead. As I approached the office, my stomach clenched with nerves. Mark had emailed to wish me luck and to *shine a light on the company*, and even Oliver had said *break a leg* before I left the house, though he didn't suggest he come along as he had when I was first approached, saying he would love to be there. We'd drifted so far apart in such a short time it took my breath away.

Driving into my parking space, I noticed a dark SUV parked nearby. A bearded man in a checked shirt and chinos was entering the warehouse with a camera around his neck. With a surge of panic, I glanced at the time on the dashboard. It was barely nine o'clock. The interview had been scheduled for eleven.

Janine greeted me with an excited hunch of her shoulders. Like me, she had made an effort with her outfit, wearing a velvet crimson dress with a white lace collar and cuffs that gave her a regal air. Despite my best attempts, I felt ordinary in my olive-green shift dress, which I'd matched with a tan belt and boots and a long, cream cardigan.

'They're early,' I said in a stage whisper.

She shrugged. 'Lucky Saskia got in at eight.'

'Is Sean here?' For reasons I couldn't explain, I was hoping he wasn't.

'He's gone to drop off some rugs for a window display,' Janine said. 'Remember that new furniture store is doing a mock-up of a posh dinner party to showcase their tables.'

I did remember and was grateful he wouldn't be on the premises during the interview.

Feeling wrong-footed, I headed up to the office to be greeted by the sight of Saskia perched on the edge of her desk, chatting to a tall woman with long red hair who I guessed was Anita, the reporter from the newspaper. Her head was thrown back as she laughed, while the man I'd seen on my way in snapped photographs and examined the display screen on his camera.

'Just checking the lighting,' he said when he saw me, face brightening into a smile. 'I'm Chris Fairleigh. You must be Nell Cosgrove.'

'Nice to meet you,' I said, trying to signal Saskia with my eyes.

Catching sight of me, she jumped up, smoothing her hands over a fitted dress in a bright jewel pink that showed off her curves. 'You look great,' I said to her, moving over and flashing a smile at Anita. 'Nell Cosgrove.'

Anita took my outstretched hand and pumped it briefly.

'I'm so sorry I'm late,' I said. 'I thought the interview was scheduled for eleven.'

Anita's wide apart blue eyes held a chill as she looked me up and down. 'You brought it forward.' She gave a tight-lipped smile. 'Apparently, you've an important meeting later this morning and this was the only time you could manage.'

'What?' My heart felt as though it was bouncing on elastic. 'I didn't—'

'I was telling Anita that nothing is more important to you than this interview,' Saskia chipped in with a placatory smile. She pulled her sleek ponytail over her shoulder. 'I think there was a mix-up with the diary.' Her smile faded. Everyone was looking at me, the light-hearted atmosphere I'd walked into ebbing away.

'I'm sorry,' I said again, trying to recall what meeting I was supposed to have booked, certain there wasn't one. I wouldn't have changed the time of the interview, but it was a measure of the newspaper's goodwill that they'd agreed. I didn't want to mess them about. 'Shall we get on with it?' *Great.* Now I sounded like a bossy head-teacher.

'Of course.' Anita's smile switched up a gear. 'We wouldn't want to hold you up.'

'Oh no, I didn't mean—'

'I'll fetch those coffees I promised, shall I?' Saskia's smile returned like a ray of sunshine and I noticed how Anita and Chris responded with friendly nods.

'Thanks, Saskia.' I wished I was the one they were offering smiles to instead of wary glances.

'No problem.' Pausing on her way to the kitchen area, she looked over her shoulder. 'The girls should be here in a minute.'

'Girls?'

'Well, Ruby said she'll definitely drop by, but I'm not sure about Poppy.'

Horror swelled in my chest. 'They're coming *here*?'

Hurrying back, Saskia came close and said in a worried undertone, 'I was going to tell you before the reporter turned up. I thought it might be a good way to get closer after . . . you know, yesterday. If Ruby saw you like this, I mean.' As she swept an arm around the room, I caught an exchange of looks between Anita and Chris. 'I texted Ruby on the off chance and she said she would call her sister.' I'd forgotten that Saskia had Ruby's number. 'You don't mind, do you? I did mention it.' Pushing up her glasses, Saskia's chin trembled. 'Oh God, I've overstepped. I'm sorry, Nell.'

'No, it's fine.' But we both knew it wasn't.

'Ruby and Poppy are your stepdaughters, is that right, Nell?'

I turned to see Anita with her head cocked, reminding me of Carla. Saskia took the opportunity to hurry away, her shoulders up around her ears.

'Yes, that's right.' I couldn't seem to gain the upper hand, stumbling a little as I crossed the floor so that my bag fell from my shoulder.

'Saskia was telling us about the set-up here.' *At least she would have put me in a favourable light.* 'I take it the family are no longer involved in the business, that Mark Bradbury left you in charge after taking early retirement due to a back injury.'

'Right again.' I clumsily retrieved my bag and made it to my desk, where I pulled out my chair and sat down. Instantly, I felt more in control. 'As you probably know, Mark was involved in a skiing accident that caused some spinal damage. He's still very much involved with the company though and checks in regularly, as does my husband, Oliver.' *There.* I'd mentioned them both, as promised. 'As you know, they founded the company together more than twenty-five years ago and, since then, it's gone from strength to strength.' My face burned, as though the heating was on full blast. Sunlight poured through the windows, turning Anita's hair to a sheet of fiery copper. Feeling sweat on my forehead, I slipped my cardigan off. 'Please, sit down,' I said.

Anita lowered herself into a wing-backed chair and crossed her long, slim legs. 'You don't mind me recording this?' Leaning forward, she placed her phone on my desk. 'I'll make notes too but replaying your words later will help bring the piece to life.'

'Of course.'

'I thought we could start up here in the office, then move downstairs, where Chris can take some shots of you in the warehouse, and perhaps with the staff if they don't mind. I'll be asking them what it's like working for you. A woman.'

Apart from Sean, I didn't think anyone would have a bad word to say, but even so, her words were somehow alarming — as was the insinuation they would prefer working for a man, especially as Anita seemed like a strong woman.

'After working with Mark and Oliver, I mean,' she clarified, as though reading my mind, though I couldn't see how that was any better.

Suppressing a sigh, I said, 'That's fine,' angling my gaze at Chris. He flapped open a white reflector and placed it on the floor by my chair.

'To bounce light at your face,' he explained with a friendly grin. 'Great hair, by the way.' I'd made more effort than usual, with a styling gel that appeared to have tamed my frizz.

'Thanks.'

'So, let's start.' Anita sounded more engaged. 'Tell me how you got to be here today.'

At last, I began to relax — *though why was it so hot?* — and was in the process of telling Anita what made our company stand out among the competition, when Saskia came back with the coffees. At the same time, there was a commotion and Ruby appeared, trailed by Poppy who looked as though she'd been up all night drinking and hadn't quite woken up. Both were rigged out in black, though Ruby had on an emerald-green choker that emphasised her pale skin.

'Hey,' she said to Saskia, who looked mortified and swiftly moved back to her desk without replying. The phone rang and she answered in a professional tone, keeping her voice low and her face averted.

'Don't mind us,' Ruby said, seeming slightly embarrassed, casting her dark eyes around as if unsure where to put herself.

'You must be Oliver Cosgrove's daughters.' Anita picked up her cup of coffee and studied Ruby over the rim. Poppy had flopped onto the floor, her back pushed up against the radiator, arms hooked around her knees. She tipped her head back, eyes closed, her skin pallid. 'What do you think of your stepmother's role here?' Chris moved past Anita and took a couple of photos of Ruby. She flashed him a smile and flicked her hair back, adopting a natural looking stance with her hands tucked into her jacket pockets.

'Ruby's an actress,' I cut in, deciding to do her a favour, but she glared at me as though I'd announced she was a serial killer.

'Ooh, what have I seen you in?' Chris asked.

When Ruby briefly shut her eyes, I realised my mistake. Now she would have to confess she wasn't famous and hadn't yet been in anything they would have seen, but before she could speak, Poppy sprang away from the radiator with a yelp of outrage.

'It's fucking boiling.'

So the heating *was* on. It explained why my face felt on fire and why Anita was fanning herself with a brochure she'd picked up.

Poppy scrabbled across the floor on all fours. 'I could have third-degree burns.'

'Poppy.' Ruby's tone was a warning. She went over to her sister and held out a hand. 'Get up,' she instructed, while my insides shrivelled. I prayed Anita wasn't mentally taking notes, and that the photos Chris was snapping were of the office layout, and not the scene unfolding.

'Hey, I've got a good headline for your interview.' Standing now, Poppy snatched her hand away from Ruby's and, swaying a little, as though she might float off, fixed Anita with a burning stare. '"Marriage-wrecking slut steals husband as well as his children's inheritance".'

'Poppy!'

'What's that supposed to mean?'

Ruby and I spoke at the same time. I briefly caught her horrified gaze before she grabbed her sister's arm and tugged her towards the stairs. 'I'm sorry, but I don't think this was a good idea,' she said.

Saskia cradled her head between her hands, lips pressed together as though to stop herself crying.

'This company would have been ours one day if you hadn't talked Dad into selling his share so you could take over.' Poppy wrenched free and lunged at my desk, eyes spitting fury. The sleeve of her top had inched up, revealing a series of barely healed cuts on her arm. 'You won't get away with it, you *bitch*.'

Spittle landed on my face. I felt welded to my chair, unable to move. 'I didn't talk him into selling his share.' My voice was feeble with shock. 'It was a mutual agreement with Mark.'

'He was doing *fine* until you came along. We *all* were.' I wanted to point out that it wasn't true, that their parents had already split up, but her tone wobbled, and she collapsed into noisy tears. 'We hate you, and so will Dad when he wakes up and realises what you're really like.'

'That's enough, Poppy.' Ruby placed an arm around her sister's shoulders and this time, Poppy let herself be led away, pausing to say in a wretched tone, 'I think I'm going to be sick,' before clamping a hand to her mouth.

Throwing me a backwards glance I couldn't read, Ruby hustled Poppy down the stairs, leaving behind a profound silence that was broken by the sound of Janine's voice, speaking gentle words I couldn't make out.

'I think we should go.' Anita got to her feet, shooting Chris a look of barely concealed excitement.

'What about taking some pictures in the warehouse?' But I knew it was futile. It might not be what they'd come for, but the newspaper had ended up with a story worthy of a tabloid and it was clear Anita couldn't wait to run it.

CHAPTER 16

Ruby

Janine held Poppy's hands. 'Deep breaths now, sweetheart,' she said, in her motherly way, and it was clear her calming presence was going some way to putting out the blazing fire inside the girl.

It hadn't been a good idea to come — was a bloody stupid idea, in fact. Ruby knew Saskia had meant well, that her heart was in the right place when she attempted to fuse the massive gap between the sisters and Nell, but it was never going to happen. Ruby should have known that.

What she hadn't expected was Poppy's toxic outburst, and she wondered now if her sister had intended to do that all along?

Together Poppy and Janine breathed in and out. 'Now this is what I always tell my Vikki, whenever she gets upset.' Janine released Poppy's hands. 'There are worse things at sea.'

'What does that even mean?' Poppy snapped, her voice still full of tension, though at least she no longer looked as though she was going to throw up.

'Things aren't as bad as they seem,' Janine clarified.

'Except they pretty much are.' Poppy rolled her watery eyes, bit at the skin around her thumbnail. 'In fact, they're a whole lot worse. Anyway, what do you know?'

Janine stroked a tendril of Poppy's damp hair from her cheek, Poppy's aggressive tone seeming to wash over her. 'Oh but I do know, sweetheart. I understand completely.'

Behind them there was a noise on the stairs, and they all turned to see Nell. 'Are you OK, Poppy?' There was a kindness in her tone, as though she was genuinely worried. 'You seem—'

'How the hell do you think I am?' Poppy cried, and without another word, she raced away, disappearing through a corridor of glittering evening dresses.

Saskia was suddenly behind Nell. 'I'm so sorry.' She was close to tears. 'This is all my fault. I've messed up big time. I thought—'

'I'm sure your intentions were good, Saskia.' Nell's voice was choked with emotion. 'But next time, please ask me when you make plans with my stepdaughters that involve me.'

Saskia turned without a word, and headed back through the door leading to the offices, a silence descending in her wake.

'Well, I've a lot to do,' Janine said after a few moments, hurrying away. 'Those beads won't sew on themselves.'.

Ruby and Nell stood, caught in the quiet, staring at each other like cowboys waiting for a shoot-out. Nell's hands hung limp at her sides, her face pale. 'They've gone,' she said. 'The journalists.'

Ruby opened her mouth and closed it again. She wanted to run and hide. This was all too much.

'God only knows what kind of story they'll print,' Nell continued. She paused for a moment, as though planning her words carefully. 'Why did you come here today Ruby? What were you hoping to prove?'

Ruby stepped backwards. This was just like the jumper debacle. She really didn't want another run-in with Nell, another confrontation. She didn't want any of this anymore. Things were out of hand, and she needed it to end.

'Why do you hate me so much?' Nell's voice was small, her arms wrapped around her body as though holding herself together.

'I don't hate you,' Ruby said, though she wasn't sure she didn't. This was the woman who had stolen the last few years of her life. 'But I'll never like you. You destroyed my family, Nell, and I will never forgive you for that.'

Instead of denying it or defending herself, Nell said, 'You could give me a chance.'

Ruby turned away. Despite feeling a snag of pity for the woman, she couldn't give her a chance — she just couldn't.

'Please, Ruby.'

Ruby swung back to face her, narrowed her eyes 'Do you actually love my dad?'

'What? Yes, of course I do.'

'Then why are you having an affair?'

'I'm not. Honestly, Ruby. I would never cheat on your father. You have to believe me.'

Ruby shook her head. 'I don't have to do anything,' she said, heading away.

She found Poppy outside by the car, sitting on the ground, cradling her knees, rocking back and forth.

'Are you OK?' Ruby said, reaching her hand down towards her sister, and pulling her to her feet. 'What the hell was that all about? It was a bit over the top, even for you.'

'I didn't plan it, if that's what you're thinking. I just thought if we came here we might catch Nellie the elephant out.'

Nellie the elephant? That was a new one. Nell was hardly an elephant. She rubbed the tension from her neck. 'I don't know what to think anymore, quite honestly. This is all getting out of hand.'

'I know, and I'm sorry. It's just seeing her kind of sparked something inside me. And it's not like I said anything we don't already know.'

'Yes, but it was in front of those reporters. You do know it will be all over the local tabloids.' Ruby placed her palm tenderly against her sister's cheek. 'I'm worried about you, lovely.'

'What? Why? I'm totally fine.' Poppy moved away, walking round to the passenger side of the car. 'Can you drop me off at the underground before you head into work?' She rubbed her arms, looked almost childlike. 'I want to go home.'

As they pulled out of the car park, Ruby glanced in the rear-view mirror. Sean stood outside the double doors of the warehouse, the orange glow of his cigarette visible against his pale skin as he took a drag. He lifted his hand in a wave.

* * *

It was gone six when Ruby pulled up outside her childhood home. Poppy's outburst that morning had played on her mind all day, and she needed to speak to her mum, hoped Fiona would listen.

'Hi, it's only me,' she called, letting herself in and stepping in through the front door, closing it behind her. 'Mum? Poppy? It's me.'

'In here.' It was Fiona, her voice echoing from the lounge.

Ruby headed into the living room. The curtains were closed. BBC News 24 bright on the TV screen, but there was no sound. Fiona looked up from where she was lying on the sofa, covered by a throw. She pulled herself up to a sitting position.

'Hello, darling, you caught me having a bit of a rest.' Her words didn't slur, and there was no sign of a bottle or glass — not like the early days — but it was clear she was still shutting herself indoors, running away from the world. Fiona rose, gave Ruby a hug, and headed into the kitchen. 'Cup of tea?'

'Please,' Ruby said, following. Fiona was wearing joggers, her loose-fitting T-shirt stained with something yellow, her hair clean but messy, dark roots showing. Tears she hadn't expected filled Ruby's eyes. How could she talk to her mum about Poppy? She suddenly felt so alone, just as she had when her dad walked out.

'Poppy said you've got a part in a play.' Fiona filled the kettle, flicking it on. Her voice was low, on a monotone, as it was most of the time. Thoughts jumped into Ruby's head of the mum before the shit hit the fan: The intelligent, bright, fun loving mum, who would take her and Poppy up to London on a whim to see art galleries and museums; the mum who organised trips abroad at a moment's notice; the mum who volunteered for The Samaritans – the strong confident role model who crumbled into a heap when Oliver left her. The mum who let a man take her power.

'It's just a small theatre, a part in an Agatha Christie play. But I'm thrilled.' Ruby lowered herself onto a stool at the breakfast bar.

'Well, good for you, darling.'

'Where's Poppy?' Ruby looked towards the kitchen door, as though expecting her sister to appear.

'Streaming on Twitch, or whatever it's called.' Fiona shook her head. 'She's always streaming. I'm not even sure what streaming is, if I'm honest.'

'She's playing her scary computer games live, and people watch her.'

Fiona narrowed her eyes as she poured hot water into mugs and stirred the coffee. 'Can anyone see her?'

Ruby nodded. 'It's what young people do these days.'

'And you're so old at twenty-six.'

Ruby smiled, taking a steaming mug from Fiona. Truth was, some days she felt as though her young years were slipping away.

'Your dad was here again today,' Fiona said after a few moments. 'The bathroom tap was leaking.' She smiled. 'He does more now than he did when he lived here. Said something about the house selling for more if it's in good repair. But I said I wasn't about to sell it, not while Poppy's still here.' Her voice cracked, her eyes wide. 'I keep wondering if he . .

.' She broke off, her eyes brimming with tears, and Ruby realised where her mum's thoughts had landed. Was her father thinking she should sell the house now Poppy was eighteen? Split the money with him?

'Dad and Nell wouldn't be having marriage counselling if they were in a good place.' Ruby was trying to give her mum hope. But was it false hope? Was there really any chance he'd return to her mum, even if he and Nell broke up?

'Ruby.' Poppy was standing in the kitchen doorway, the sleeves of her sweatshirt pulled up. 'I thought I heard your voice.'

Ruby's eyes went straight to the small cuts on Poppy's arms. She was self-harming again. There was no doubt of that. She'd seen the same thing before years ago, though those wounds were now scars.

Fiona took a gulp of her coffee, seeming oblivious to the state her daughter was in. Ruby needed to talk to her father. She needed his help. There was no way she could cope alone if her sister spiralled downwards — not again.

CHAPTER 17

Nell

'I know how it sounds, but someone is trying to ruin my life and I've no idea who it is,' I said. Carla had listened, without comment, while I poured out all that had happened since our last meeting. 'As if it's not enough to make it seem like I'm having an affair, whoever it is wants me to lose my job.' I paused for breath, images filling my mind: Poppy's fury-filled face when I asked her how she was feeling; Ruby's shocked expression; Anita's smile as she left — knowing and gleeful. Janine, soothing Poppy as though she was still a child before hurrying away, leaving me to face Ruby's wretched expression. I wished I hadn't asked her why she hated me so much. It made me seem insecure and needy — something I'd never been until I married Oliver. *You shouldn't ask questions you won't like the answers to* my father would have said. He was right.

When she accused me of destroying her family, I'd wanted to remind her Oliver had chosen to leave Fiona before he even met me and would never have returned, but I knew it was futile. It didn't fit her narrative. Plus, I would never know that for certain — whether, if he hadn't met me, the lure of his old, familiar life would have been too great to resist.

As Ruby stalked off, Sean had appeared, a cigarette gripped between finger and thumb, watching her as she left with her sister. He wasn't supposed to smoke on the premises, but I hadn't felt up to reprimanding him. It seemed like the least of my worries.

Saskia had been overcome with remorse, and I felt bad for snapping at her. I told her to take the afternoon off. She didn't resist, working in pale-lipped silence until lunchtime when she quietly brought me a mug of coffee before slipping out with a murmured, *See you tomorrow?* as if unsure she would be welcome.

I nodded, staying focused on the copy I was pretending to write for the website, all the while turning over the morning's events in my mind, wondering whether I should contact Anita and try to explain Poppy's attack. Knowing it would probably only increase speculation, I decided against it, waiting until I could escape and talk to Carla.

'I have literally no idea what's going on, only that my life is falling apart,' I finished, emotion wheeling through me.

Carla's eyes were full of sympathy, as though my tale of woe had nudged her away from neutrality. It was worse somehow, giving credence to my worries. The wrinkle of concern in her voice when she said, 'Some of the things you've mentioned, Nell — the ruined costume, your stolen sweater — you should speak to the police,' sent a chill through me.

'I would rather not involve them.' Forcing myself to calm down, I took a breath before saying, 'If Oliver's daughters are involved — and I think they might be — it would be better to sort it out in person.'

'You're certain it's them?'

'Well . . . not certain, no.' Sean leapt into my head, his comment about the *Cosgrove Curse*. Could he be trying to get at Oliver by breaking us up, the way Oliver had ended Sean's relationship with Ruby? Oliver told me he'd warned Sean off, saying he wasn't right for his daughter, and I'd had to agree with him. But Sean was with Vikki now, seemingly happy, so why would he go to these lengths?

'I don't think my life is at risk,' I went on, as Carla's mouth puckered in consternation. 'Just my marriage and reputation.'

'Ah, well. When you put it like that.' At Carla's dry tone, I gave a reluctant smile.

'I know it sounds bad, but it's not a police matter.'

'What if things escalate?'

My heart gave a hard, warning beat. 'Escalate?'

'Nell . . .' Carla leaned forwards, her face earnest. The silver chain round her neck swung away from her buttoned-up cardigan, the attached letter C catching the light from the lamp by her chair. 'Have you talked to Oliver?'

His name seemed to conjure his presence, inserting itself between us. 'I've tried.' I twisted my wedding ring round and round my finger. 'It's tricky, because if I sound as though I'm accusing his daughter of something . . .' my words tapered off. 'I still can't believe Poppy accused me of stealing their inheritance, by talking him into giving up the company. I'm not interested in his money, would never do such a thing. Leaving Classic Props was his idea,' I said, voice rising. 'I'm worried he wouldn't believe me if I told him what Poppy said.' *Especially as it's becoming increasingly obvious that he doesn't know his daughters very well. Or, doesn't want to know.*

Carla nodded, as though she'd suspected as much, her eyes clouded with worry. 'Nell, have you heard of gaslighting?'

My head pulled back. 'Yes, but that's not Oliver.' I was horrified by the insinuation. 'He's not trying to convince me I'm imagining things, it's more that he doesn't know what to think, or whether to believe I'm not having an affair, for instance. I can hardly blame him for that when he's seen flowers, and those texts I received when we were here.'

Carla sat back, her face smoothing out. 'And you suspect that everything that's happened is linked to you being his wife, that — forgive me if I've got this wrong,' — her eyes darted to her notes — 'this person, or persons, would leave you alone if you and Oliver broke up?'

'I think the aim of the . . . campaign, or whatever you want to call it, is to break up my marriage, so, yes.' Carla's meaningful silence prompted me to add, 'But of course, I'm not giving up. Apart from the fact that I love my husband, that would be letting whoever it is win and no way am I going to let that happen.'

A shadow passed over Carla's face, quickly masked by a smile. 'Of course not.' She probably thought I was deluded, had heard this sort of thing before. A woman unable to accept her marriage was over, clinging on in denial of the facts — just like Fiona. *Why stay when the trust has gone?* But more than anything, I wanted to prove to Oliver that I *was* trustworthy.

'Do you trust him?'

'Of course.' I said it without hesitation, but a tremor inside gave the lie to my certainty. I did trust him only . . . he was out of the house so early, and home so late these days, and I'd caught him on that phone call to — what was the man's name? Birdie? *John Bird.* Oliver's response had been glib, yet there'd been something intimate in his tone, more than seemed appropriate for a business contact.

It was as though sitting opposite Carla, an unconsciously sceptical arch to her eyebrow, the only sounds the occasional rumble of a car outside, had allowed a doubt, couched in the back of my mind, to grow.

Out of nowhere, I was suffused with a wave of nostalgia for the early days with Oliver, talking about music, our favourite TV shows, as we got to know each other. I looked Carla in the eye. 'Oliver would never betray me,' I said firmly. 'That's not the issue, or why I'm here. I want us to find a path back to each other. Can you help with that?'

Her gaze landed on the empty seat beside me. 'My impression was that you were unhappy, Nell. There's a lot going on in your life right now. I'd like us to explore that a little more.'

Her words jarred. I had the sensation I'd taken the wrong path and got lost. 'Actually, I think I've talked enough for now.' Anxiety tightened my stomach. 'You're right, it's Oliver I should be discussing this with. Thank you for pointing that out.'

Alarm flitted over her face. 'Nell, I didn't say—'

'I'm sorry, I have to go.'

Carla was on her feet, but I was quicker, pulling open the door and then running downstairs.

'Nell, wait!'

I drove quickly, as keen to get away as I'd been to talk to Carla less than an hour ago. It was almost seven-thirty, the roads quiet. I passed a group of skateboarding teenagers in low-slung jeans and realised I was driving the wrong way, towards Finsbury Park. Pulling into the nearest side road, about to swing the car around, I spotted a familiar figure on the opposite side of the street. *Saskia.* Her hair was in a high ponytail, and she was dressed more casually than she did for work in jeans and a black leather jacket with low-heeled boots. Her arm was linked through her male companion's, and she was laughing at something he'd said, gazing up at him. It must be her fiancé, Alex. He was tall, broad-shouldered and attractive, and looking at her with obvious affection. I was stung with envy. *That used to be Oliver and me.*

I almost tooted the horn, then realised Saskia might wonder what I was doing here, instead of being at home — plus, we hadn't exactly parted on the friendliest of terms. Best leave before I was spotted.

It struck me as I drove home that I didn't know much about Saskia. Perhaps it was an attempt to avoid going over everything else, but when I got in and realised the house was empty — *had Oliver told me he would be late home?* — I made a bowl of pasta and smothered it in grated cheese, and once seated at the kitchen table opened Facebook on my phone.

Saskia French yielded several results, but her profile was instantly recognisable, even without her glasses. I smiled at her little show of vanity. Her eyes looked bigger, but her face was somehow vulnerable, a scattering of freckles across the bridge of her nose. Her settings were private, but she'd been tagged in a couple of photos. In one, she looked quite different, a shot taken at a beach party, judging by the background. Her hair was blonde, and she was wearing a bikini top and a tie-dyed skirt, raising a beer bottle to the camera. In the other, there was an arm around her shoulders, the other person out of shot — female, judging by the neatly manicured nails — above a caption by the person who'd posted the picture, someone called Hannah Jones. *Sharing my birthday with old friends!!*

There weren't any profile photos of Saskia with Alex, which seemed unusual — but maybe she was a private person, like I was, preferring not to flaunt her relationships. I looked for some mention of her engagement, remembering Alex had proposed by placing a ring among a bouquet of flowers — surely worthy of a social media post, but there was nothing. Not that it mattered. My own ring was a glittering, pear-shaped diamond I'd been almost embarrassed to wear and wouldn't have dreamt of showing off online.

On a whim, I opened Instagram while eating my pasta and found her under the username SaskiaSunshine21. Among the photos of sunsets, a cute, curly-haired dog belonging to a friend, and flowers in *Gran's garden*, I landed on what I was looking for: pictures of her with the man I'd spotted earlier, their faces squashed together, one captioned *he has my heart*!! Only one though, and apart from a couple of random shots of a flat-looking landscape in muted colours and another of an old windmill, there was nothing else.

The front door slammed. I switched off my phone, leaping to my feet so fast my pasta bowl skidded across the table. Outside, the sky was a dusky blue, casting the kitchen into shadow. I headed into the hallway to greet Oliver with a kiss, hoping it might open a line of communication between us, but when I put my arms around him, he took them in his hands and placed them forcibly at my sides. 'Sorry, Nell. I've had a busy day and need a shower.'

Trying not to show how hurt I was, I waited for him to ask how the interview had gone — he hadn't even texted me about it — and when he shrugged off his jacket and headed for the stairs, without saying a word, I burst out, 'Ruby and Poppy gate-crashed the interview with me this morning. Poppy said some awful things.'

'I know.' He swivelled to stare at me, his face the same milky-white as his shirt, his expression fixed. *So that's why he'd rejected my kiss.* 'Ruby called to say how sorry she was.'

'It should have been Poppy calling, and it's *me* she should apologise to.'

His gaze was as cool and detached as a surgeon's. 'Maybe she and Ruby were right to not trust you.'

'*What?*'

He softened then, as though regretting his words, and bowed his head. 'Nell . . . I don't know what's going on with you.'

'Nothing's going on with me.' My mind raced, jumpy with nerves. 'Don't you care what the interview will look like, how awful I'm going to come across if they print what Poppy said?'

He hesitated, seemed about to take a step towards me then changed his mind. 'Look, can I have a shower first, and then we'll talk it through?'

'Fine.' My jaw was rigid with frustration. 'Would you like some pasta?'

'I've already eaten, thanks.' *Where and who with?* I didn't say it.

I turned back to the kitchen and switched on the lights, emotion rising like dough in my chest, expanding to fill my limbs. *How had we come to this?*

A message pinged onto my phone, making me jump. I hardly dared look, dreading another anonymous message, but a glance at the screen revealed it was from Ruby. It was the first time she'd contacted me since I gave her my number when we first met — an awkward meeting in a wine bar with Oliver, me thinking initially we might be friends, though her frosty smile and Poppy's incredulous snigger should have told me it was never going to happen.

I'm sorry about this morning. Ruby.

It was something. More than I would have expected.

Thank you. Not your fault, though. I hope Poppy's feeling better. Nell x

A flame of hope surged. Maybe Ruby would talk to Poppy, get her to call the paper and retract her outburst.

I waited, but when there was no response, I decided to make coffee for when Oliver had finished in the shower. We could sit in the window seat in the living room and watch the sun set, or take our drinks up to bed and talk there. It had been ages since we'd done anything like that, and who cared if I was the one to instigate it? It had to be worth a try, to get through to Oliver.

I'd barely got the clean mugs out of the dishwasher, when I heard footfall on the stairs and Oliver strode into the kitchen, a towel around his waist, water droplets on his shoulders. 'What's this all about?'

'Now what have I done?' I aimed for levity to hide a leap of fear at his expression.

He placed a shiny orange and white flyer onto the countertop. I twisted my head to read the words: *Life Insurance for the ones you love*, alongside an image of a man with his arms looped around an attractive woman, supposedly his wife. Iciness spread across my chest.

'Oliver, I swear I've never seen it before, I don't—'

'And this.' Something else was placed down — a photo. 'I'm seriously worried now, Nell.'

I stared in horror at the picture. It was a smaller replica of the wedding photo in the living room, which normally resided on my bedside table. No longer in its frame, it had been ripped in half, but worse than that, Oliver's face had been scratched out.

CHAPTER 18

Ruby

The fluorescent numbers on the clock on the bedside unit glowed, changing to 3 a.m. Anxiety always messed with Ruby's sleep. It had happened when she was living with Sean. Not at first. It was a gradual thing, the realisation he was controlling her little by little, and her life outside of him and her was getting smaller and smaller. The warning signs began appearing like red flags, and that's when sleep started to escape her. It happened when her parents broke up too — sharp, raw thoughts preventing the comfort of sleep — the sound of her mum crying on the other side of the wall, making her wish she was a million miles away.

And now her brain wouldn't shut down . . . Poppy . . . Nell . . . Sean . . . Poppy . . . Nell . . . Sean . . . over and over and over.

Tears were close. It was clear Poppy was self-harming, even though her sister had covered her arms quickly when she saw where Ruby's eyes had landed. She needed to talk to her sister. Maybe move back home. After all, who else was going to care for Poppy? Their mother was still lost in her own world, and didn't seem to notice Poppy's pain, too obsessed with her own.

Ruby squeezed her eyes closed. She must stop going along with Poppy's vendetta against Nell. Try to quell her sister's anger. Ruby had texted Nell to say sorry for what happened. It was a start. If she expected Poppy to let go of her anger, she had to let go of hers.

She rose at 5 a.m., still unable to sleep, and made her way into the kitchen. Already the area outside was noisy with London traffic. A radio blared somewhere in the block of flats, and pipes clanged upstairs as someone took a shower. This wasn't home. Nobody but the man in the flat above her had spoken to her since she moved in. If this was independence she didn't like it that much. When she'd moved out when she was younger, she had shared houses or flats with friends, and later with Sean. But this was different. She was lonely here.

She made a mug of tea and as she cut across the small hallway on the way to the lounge, she spotted an envelope on the mat. She bent to pick it up, seeing her name on the front in swirly handwriting. *Who knows I'm here?*

She sat down on the sofa, opened it, and pulled out a folded piece of paper. In the same swirly hand was a short note:

Stay away from Sean. He's taken.

Ruby flopped her head back and closed her eyes. This was all she needed. Another layer of anxiety settled on her chest. Who the hell was the letter from? She would have no trouble obeying the sender's wishes — but it was still unnerving. She forced back tears. It wasn't the letter itself that was making her emotional; it was the realisation that she had so few people to turn to.

She picked up her phone, thoughts of Saskia pushing to the surface: *The beginnings of a friendship*. Perhaps they could meet up. She would be someone to talk to, at least. The kind of person she could confide in. She opened up her phone address book, and was about to call her, when she remembered how early it was. She took a deep breath. Maybe it wasn't such a good idea, anyway. How well did she really know Saskia?

Instead she punched in a quick text to Oliver:

Hey, Dad. If you are about today, can we meet up? Ruby x

The reply was almost instant. Oliver often rose early.

Sounds good. Usual place for breakfast, nine o'clock? Dad x

Seeing his text gave Ruby a virtual hug, and the worries of the middle of the night began ebbing away. She would tell him her concerns about Poppy, show him the note. Everything would be OK.

* * *

Ruby was already sitting in the café drinking an Americano, when Oliver appeared. He playfully poked his tongue out at her through the window.

Once inside he ordered a cup of coffee from the woman at the counter — obviously flirting with her, making her laugh.

'Shall I order breakfast?' he called over to Ruby, and she nodded and smiled, wondering if Nell knew he was meeting her.

He finally approached, kissed her cheek, and sat down opposite.

'I wanted to talk to you about Poppy,' she said, desperate to set her worries free. 'I'm concerned about her.'

'Me too.' His brow crinkled 'I heard what happened yesterday at Classics.'

'Her dislike for Nell is getting out of hand, Dad.'

He dragged his fingers through his hair, furrowed his forehead. 'But I thought you girls were starting to bond with Nell.'

'What? Christ, Dad, sometimes I think you go around with your eyes closed.' Ruby shook her head. 'We've both tried for your sake, but . . .' Her words petered away. It wasn't even true. Neither of them had tried for his sake or otherwise. 'It isn't easy. Not when Mum is still so low.' She paused for a moment, as a waiter brought over Oliver's coffee. 'Why do you visit her?' she added, once the man had gone.

'Who? Your mum?'

'No, Kate Middleton.'

Oliver didn't smile. He picked up his coffee, took a sip. 'I feel bad, I suppose, for letting her down. And the house, it's . . .' He stopped mid-sentence.

'Do you still have feelings for her?' Ruby knew she was crossing a line, but she had to know.

'She's yours and Poppy's mum. I guess I will always care about her. But you have to know we'll never get back together, sweetheart. If that's what you're hoping for.' He placed his hand over Ruby's.

After a moment Ruby pulled her hand away, feeling close to tears. Was this the reality of it? Would they never get back together even if he broke up with Nell? Had she really been that naïve? 'You're giving Mum false hope, by going round there.' *And me and Poppy.* 'You need to make your intentions clearer.' A silence fell between them as their breakfast arrived. Ruby looked down at the poached egg and two slices of bacon, no longer hungry.

'I thought I had made them clear enough,' Oliver said, once the waiter had disappeared. 'I'm married to Nell now, surely that speaks for itself.'

But you're going to marriage counselling. Ruby took a deep breath, picked up her fork, and poked the egg, staring as the yolk erupted. 'Poppy's convinced you'll get back with Mum.' *I was too.* 'If you did, it would be a real turning point for Poppy.'

Ruby watched as her dad shovelled a mushroom into his mouth, regretting immediately that she was resorting to emotional blackmail.

He chewed for some moments before swallowing, and lowered his cutlery. 'I don't know what to say, Ruby. Poppy's clearly not thinking straight.'

'And she needs help, Dad. She needs you to talk to her.' She paused for a moment. 'She's self-harming, like she did before, remember? She hasn't been coping too well since I moved out.'

'Maybe you could encourage her to see someone.'

'Or you could talk to her.' It came out sharp. 'She needs one of her parents to take some responsibility.'

'Ouch.'

'Sorry, but—'

'Your sister's a live wire, Ruby, that's all.'

Calling Poppy a live wire when she was a child was fine, but now it felt dismissive — irresponsible. 'You could at least try.'

He narrowed his eyes. 'Do you know if Poppy has been in my house, Ruby?'

'What?' That wasn't what she was expecting to hear. She felt herself redden. Guilt rising. Why would he even ask that? Had someone seen them go into the house? Told him.

He rummaged in his jacket pocket and brought out a photo of his wedding day. The side with Nell was untouched, but Oliver's face had been scratched out.

Ruby stared down at the photo. 'You think Poppy did this?'

'I don't know who did it.' Oliver tucked it back in his pocket, and continued with his breakfast as though unfazed by the photo. 'I found it in my bedside drawer, along with . . .'

'Along with what?'

'It's just, after hearing about Poppy's outburst, and now you're saying she's self-harming again, I thought she might . . .' He picked up his mug, took a long gulp of his drink. 'Like you, I'm worried about her, that's all.'

'Nell might have done it,' Ruby said, though not really believing it. *Why would she?*

He shrugged. 'Actually, I'm a bit worried about her too.' He shook his head, looking down. 'She's not herself, doesn't seem to be coping at work.'

Ruby stared at her dad for a long moment, before closing her eyes briefly, needing to focus. Part of her wanted to confess that she and Poppy had been in his house. But then she knew Poppy hadn't touched any photos. Well, not unless she'd been back to the house on her own since they went together. Oh, God, this was too much. She would talk to Poppy. Warn her that their dad was suspicious, that she needed to be careful. She would suggest her sister saw a doctor. Move back home to support her. But what about the show? Her chance to get back on the stage? She would never be able to travel from Richmond to Islington each day.

'Are you going to eat that hash brown?' Oliver's fork hovered over her breakfast, ready to stab her food. Nothing seemed to affect his appetite.

She shoved the plate across the table towards him, and rose to her feet. 'Fill your boots. I've got to get to work.'

'Ruby!' He called after her, as she raced across the café and out through the door without looking back.

As she hurried down the road, she pulled out the anonymous letter she'd received. It wasn't that she'd forgotten to show it to her dad, it was more that she felt it was a waste of time. He wasn't there for her, not really, and he definitely wasn't there for Poppy. In fact, she wondered now if he ever had been.

She scanned the words once more:

Stay away from Sean. He's taken.

Surely only one person could have sent it. It had to be from his new partner, Vikki.

CHAPTER 19

Nell

When Saskia arrived at work the following morning, I felt a rush of relief. Part of me hadn't expected her back after the events of the day before. She was pale but composed, her smile hesitant as she pushed her bag into her desk drawer. 'Everything OK?'

'Fine,' I lied, attempting an answering smile. I knew I looked tired, despite using concealer to hide the shadows under my eyes. The scene with Oliver last night had kept me awake until the small hours. He had seemed convinced in the end that I hadn't defaced our wedding photo or looked into taking out a life insurance policy on him, despite the apparent evidence lying between us.

'Where did you even find these?' I'd managed, trying to take in the reality of his scratched-out face and the flyer he'd thrown in front of me.

'In the drawer of my bedside table. It was open slightly, and I spotted the edge of the flyer, and when I looked inside I saw the photo.'

I turned the picture over with shaking hands, unable to look at his ruined image any longer. 'If I *had* done this, why would I have left them where you could find them?'

'I don't know, Nell.' Puzzlement vied with anger. 'Are you sending me some kind of message?'

'Message?'

'That you don't want us to be married anymore?' His fingers drummed the worktop as though channelling his feelings. 'That you want me *dead?'*

'Dead?' I was an echo, my mind scrambling to catch up. 'Oliver, if I didn't want to be with you, I would ask for a divorce, not spend a fortune on counselling while playing ridiculous mind games.' Brushing aside the terrifying question of who had done this — *Poppy, Sean? Ruby?* — I swallowed the frustrated tears that threatened. 'You *know* me, Oliver. None of this is my doing.'

His brow creased with bafflement. 'Maybe I don't know you as well as I thought I did.'

His words sent a shock wave through me. 'Oliver, *please.*' I hated the tremulous note in my voice. Where was the anger, the outrage? Oliver doubted me, that much was obvious. It was in the slide of his gaze across my face, as though I was an intruder, and the stiffening of his shoulders when I touched him. *Someone wanted this.*

'Remember our first Christmas, just the two of us?' Softening my voice, I slid my arms around his neck, wanting to remind him of happier times. 'That enormous turkey you cooked and how we thought we should walk it off afterwards, and it started snowing?' I'd suggested his daughters join us, but they wanted to spend the day with their mother, and part of me was relieved. There had been something magical about that day that sustained me through a long chat on the phone with Mum, who had spent Christmas in Wales with her brother and his family, and a visit to Oliver's mother's — *you do know Fiona spent the day in bed, Oliver?* — on Boxing Day. 'We stayed out until we couldn't feel our fingers anymore because you wanted a snowball fight, but it didn't settle.' *Didn't settle.* The words seemed meaningful somehow.

Oliver pulled away, a nerve twitching in his jaw. 'Things change, Nell. *You've* changed.'

I strained to think how and when, to pinpoint where I'd gone wrong. 'I want the same things I did back then. All this stuff . . .' I gestured to the photo, the stupid flyer. 'Why won't you see that somebody is deliberately doing this? They want us at each other's throats.'

'By someone, you mean my daughters?'

'It's less far-fetched than you blaming me.'

'I'm not sure how much more I can take, Nell.'

I shrank from the detachment in his gaze.

'I'm going to my study,' he said wearily. 'I need to think.'

I'd held my body still, feigning sleep when he finally came to bed, but he didn't attempt to touch me. I could barely remember the last time he had.

* * *

'Do you know when the feature will go live?'

Saskia's query broke my spinning thoughts. 'Around lunchtime.' I gave an internal shudder. I'd been trying not to think about it, to resist checking the article hadn't gone up on the newspaper's website already. 'I'm not sure I dare look.'

'Won't you get copy approval first?'

I shook my head. 'I didn't think to ask for it. Naïve, really, but when I agreed to be interviewed, I had no idea how it was going to go. Even if I did ask, I doubt they'll change anything.'

'You could sue them if they're slanderous.' Saskia adjusted her glasses, patches of red on her cheeks. 'It's not fair.'

Gratified she seemed annoyed on my behalf, my smile was genuine this time. 'Probably better to ride it out,' I said. 'But I'll cross that bridge later.' I glanced at her engagement ring as it caught the light and remembered seeing her with

Alex the night before, and how carefree and happy she had looked. 'Sorry you've been dragged into this. Not quite the job you were expecting, I'm sure.'

'It's been . . . interesting.' When a flash of humour brightened her face, my relief intensified.

'I'm glad you're here, Saskia.' I realised I meant it, in spite of everything. 'At the moment, it feels as if you're the only person on my side.'

She shifted in her swivel chair, getting comfortable. 'What about your mum?'

'Mothers are conditioned to love their children, no matter what.' When a shadow crossed her face, I could have kicked myself. I didn't know anything about her home life. 'Sorry if that was insensitive.'

'I lost my parents when I was eighteen.' She tightened her ponytail — a tic I was starting to recognise as a self-soothing gesture. 'Car accident.'

'That's awful, Saskia. I'm so sorry.' The thought of it brought a tightness to my throat. At eighteen, I had taken my parents for granted in the best possible way, cushioned by their loving presence, and their unconditional support. 'You must miss them so much.'

Her hands gripped the edge of the desk, as if to steady herself. The loss was plainly still raw. 'They were really happy together.' Her voice sounded small and tight. 'That's the kind of marriage I want.'

I was glad now that I had seen the way her fiancé looked at her. 'And I'm sure you'll have it,' I said, gently.

She nodded, the movement decisive. 'I will.'

I imagined her saying those two words as part of her wedding vows — as I had with Oliver — and felt a glimmer of apprehension that her expectations might be unrealistic. Then again, I was hardly in a position to give relationship advice.

'It's what I want too,' I said. 'The sort of marriage my parents had before my dad died.' Saskia's lips pursed, as if unsure whether to ask what happened. 'Heart attack,' I clarified, the words bringing a twist of pain.

'I'm sorry.' Her hands released their grip on the desk, and she switched on her computer. 'But you and Oliver aren't really happy, are you?'

Her bluntness threw me, but there was no point denying it. 'Not at the moment, no.' I felt the burn of humiliation. 'But I'm working on it. I'll keep going until we get back to where we were a couple of years ago. Six months ago, even.' I was saying too much, as usual. Saskia looked embarrassed, moving the mouse mat about, her neatly trimmed nails making little scratching sounds. I must sound like an idiot, in denial about the true state of my relationship, but Saskia couldn't know how determined I was when I put my mind to something. Oliver might be doubting me, his daughters might hate me, his ex-wife too — enough to want to break me — but if anything, my resolve to fix things was stronger than ever. I had never been the type to give up at the first hurdle, or even the tenth, and wasn't about to start now.

'Maybe you should both take a day off work and spend some time together,' Saskia suggested, stroking a tendril of hair behind her ear. 'I can manage this place.'

I'd thought about it earlier, waking from a fitful sleep and hearing Oliver moving about downstairs. I'd registered surprise that he hadn't already left to meet a client, but when I entered the kitchen he was putting his jacket on and announced he was meeting Ruby for breakfast. No kiss goodbye. He had barely looked me in the eye.

'He's very busy, and I would rather be at work if he's not at home.'

When Saskia tried to hide a pitying look, I realised how sad it sounded — as if I didn't know how to fill my time without my husband. 'I do love my job.'

'I can see that.' A playful gleam entered her eyes. 'So, what's on the agenda this morning?'

Despite being occupied for the next few hours, my mind kept returning to the interview, and by midday I couldn't wait any longer.

While Saskia was down in the warehouse, checking in new stock with Janine, I opened my email, half-expecting a message from Anita with a link to the newspaper's webpage, but there was nothing. Nerves prickling, I clicked onto the site. Shock thudded through me. My interview was the main feature.

Eyes darting back and forth, I took in a well-lit photo of me sitting behind my desk. Poppy was leaning over it, her face captured in a mask of anger, one finger jabbing the air near my nose. My expression was frozen, wide-eyed, yet frowning — a portrait of stony disapproval under the heading:

Local businesswoman accused of stealing children's inheritance.

As I skim-read the paragraph underneath, heat flushed up my neck. Poppy's eruption was the leading paragraph, including the part about my supposed husband-stealing. A link beneath encouraged the public to read more. I did. It wasn't pretty. Much less had been made of my achievements at Classic Costumes and Props after taking over from Mark Bradbury who had *retired due to injury after an accident*, and *husband, Oliver Cosgrove, son of respected wine merchant Leonard Cosgrove,* and more of the speculation that I somehow persuaded Oliver to relinquish co-ownership of the company with my own bid for power after seducing him away from his wife and mother of his daughters.

It became clear before our interview had even started that the real story here is one of betrayal — a wife discarded, two daughters torn between their parents, a new wife struggling to hold onto the role she has — some would say — ruthlessly carved out after her former career in wedding planning failed. It's obvious there is no love lost between the girls and their new stepmother. The fractures are clear to see, which begs the question: is success at any cost really worth it?

Anger shot through me. Anita hadn't bothered to ask for my side of the story; had made up her own, almost fictionalised version. So much for women supporting other women.

There was another photograph, an old one of Oliver with Fiona and the girls when they were younger. Poppy's hair was shorter and twisted into bunches, Ruby's loose around her shoulders, a contrast to Fiona's glossy, blonde bob. Oliver's arms encircled them from behind and their faces were smiling for the camera in a picture of contentment. I hadn't seen it before, and the sight was a stab in the ribs, a reminder of all that I didn't share with Oliver; parenthood, and everything that went with raising a family.

I wondered where Anita had found the image, and remembered there had been a few features about Oliver, the company, and his family over the years. It wouldn't have been hard to find the picture online. *Happier times for the Cosgroves* was the caption. I shook my head in disbelief. I felt sure a man in my position would never have been painted like this, or have his integrity questioned. The injustice burned inside my chest.

Scrolling down, I landed on another photo, this one of Saskia behind her desk, smiling squarely at the camera. Chris had obviously put her at ease. The image of me conveyed a negative tone, while Saskia radiated calm efficiency, the smooth planes of her face and gleam of her hair at odds with my clenched expression and the hint of frizz at my hairline, as if I was about to come undone.

An oasis of calm, PA Saskia French, twenty-eight, continued to work while the storm raged around her. Asked whether she could see herself in Nell's position one day, Saskia laughed and said that while she loves to work — and that should the opportunity present itself, she would accept more responsibility — she doesn't buy into the oft-quoted belief that women can have it all. 'Something, or usually someone, suffers,' she said. 'If I had to choose, it would be family, my loved ones, every time. No one on their deathbed ever said, "I wish I'd spent more time at the office". At least, not that I know of!'

Maybe Nell Cosgrove should take note. Rumours have it her relationship is suffering, and the couple are receiving marriage counselling. My anger deepened. How did she know? *Has Nell's swift rise at Classic Costume and Props been worth it?*

'Oh my God, they've twisted everything.' I had been aware of Saskia's return and how, drawn no doubt by the look on my face, she'd come to stand at my shoulder to read the article. 'I had no idea they were going to quote anything I said, I promise, Nell. We were chatting before you came in and the photographer was taking some test shots.' I could hear her breaths, short and sharp, smell her vanilla perfume, and then she was moving away, back to her desk. Seeing her pull open a drawer and take out her bag, I said, 'What are you doing?'

'This is all my fault.' Her voice was shaky, and her chin trembled. Janine appeared at the top of the stairs, a sheaf of thick fabric over one arm. She took one look at us both and retreated. 'I'm supposed to be here to make your life easier, Nell, but things have got worse because of me.' She unzipped her bag and closed it again, clearly fighting her emotions. 'I think I should leave.'

'What?' I rose, feeling untethered. 'Don't be silly,' I said, even as part of me acknowledged that she was right, things *had* worsened, and she should never have invited Ruby and Poppy here — but things hadn't been great even before she arrived. 'You weren't to know they were going to use your words against you,' I insisted. 'Anita was here for a story, and she got one.'

'I hate the way they've put you down, as if you haven't worked hard to be where you are.'

'I hate it too.' I curled my hands into fists and rested them on my desk. 'It's nothing but gossip, and a shame Anita wasn't championing working women, but it's done now. Hopefully, it'll blow over.' Saskia sniffed and nodded, pulling a tissue from the sleeve of her blouse. 'In the meantime, we've work to do.'

'If you're sure?'

'I'm positive.' I strove to sound reassuring, in control. 'Shall I go and make us some coffee?'

'I'll do it.' With a watery smile, she dabbed at her eyes under her glasses. 'Thank you, Nell.'

When she had gone to the kitchen, I dropped back down in my chair and let out a breath of despair. I would email Anita to let her know what I thought of the piece, of the cheap shots she'd fired without giving me the right to reply. As I went to click off the page, a link in the sidebar caught my eye. One of the tabloid newspapers had picked up on the story, running with the headline:

London costume hire company at centre of family scandal.

My heart lurched as I read it. They'd regurgitated the whole story, with added details about some of the companies who used our services. *Unlike the plot of a film by Finlay Productions — a regular client of Classic Costumes and Props — this drama looks set to continue.* Anita must have alerted them, perhaps hoping to boost her own career with a commission from a national paper. The irony made me feel sick.

'Saskia, I'm sorry, but I don't feel well,' I said, when she returned with the coffees. 'Can you hold the fort?'

She looked briefly startled as she put down my mug. 'Of course,' she said, rallying. 'You go. I'll be fine.'

All I could think as I sped outside, ignoring Janine's cry of 'Nell, wait!' and Sean's curious, cool green gaze as I dived into my car, was that I had to talk to Oliver before he got wind of the article and saw for himself what a bad light it cast me in. I imagined his anger, him getting onto the phone to the newspaper, tearing a strip off them for misrepresenting me. *Seduced him away from his wife.* I wanted to scream.

Oliver's car was parked on the drive when I got home, a small crate of wine on the ground beside it, as though he'd got distracted before taking it inside. The front door was slightly ajar. I stepped inside and heard voices, muffled by the walls, instantly recognising the pitch of Oliver's tone, coming from his study. Heart pummelling my chest, I edged down the hallway, pausing as I realised his visitor was Poppy.

'Please, Daddy,' she was saying. 'Let me stay here for a while, just a few nights. I don't want to be at Mum's. She's so miserable all the time.'

I thought of the cuts on Poppy's arms I'd glimpsed the day before and — despite myself — felt a surge of pity.

'I promise I won't get in the way.'

'Don't you have friends you can go to?'

'I told you, no, and Ruby's sick of me.'

'Your sister loves you, we all do.' Oliver sounded surprisingly fraught — unprepared for a confrontation with his younger daughter. He hated being disturbed when he was working. She must have turned up out of the blue. 'And anyway, your mum needs you.'

'That's the problem.' Poppy's tone grew sullen. 'I'm sick of her needing me. She needs *you*.'

'Not this again.' I pictured him rubbing the crease between his eyebrows. 'Look sweetheart, I'm really busy—'

'It's her, isn't it?' I stiffened. '*Nell.* She doesn't want me here.'

'She's pretty angry about what you said yesterday at the office.' He didn't deny Poppy's assertion that I wouldn't want her to stay and with piercing clarity, I realised he was out of his depth. He didn't know how to cope with Poppy and her 'issues' as he called them. *Did he even realise they were linked to his break-up with Fiona?*

'I didn't say anything that wasn't true.' Defiant now. 'God's sake, Dad, look at her properly, see her for what she is.'

'What exactly do you mean?'

'She's taken over your company, and now she's having an affair. It's obvious, and I don't know why you can't see it, Dad. Mum would never cheat on you, she loves you.'

In the beat of silence that followed I held my breath, feeling as if I was standing on the edge of a cliff — waiting for him to tell her that he would never go back to Fiona, that Poppy had to accept their relationship was over.

'I'm going to call your sister,' he said instead.

Disappointment flooded through me. Even with our own relationship under threat, his instinct had been to protect Poppy, and while I understood that, I'd hoped he might defend me too.

My phone pinged in my bag, startling me. I couldn't face the pair of them with my thoughts so scattered. I wouldn't know what to say. I pulled out my mobile to see a voicemail alert. Carla.

I was worried after you left our last session so suddenly, Nell. Please call and we'll arrange another time.

I was overwhelmed with an urge to speak to her; to hear her soothing voice, her calm reassurances. I could talk to her about Poppy, then see if Oliver — or Ruby — could persuade her to get some help. I slipped into the kitchen, pausing as I noticed the cupboard under the sink was half-open. About to close it, I glanced inside to see a six-pack of bottled beers nestled beside the cleaning equipment — the beers I'd bought for Ruby and Poppy that had gone missing from the fridge. *Weird.* I definitely hadn't put them there. Unease slid through me, as I shut the door, jumping when a piercing shriek cut through the air.

'I *hate* you, and that bitch you married!' Footsteps thundered down the hall and the slam of the front door reverberated through the house.

I stood in frozen silence for several seconds, Poppy's words ringing in my ears.

There was no sound from Oliver as I moved back into the hallway, then I heard the low hum of his voice, talking to someone on the phone. *Business as usual.*

Tears blocked my throat. Unwilling to face him, or even let him know I was home, I silently left the house, half-expecting to see Poppy — she must have got a taxi here — but there was no sign of her.

I drove back to work, something ominous hovering like a shadow at the edge of my mind. I barely had time to sit at my desk, or acknowledge Saskia's quietly spoken, 'Is everything OK?' when the work phone rang.

She answered, casting me a worried look. 'It's Mark. He wants to talk to you.'

CHAPTER 20

Ruby

Ruby bumped her van onto the kerb in the narrow street behind Sharma's Sandwiches, as a text appeared on her phone.

Poppy is out of control. We need to talk. Dad X

She took a deep breath, and pressed his number, pinned the phone against her ear. 'Hey,' she said when he answered.

'Poppy was round here yesterday,' he said, without so much as a hello. 'Shouting the odds about Nell. Asking to stay here, of all things.' His breath was raspy, as though he was walking fast. But it was more than that, his tone had a cold harshness she hadn't heard in a long time.

'Why isn't she staying at Mum's?'

'She says she's sick of being needed by her.'

Ruby's stomach tipped. *She's sick of being needed.* 'So can she stay with you for a bit?'

'Christ, Ruby, you know that isn't practical.' There was a hint of desperation in his tone now. He would get like this when she was younger, whenever he was asked to do something he didn't want to do. 'Think about it, Ruby — she hates Nell. How do you think that would work out?'

'But Poppy needs your support, Dad.' Her voice broke off. Her sister was the victim here, and nobody seemed to want to help her.

'She's eighteen, Ruby, not a child.'

'Oh, come on, Dad, you know Poppy is still a child in so many ways. I told you how bad things are, about her self-harming. I mean she must be desperate if she's come to you.'

'What's that supposed to mean?'

'Nothing. It doesn't mean anything.' She shook her head, closed her eyes feeling helpless. 'All I'm saying is, if she's willing to move in with you and Nell—'

'Maybe she could stay with you?' His voice was softer now. 'She loves you so much, Ruby.'

Emotional blackmail. 'My place is a hamster hutch, Dad, and there's barely room to swing one.' Guilt surged. This was turning into pass the buck, and she hated the way that made her feel. 'OK. I'll talk to her. I'll go round to Mum's, find out why she's not happy there, and try to work out what to do for the best.'

'Great. Thanks, Ruby. You're a princess.' And then he was gone, not allowing her a moment to pass that buck back to him.

She quickly keyed in a text to Poppy:

I'll be round to Mum's later. Hope you're OK X

She had to help her sister, but moving back home was a step backwards. She'd already given up so much for Poppy and her mum. Was it wrong to want to put herself first for once? She would talk to her mum and sister later. Discover if Poppy had destroyed their dad's and Nell's wedding photo, confront her about the self-harming, offer to go with her to the doctors, maybe arrange some counselling. And hopefully she could make their mum see how bad things were with

Poppy. Maybe her dad should come too. She would message him. Ask him to. Her parents needed to help her deal with this before it got any worse.

* * *

Ruby hung the van keys on one of the hooks near the door at the back of the shop, and was about to leave, when Benita appeared.

'Have you seen the article in the local paper?' She handed Ruby the latest edition. 'It's all about Nell, and there's a photo of you when you were younger.'

Ruby stared down at the article, her heart thudding. 'Oh God, this is awful.'

'Is it? I thought you hated Nell. I thought you'd be pleased.'

Hate is a strong emotion. 'I don't do hate anymore.' Ruby scanned the words. 'Surely this is slander?'

'Only if it isn't true.' Benita's eyes widened. 'Is it true?'

'I guess so, but it's still a bit harsh.' Ruby took in the photo, *Happier times for the Cosgroves,* her mind drifting back to when they were all together. 'Nell doesn't deserve this. Nobody does.'

'Well you've changed your tune.' The bell rang in the shop, and Benita turned and headed away.

Ruby folded the paper and made her way outside into the cool air. Nell was having a rough ride, and the truth was Ruby couldn't help but feel sorry for her.

* * *

'Poppy's not here, she didn't come home last night.' Fiona took a bottle of red wine from the cupboard, unscrewed the lid.

Ruby watched as her mother poured two large glasses, her heart sinking. She thought her mum had stopped drinking. 'That's not like her to stay out all night, is it?'

'She texted to say she's staying with a friend.'

'What friend? She hasn't got any friends as far as I know.'

Fiona picked up one of the glasses, took a gulp.

'I've heard nothing from her all day, Mum. Her phone keeps going to voicemail.'

'Stop panicking, Ruby.'

'I'm not panicking.' She glared at the brimming glass on the work surface. 'And I really don't want any wine, Mum. I'm driving.'

'You don't have to take that attitude.'

'What attitude?' She rubbed her hand over her mouth a couple of times, trying not to get angry. 'Dad said Poppy was in a right state yesterday. You must have noticed how she's been since I left.'

Fiona carried her glass through to the lounge, and Ruby followed. 'Mum, are you even listening to me?'

'Of course I am.' Fiona sat down, patted the sofa next to her.

But Ruby remained standing, began pacing the room, glancing out of the window. There was no sign of her father. Not that he'd agreed to come. In fact, he hadn't even replied to her message.

'We had a bit of a disagreement.' Fiona took a gulp of her drink, her voice calm. 'Poppy said I depended on her too much. Which, of course, I do not.'

Ruby stopped pacing and stared at her mother. Fiona had depended on Ruby, so why not Poppy? She imagined for a moment Poppy and Fiona moving around the huge house, swaying to and fro, like broken reeds, unable to prop each other up.

She pulled out her phone, tried her sister's number again, but again it went straight to voicemail. 'Call me, Poppy. We're getting worried about you.'

'I don't know why you're so worried, Ruby.' Fiona took another gulp of her drink, red stains appearing at the corner of her mouth like The Joker. 'Poppy has every right to go out.'

'But she doesn't go out though, does she, Mum? Especially overnight. She spends most of her time on her bloody computer. Twitching, or whatever she does up in her room. And it's not only that, it's everything else. Like the terrible scene she made in front of that journalist.'

'Oh yes.' Fiona smiled, leaned forward and picked up her phone. 'Poppy sent me the link to the article.' She stared at the screen for some moments.' 'I've always liked this picture of us,' she said.

'Why are you like this, Mum?' Ruby said slowly, tears building behind her eyes. Once upon a time she would have turned to her mother about everything that'd been happening. 'You never used to be.'

Before Fiona could respond, Ruby's phone rang.

'Hi,' Ruby said into the phone, trying to disguise her emotions.

'Ruby?'

'Yes.'

'It's Saskia. The thing is, I've found Poppy's phone. It was on the floor near the entrance to Classics. I think she must have lost it. Could you let her know I've found it?'

Ruby's heart banged against her ribs. Where was her sister? She opened her mouth, about to confide in Saskia that Poppy hadn't been home, but thought better of it. The lost phone at least explained why she'd been ignoring her calls. 'Thanks, Saskia. Could you keep hold of it. I'll collect it when I'm on my round tomorrow.'

CHAPTER 21

Nell

'I really don't need this, Nell.' Oliver was watching me from the doorway. 'I've had a right day of it with Ruby bombarding my phone.'

I stopped pacing the living room and stood in front of the fire I'd lit after arriving home from work earlier, chilled by my conversation with Mark. 'Why would you even speak to him?'

'I've explained quite clearly already.' Oliver spoke with forced patience, leaning against the frame with his arms folded. 'I wanted to give Mark a heads-up about that awful feature in the news.'

'The *news*?' I let out a humourless laugh. 'It was one local paper and the gutter press.'

'I thought he should hear it from one of us.' Oliver held up a hand as I started to speak. 'You seemed to have enough on your plate.'

'Oh, so you were doing me a favour?' His betrayal stung and I wanted to hit back. 'You don't even work there anymore.'

Oliver's expression hardened. 'Mark is my closest friend.' His voice was ominously quiet. 'In case you've forgotten, we ran that place together for more than twenty-five years.' *As if he would let me forget.* 'Also, that feature included a photo of my family, which means I have a right to say what I think.'

I stared, not liking his tone — or the implication that 'family' didn't include me. 'He's put me on gardening leave,' I pushed the words past a knot in my throat. 'He doesn't trust me to be there anymore.'

'Only until things blow over.'

I dropped onto the sofa, my limbs heavy. Mark's words bounced around my skull — his disappointment after hearing from Oliver what had happened; his concern that business might be affected during a critical time. He'd heard a new prop hire company were starting up not far from us, funded by an actor, though it was the first I'd heard of it. He didn't sound so much angry as confused, which made me feel even worse. My face had burned under Saskia's curious gaze.

'It's nothing I can't handle, Mark.' I'd tried not to sound desperate. 'I think someone is trying to sabotage me and the company, but I'll get to the bottom of it.'

Mark's silence had spoken volumes and my heart dropped like a stone.

'Nell, if that's true — and I really hope it isn't — it might be a good idea for you to take some time off.'

'Time off?' I'd registered Saskia's stillness, the way her eyes filled with horrified sympathy. 'Honestly, Mark, there's no need for that. I can deal with it, I promise, I just—'

'It isn't a request, Nell.' There had been kindness in his tone, even a hint of apology. He knew I loved my job and was good at it — usually. 'It's for the best, until whatever this is has passed, and the fallout has died down.'

'But Mark—'

'I gather Saskia has settled in well, and of course I'll be there too.'

My stomach pitched. 'You're coming back?'

'Just for now.'

'Right.' I tried to hold onto whatever shred of dignity I had left. 'How long will that be?'

'Let's see how it goes.' After a pause, he added softly, 'Effective immediately, Nell. I'm on my way over.'

It was pointless arguing. Mark owned the company, and, in his eyes, I'd messed up. He wanted me out — at least for a while.

As I grabbed my jacket and bag, I felt the heat of blame, and a heavy weight settled in my chest. I'd barely been in the office for half an hour.

Saskia rose, her face flushed. 'You're not leaving me here?'

'No choice,' I said too brightly, blinking away tears. 'You'll be fine with Mark, he's a good boss, and you know what you're doing.'

'But it's not fair.' She hurried over, eyes gleaming behind her glasses. 'You should fight your corner, Nell.'

'How, when I don't know who, or what, I'm fighting?'

Her hand fell away from my arm. 'I'm leaving too, then.'

Alarmed, I watched her rush back to her desk. The phone was ringing but she ignored it, pulling her trench coat on. 'No,' I said, firmly. 'I appreciate the gesture, Saskia, but it won't help. The best thing you can do is to keep things running smoothly here.' I straightened my shoulders. 'I'm only a phone call or email away. If anyone asks, tell them . . .' my voice cracked. 'Tell them whatever you have to. The business is all that matters.'

I hadn't waited for her reply, or for Mark to arrive, not wanting him to see me in this state, leaving him a voicemail instead as I hurried to my car.

I'm sorry you feel I've let you down, Mark, but I'm not going to let it lie. I'll get to the bottom of what's going on and put it right.

The first thing I'd done back home was confront Oliver, busy on the phone in his study.

'So, what am I supposed to do?' I asked him now.

'This isn't only about you, Nell.' He observed me with a look of calculation. 'Do you realise how selfish you sound?'

'Selfish?' I swivelled to look at him more closely and saw he was deadly serious. 'This is happening to *me*, Oliver. I've practically lost my job, had my reputation trashed, been called a gold-digging *slut* by your daughter, been accused of having an affair, and you're calling me *selfish?'*

'Not everything is about work, and Poppy was being . . .' he twirled a wrist in the air. 'Poppy,' he concluded, tiredly.

'That doesn't make it acceptable.' I jumped as a log cracked in the grate, spitting an ember onto the rug. Feeling overheated, I watched it glow and fade before returning my gaze to Oliver. 'This is why I've been making an effort, lately. Taking on Saskia, going to counselling, inviting the girls for dinner, trying to be home more. I don't see *you* doing much. You haven't even cut down on your working hours.'

'That's different. I'm still building my client base.' He gave a dismissive shake of his head. 'You know how it is, Nell. Without a decent income, we wouldn't be able to afford this place—'

'I don't care if we live somewhere smaller, less expensive. It would be worth it to see each other more.'

'Well, I do care.'

'Even at the expense of our marriage?' I couldn't understand why he wasn't tearing down walls to repair things between us, to get to the bottom of all the strange things that were happening. How could he care more about having a big, fancy house?

'It's important to me to have a lovely home for us.' He lowered his head, shaking it from side to side, and I tried to understand that his need to provide materially was one of his ways of showing love. 'I have to go out,' he said to the floor. 'Maybe you should try to relax.'

Relax? I looked at him, seeking the man who had spread a picnic rug in the garden the weekend after we moved in, where we ate the feast he'd provided and toasted our new home with champagne, before lying back to look at the sky, holding hands. 'What's happening to us, Oliver?'

Before he could reply, his phone rang. Not looking at me, he pulled it from his trouser pocket. 'Oliver Cosgrove.' His face darkened as he listened. 'Missing?'

I got to my feet while he listened some more, a frown cutting between his eyebrows.

'Thanks for letting me know,' he said at last. 'Keep me posted.'

'What is it?'

'That was Ruby. Apparently Poppy's gone missing. Her phone was found outside Classics. Saskia found it and called Ruby to let her know.' I immediately thought of the red paint, and the ruined costume — the shadowy glimpse of a hooded figure on camera. 'It seems Poppy didn't go home last night and Ruby's worried.'

'Naturally.' I was surprised he didn't sound more concerned.

'It's the sort of thing Poppy does.' Irritation flashed over his face. 'Attention-seeking, that's all. She'll be in the summerhouse at Fiona's or hiding in Ruby's closet.'

'But—'

'She wants everyone out there, looking for her.'

'So, that's what we should be doing.' I couldn't understand his lack of urgency. 'Oliver, she's not well.'

He screwed up his eyes, as if I was a riddle he couldn't solve. 'You don't know my daughter like I do, Nell. She's done this before. I'm telling you, she'll be fine.' His phone rang again, and Fiona's name flashed up.

Oliver declined the call and thrust his phone back in his pocket, simultaneously reaching for his wallet and keys on the table by the front door.

'You're still going out?'

He closed his eyes and pinched the bridge of his nose. 'I'll be back in a couple of hours,' he said with resigned weariness. 'It'll be fine, Nell. Don't worry.'

He opened the door. Outside, greyish daylight filtered through a sheet of cloud. Before I could move he'd gone, the door slamming behind him. Seconds later came the sound of his car engine revving.

A tear tracked down my cheek. I brushed it away impatiently. Oliver wasn't right, he couldn't be. I wasn't being selfish. And regardless of whether Poppy's behaviour was attention-seeking, the fact was, she hadn't gone home and didn't have her phone, worrying Ruby enough to call her father, and he'd done nothing.

I wandered into the kitchen to put the kettle on, noticing a container of milk on the counter that I was sure hadn't been there before.

What if Poppy was here, hiding somewhere?

I flew upstairs. 'Poppy! It's OK, you can come out now.' I barged into each room, but the only sound was my ragged breathing, the only sight my face in the bathroom mirror, blotchy with anxiety. In the bedroom, I pulled open the wardrobe, then, recalling the ruined photo and insurance flyer Oliver had found, looked inside the drawer of his bedside cabinet, which was almost empty now. About to close it and resume my search for Poppy, I heard something above — a creak, like someone stepping on a floorboard. I froze, glancing up. Had it come from the loft, the one place I rarely ventured beyond putting away the Christmas decorations?

I held my breath, straining for further sounds, and jumped when a gust of wind blew rain against the windowpanes. It was only the weather, which sometimes created strange sounds in and around the old building. It couldn't make up its mind, sunny one minute, raining the next, adding to my feeling of dislocation.

Close to tears, I ran back downstairs and located my phone. I should talk to Ruby, but when I tried her number it went straight to voicemail. I opened my mouth to leave a message but wasn't sure what to say and ended the call instead. *Could today get any worse?* I imagined Oliver driving off as though he didn't have a worry in the world, oblivious to the danger his daughter could be in. Despite the blazing fire, I felt cold at my centre. Maybe everything that was happening wasn't intended to ruin my reputation, or the business Oliver had helped to build. Perhaps someone wanted to show me Oliver wasn't the man — the father — I thought he was. I allowed myself a minute to let the realisation to take root, then called another number.

'Carla,' I said when she picked up. 'Can I come and see you?'

CHAPTER 22

Ruby

Fiona was filling her wine glass, as Ruby entered the kitchen. She'd been upstairs searching for Poppy. Once, just after Oliver left, they'd found her sister wedged at the back of the wardrobe, her arms wrapped round her legs, her face pale with distress.

'She's done this before.' Fiona sighed deeply. 'She'll be hiding somewhere, you'll see.'

'Even if that's true, it's still a cry for help, and you and Dad need to answer that cry.'

'She was always a difficult child.' Fiona picked up her glass, put it to her lips, and then returned it to the work surface, as though thinking better of it. 'Your father pandered to her.' She shook her head. 'Anything for a quiet life.'

Ruby didn't remember it like that. Yes, Poppy was perhaps a bit hyper, but she was always a loveable child. They were a happy family, weren't they? Before Nell ruined it all.

'We found her in the summerhouse once, remember?' Fiona's voice cracked. 'We need to look there now.' Her eyes shimmered with tears. 'She's probably hiding, waiting for us to find her.'

A memory flooded in of Poppy's sixteenth birthday: A friend had come over for a sleepover, a rarity for Poppy, and they were sharing pizza and watching a film. Oliver had moved out a few months before, after telling the girls that he and their mother needed some time apart. But he was back at the house that day, had brought Poppy a gift. It was around ten o'clock that Poppy's friend came downstairs and told Ruby and her parents that Poppy had disappeared. She'd apparently gone to get some more popcorn, and hadn't returned.

They'd eventually found Poppy curled up like a foetus, sobbing in the summerhouse.

It was the night everything changed.

'He was talking to some woman on his phone,' Poppy had yelled through her tears, when Ruby found her.

'Who?' Ruby had crouched down by her sister, pulled her close.

'Dad. He was on his phone in the porch. Talking to her. He's having an affair. He doesn't love us anymore. He's never coming back, is he?'

It wasn't long after that, that Oliver started seeing Nell, and Poppy began to self-harm, abandoning her friend, a dark place swallowing her. She would often disappear, walking the streets in bare feet in the middle of winter or in the pouring rain. Sometimes she would shut herself away for hours. Fiona, oblivious, it seemed, to how desperate Poppy was, how her daughter was spiralling downwards, instead drowning her own sadness with alcohol. Eventually Ruby moved back home, and things slowly improved, though they were never the same again.

'I'll check the summerhouse.' Ruby moved towards the back door. 'And then I'm going to Classics. That's where Saskia found Poppy's phone. She could still be there somewhere. And if she's not, we need to call the police.'

'She'll be hiding somewhere,' Fiona repeated, her eyes trancelike on the window. 'Just like she used to.'

'You can't see it, can you, Mum?' Ruby was shocked by how firm she sounded, how angry she suddenly felt. This was her mum, and yet Ruby felt as though she was the parent. She'd never had the courage to confront Fiona before, too afraid of sending her reeling back to the dark place she'd occupied after her marriage collapsed, but now . . .

Fiona turned to face Ruby. 'See what?'

'The damage — the pain you've caused.'

'*I've* caused!' Fiona pressed her hand against her chest. 'It wasn't me who deserted our family.'

'But you did, didn't you, Mum? You left us too. You haven't been here for Poppy or me for over two years. Always wallowing in self-pity. Drinking too much. Why have you let Dad do this to you? Why have you done this to yourself? To us.'

More tears filled Fiona's eyes, and Ruby wished she could retract what she'd said. Her mum needed her support, not her cruel words, however true they were. If Fiona had acted differently, been stronger for Poppy when she needed her most — been there for her now, maybe this wouldn't be happening. She reached out to touch her mum's arm. 'Sorry.'

Her mum didn't respond, she simply tipped her wine down the sink and walked away. It was a start.

Ruby opened the back door and made her way down the garden. The lawn had been recently mowed, the borders neat and tidy. Had her dad been round again?

Ruby cupped her hand over her eyes and peered into the summerhouse. Unused deckchairs were propped against the walls alongside a picnic basket covered in cobwebs, and various tools, but there was no sign of her sister.

'Where are you, Poppy?' she whispered, turning to see her mum staring out of her bedroom window. Within moments she'd whipped the curtain across the glass. 'It looks like it's all on me again,' Ruby said, before springing towards the gate, desperate to find her sister and make sure she was safe.

It was dark by the time she arrived at Classics Props. There was a Fiat 500 in the car park she didn't recognise, and the lights in the offices were out. The warehouse side door stood ajar.

She got out of her car and headed towards the building, looking about her, wondering exactly where Saskia had found Poppy's phone. How had her sister come to lose it, when it was normally glued to her hand?

She stepped inside the door to find the whole area in darkness. 'Hello,' she called, moving her hand across the wall to switch on the lights.

She headed through the loading bay and into the warehouse. Janine's room was a blur of shadows, but she could see someone up ahead, facing side on, looking out of a window in the dimly lit area that housed Edwardian props. *Poppy?* Whoever it was had long dark hair, was small and slim. Ruby moved closer, disturbed suddenly by footsteps racing up behind her. She swung round.

'Sean!' Her heart thudded. 'You scared the hell out of me.'

'What are you doing here, Ruby?'

She glanced back, but whoever had been standing by the window had gone. 'I'm looking for Poppy. Have you seen her?'

He narrowed his eyes. 'Nope. Why would she be here?'

She was about to tell him about the phone, but decided he didn't need to know. She looked towards the window once more. 'I thought I saw her . . . someone.' Had she imagined it?

'I'm about to lock up, Ruby. You need to go. You could have been locked in — and it's pretty creepy in here at night.' It sounded like a threat.

'I need to check Poppy isn't here first. I'll just give the place a quick search.'

'Fine. But if you're more than five minutes, I'll have to lock you in.' He jangled his keys and smiled.

Sudden footsteps approached making Ruby's heart jump further. She turned to see Vikki, Janine's daughter, her long dark hair shining under the overhead lights. It must have been her she saw by the window.

'Ruby,' the young woman said, sliding her arm through Sean's elbow, as if marking her territory. 'What are you doing here? Your dad sold his shares in the place, didn't he?' She smiled up at Sean, whose expression was cold, his eyes on Ruby. 'Surely you're not allowed on the premises anymore.'

'She's looking for her sister,' Sean said, before Ruby could respond. 'Thinks she's somewhere in the building.'

'Well, there's nobody here.' Vikki looked about her. 'And I'm afraid we really need to leave. We're going out for a pizza with Mum and I'm starving.'

Ruby looked about her. It was clear she couldn't stay. That if she did, Sean would lock her in, and that wouldn't help Poppy. 'OK, fine,' she said, heading for the exit.

Once back in her car she watched the couple from a distance walking towards the Fiat 500 she'd seen earlier, Vikki staring up at Sean with obvious adoration. A surge of pity ran through her, that the young woman clearly thought she'd found her dream man. Should she warn her? Warn Janine? But then Janine already knew. She'd seen how Sean had behaved when Ruby tried to break up with him.

Ruby's mind wouldn't settle as she drove to Marlow, her body fizzing with anxiety. She would call the police, but first she needed her father's support. She tried his number a couple of times, but it kept going straight to voicemail.

Oliver's vintage Saab wasn't on the drive of The Coach House when she pulled up, but Nell's car was there, and an amber light glowed from the bay window. She took a deep breath and killed the engine. Nell would know where her father was, wouldn't she? She had to ask her, for Poppy's sake.

She took a deep breath and climbed out of the car, approached, and rang the doorbell.

It was some moments before the door opened.

'Nell,' Ruby said, taking in the paleness of the woman's skin, her bloodshot eyes. 'The thing is . . . Poppy's missing.'

'Yes, I know,' Nell said. 'You'd better come in.'

CHAPTER 23

Nell

'I think even his eldest daughter is starting to see him in a different light,' I said to Carla the following morning, uneasy at bringing Ruby into the one-sided torrent of words I'd just unleashed. I wanted to add weight to my theory that Oliver was showing himself in a bad light at the moment. 'He and his ex-wife Fiona let Ruby deal with Poppy, which is a big responsibility for her. Maybe it's always been that way. They insist it's typical behaviour for Poppy and don't take her seriously, and, perhaps it is, but the girl still needs help. If they'd paid her a bit more attention in the first place, she might not have vanished.' Running out of steam, I sagged back on the sofa, fingers picking at a thread on the hem of the shirt I'd thrown on after Carla called me at 8 a.m. suggesting I visit before her first client of the day.

'Can I ask, are the police involved?' She was plainly struggling to hide her concern, her fair eyebrows gathered. 'How long has Poppy been gone?'

'Not long and, no, not yet. Oliver spoke to Ruby last night and seemed to convince her that no harm would come to Poppy, and to wait.'

I'd been shocked when Ruby turned up the day before, embarrassed for her to see me puffy-faced, eyes swollen from crying. Convinced she was there either to see Oliver, or have a go at me about the newspaper article, I was surprised when she said quietly, 'Can I come in? I'm worried about my sister.'

She hadn't expressed disappointment that Oliver wasn't there, instead saying with a sigh of resignation, 'I didn't think he would be, if I'm honest.'

Carla was silent, waiting for me to go on. 'Ruby and I talked yesterday. She came to see me,' I said. 'It felt like a breakthrough, actually, but a shame it was under those circumstances.'

Carla's head tilted. Her gaze was steady, her hands knotted tightly in her lap. 'Did you come to any conclusions?'

'I believe Ruby did.' I remembered the look on her face as she dropped into the fireside armchair that Oliver tended to occupy when he was home — though I couldn't recall the last time he'd sat in it. She'd looked drawn, her wide eyes troubled as she recounted Poppy's behaviour over the past few years.

'She's getting worse,' she said flatly. 'That scene in front of the journalist . . .' she shook her head, her hair falling forward. 'It's as if she's stopped seeing the bigger picture and is completely focused on getting Dad home whatever the cost only . . .' she paused again, glancing at me perched awkwardly on the sofa opposite with a balled-up tissue in my hand. 'That's not going to happen, because you're never going to leave him.'

'Do you really think it would solve everything if I did?' I hadn't bothered sugar-coating the words, knowing we were past that point.

Ruby's half-smile was sad. 'No, I suppose not.'

'You shouldn't be left in charge of your sister's mental health.'

'Who else is there?' She snapped the words out. 'It turns out my parents are too wrapped up in themselves to care.'

'You know their marriage can't have been good in the first place, or your father would never have left.'

Ruby's head jolted up. 'You don't know anything about their marriage, you weren't there.' She hesitated, and when I didn't speak, continued in a lower voice. 'I'm sure they had ups and downs like most married couples, but nothing worth breaking up for.'

'They were probably trying to protect you and Poppy. You can't know what they were like when the pair of you weren't around.' I didn't want to burst her bubble by revealing how needy Fiona had been, according to Oliver, or how much of his money she'd spent over the course of their marriage in order to fill the long days when the girls were at school. How she'd relied heavily on Oliver to support her, despite having her own business.

'All I know is they loved each other, and Mum would have Dad back in a heartbeat.'

'Why would she want a husband who has chosen someone else?'

'You happened to be there,' Ruby said. 'They were having a low patch, and he got carried away.'

Ouch. 'But he'd already left her by then.'

'You know, Mum only agreed to a divorce because she thought he'd come back when he'd got you out of his system.' Her mouth turned down. 'Sad, really.'

There was nothing I could say to that. Fiona loved Oliver, however much I wished it wasn't true, and Ruby was caught in the middle.

'I can't understand why your dad isn't out there looking for Poppy,' I said, tears rising once more. 'I thought that parental love overrode everything else, and he would be pulling his hair out.'

'You know, he was such a great dad for a lot of the time when we were growing up.' Ruby's gaze grew wistful, looking past me at the small gallery of photos he'd set up on the mantelpiece when we moved in. 'He did all the stuff dads are supposed to; taught us to ride our bikes, gave us piggybacks, set up a tent in the garden in the summer so we could sleep outside, gave great advice . . . made us laugh. He could be so funny. Maybe it was easier when we were younger.' She sat back, shoulders slumped. 'But there were times when he was kind of absent even when he was there — work stuff probably. The business was a huge part of his life,' — her eyes slid towards me and away, and I read *the business you stole* in her expression — 'and I think when that happened we would do anything, say anything, to get him back and turn him into our dad again, when we felt like the most special people on the planet.' She paused. 'Poppy particularly found it hard to deal with his attention being elsewhere. As she got older she did silly things to get him to notice her. It's as if she never quite grew up.'

I remembered the shine of Oliver's attention so clearly; how he could make you feel like the only interesting person in the room and the way, at my interview, he got me to open up about my dad's death, my sorrow over losing my previous job, and the way his kindness seemed to enfold me like a reassuring hug. And I understood now how ice-cold the shock of his withdrawal could be. 'I'm so sorry,' I said, feeling helpless. 'I wish things were different.'

Ruby looked at me as if seeing me properly for the first time. Her eyes shone with tears. 'It's not that my parents don't love us.' I noticed how she included their mother and felt a fresh stab of pain that I'd unwittingly been the catalyst for Fiona's and Poppy's breakdowns. 'I think they want to pretend Poppy isn't really missing because it makes them feel like bad parents. Either that, or going on past experience, they really do expect Poppy to turn up and be fine, or they know I'll take care of her, so they don't have to get too involved. I'm sure they would both prefer it if we were toddlers again and easier to control.'

Ruby spoke with the air of someone finally realising a truth that she had long denied to herself. As if the new knowledge had made her vulnerable, she jumped to her feet, patting the pockets of her leather jacket. 'I'd better go.'

'You don't have to.' I rose too, wanting to hold onto whatever it was that had prompted her to finally talk to me like a human being. 'Stay and have something to drink or eat. I haven't had dinner yet—'

'I'm not going to sit around eating and drinking when my sister's missing,' she broke in, but her gaze was slightly less hostile. 'Let me know if she turns up here, won't you?'

'Of course,' I stammered, flooded with guilt at my thoughtless invitation. 'I'm sorry, Ruby. And you'll let me know when you find her?'

She gave a curt nod, pulling a car key from her pocket. 'Where *is* my dad, by the way?'

'A . . . a meeting, I think.'

Her eyebrows rose in a very Oliver-like way. 'You think?'

My cheeks grew warm. 'He wasn't specific.' With an impulse to stick up for him, I added, 'Your dad was in a bit of a state after your call.'

'Not enough of a state to miss his meeting.'

'Ruby, is Poppy . . . has she . . . ?' I tried to find the words to ask whether Poppy was the one trying to ruin things for me and Oliver, but even if she was, would Ruby tell me? Instead, I said quickly, 'I thought she might have been in the house. I don't know why, but I've looked everywhere and she's not here.'

Back in the moment, I looked at Carla. Her expression was rapt, as if my story was far more intriguing than the ones she normally heard. 'Ruby looked as if she was going to tell me it was true,' I told her. 'That Poppy *had* been in the house, but she changed her mind and walked out looking . . . I don't know. Spent, I suppose. And when Oliver got back — I'd fallen asleep on the sofa — he didn't seem interested in Ruby's visit. He said he'd spoken to her on the phone and then he asked if I was coming to bed.'

'And did you?'

Carla's expression was almost impersonal as she asked what must be a routine question. It would be natural to query whether I was happy to go to bed with a husband giving every impression he didn't care about his family.

'No, I didn't.' I tried to rub the tension from my neck, where the muscles felt rigid. 'I stayed on the sofa, and I pretended to be asleep when he left me a cup of coffee before leaving this morning. I couldn't face him.' I covered my face with my hands. 'And I can't go to work because I've been put on leave.'

Carla waited while I composed myself, pulling a tissue from the box on the table and handing it to me. I swiped it over my eyes. I was so tired of crying, of feeling like the bad guy.

'You don't like relinquishing control at work?'

'I'm not a control freak,' I protested, looking her square in the eyes. 'I love my job, but not to the detriment of everything else.' *Was that true?* 'But I resent having to leave when I haven't done anything wrong.'

'Would you say the business is in safe hands?'

'Of course. Mark — he's the owner — is probably happy to be in charge again, and my assistant is more than capable.'

'Too capable?' Carla let a moment's silence lapse.

'I'm not worried about her taking over if that's what you mean.' *Was I?* 'I just want my life to be how it was before . . .'

Carla seemed to be having difficulty forming words, perhaps waiting for me to fill the gap. 'Before . . . ?' she finally prompted.

'Before all *this*.' I gestured with my hands, glancing at my watch. It must be almost time for Carla's next client. What was I going to do with the rest of my day? I could visit Mum, but it would be hard keeping everything from her when she could read me so well. 'If I was a friend or relative, what would you advise me to do?'

Carla's expression stilled. 'We're not supposed to give advice.' Her tone was gently reproving, but something in her gaze told me she wanted to. After pausing for a second, she went on, 'Why are you fighting to stay with your husband when you clearly feel he's letting down the people he's supposed to love?'

'Because we married for better or worse. I can't give up on our relationship because he doesn't react to some situations the same way I would.'

'Why did you marry him, Nell?'

'I fell in love with him.' The words came automatically, but somehow I didn't feel them as intensely as I had a month ago. 'He was everything I wanted, though my mum worried about him being older and thought I was rushing into it. I knew he was still married when we first met and had children, of course I did. I suppose knowing his daughters weren't toddlers made it easier somehow, that the impact of the divorce on them would be . . . less.' I paused and looked at my hands. 'I was wrong.'

'So, what will you do next?'

Carla's simple question uncluttered my head.

'I'm going back to work.' As soon as I said it, the paralysing feeling of powerlessness eased a little. 'Running away makes me look guilty. I'll talk to Mark and make it clear I'm not backing down, that I'm not scared. Let whoever it is come for me in person and see how far they get.' Something flickered across Carla's face and her pen slid to the floor. 'And as for my marriage, I'll keep on being there for Oliver, waiting for when he's ready to talk.'

'Nell, it might not be that simple.' Carla was rising, holding out a hand. 'Not everyone will fall in with your plans—'

'Thanks for seeing me, Carla. You've really helped, but I have to go.'

CHAPTER 24

Nell

Driving to work, my resolve faltered. Would Mark be angry and insist on sending me home, like a naughty child? But we'd had a good relationship before he left the company — still did, or so I'd thought.

I was sure I could talk him round, and Saskia and Janine would back me up. Did I have a legal case? *Probably not.* And I didn't want things going that far, anyway.

As I got out of my car, wishing for once I'd dressed more smartly, Janine hurried over with a smile lighting up her face. 'I'm so glad you're here, Nell.'

In spite of everything, I smiled back. 'I'm glad someone is.'

'The phone's been ringing non-stop.' The words burst out of her. 'I was going to call you. Customers have read that article, and they're on your side! Bookings are up already.' She nodded furiously and pointed to where Sean and a couple of other drivers were loading a van with a pair of walnut bookcases. 'Honestly, you've nothing to worry about.' She gave an excited laugh. 'If anything, that journalist has put this place even more firmly on the map.'

'That's . . . crazy.' My heart started beating fast. Surely Mark couldn't force me to stay away now. 'Thanks, Janine.'

'Nothing to do with me, love.' She spread her hands, head on one side as if seeing me in a different light. 'You're clearly very well thought of.'

'I need to convince Mark of that.' I gave her arm a grateful squeeze. 'Thanks,' I repeated. About to head up to the office, feeling as if a weight had rolled off my shoulders, I paused. Saskia was bowling down the stairs, heels clattering, and she swept me outside with a firm grip on my elbow. Tendrils of hair had escaped her ponytail and her glasses were smeared. She looked on the verge of tears.

'It's OK, Saskia.' I gave a half-laugh. 'Janine just told me things aren't as bad as I thought.' I looked over my shoulder, but Janine had slipped back into the warehouse. 'I was going to talk to Mark.'

'Don't bother.' She almost choked on a sob. 'I told him you should be here. I wanted him to call you and tell you how much support you've had, but he . . .' she hesitated, glancing up at the windows, as if Mark might be watching us. 'He seems kind of power crazy,' she said in a loud whisper, shuffling further towards where the cars were parked, out of sight of the office. 'It's as if now he's back, he doesn't want to let go again. He actually said that for him . . .' she broke off and pressed her lips together.

'What?' I wanted to shake the words out of her. 'Tell me, Saskia.'

'He said, for him, you leaving was the best thing that could have happened, because he wants to come back and be in charge again permanently.' She lifted her glasses and rubbed shaky fingertips across her cheeks. 'He doesn't want you here.'

'*What?*' Confusion fought with anger. Had this been Mark's plan all along? He wanted me out, so he could come back for good. 'I'll speak to him,' I said. 'You must have got it wrong.'

'I haven't, I—' Saskia retched suddenly and clapped a hand to her mouth.

I gripped her upper arms to stop her crumpling. 'Are you OK?'

She straightened but looked as if she might be sick any second. 'Between you and me, Nell, I'm pregnant.'

'Oh!' I let go of her, trying to absorb this deluge of new information. 'That's . . . congratulations.'

'Please can you give me a lift home?' Her eyes filled once more. 'I feel so ill, and this stuff with Mark . . .' She gave a muffled sob. 'I can't be here at the moment.'

I craned to look at the warehouse, wanting desperately to be inside, having it out with Mark, but Saskia was in no fit state to be left alone.

'When I heard your voice, I grabbed my bag and made a run for it.' She inhaled a shaky breath. 'I wanted to warn you what Mark had said before you came in and then I was going to go home, but I don't fancy my chances on the tube.' She pressed a hand to her mouth again, closing her eyes.

'Don't worry,' I said, making up my mind. 'Where do you live again?'

'Finsbury Park.'

It wasn't far. Mark would have to wait. 'OK.' I ushered her to my car as her colour drained once more. 'Let's get you home.'

Saskia retched a couple of times on the drive there, but thankfully wasn't sick. Her face was waxy, a sheen of perspiration on her pale skin.

'I don't want to be on my own,' she confessed when I pulled up in front of a bland, two-storey building on a quiet side street lined with spindly trees. 'Will you come in?'

Seeing the shimmer of tears in her eyes, a sisterly warmth rose inside me. 'I'll have a quick coffee,' I said. 'Maybe you should call Alex so you're not here on your own.'

She didn't answer as I followed her inside and up a flight of beige-carpeted stairs into a small entrance that led to a sitting and dining area. The black and white décor was brightened by colourful cushions on the two-seater sofa and matching armchair, and a collection of decorative glassware on the windowsill. 'It's nice,' I said, though it was too austere for my taste. I looked for signs of a male presence, but the place was so tidy it was hard to believe anyone lived there at all. I wondered how she afforded a flat in London but didn't like to ask. Perhaps there had been an inheritance from her parents and — more recently — her grandmother. It could explain why she hadn't yet sorted out giving me her P45 or bank details. Perhaps she didn't need the money, and it wasn't a priority.

Saskia slipped off her coat and hurried through an adjoining door I guessed was the bathroom where I heard the sound of running water and the toilet flushing.

Through another door, I glimpsed a neatly-made bed, and a treadmill next to a couple of heavy looking weights. Perhaps Alex worked out.

Gazing round the living room, I spotted a row of photos on a bookshelf and wandered over. One was the picture of Saskia and Alex I'd seen on Instagram, in a silver frame, and next to that a slightly faded, eighties-style wedding photo of a couple who must be her parents. Saskia clearly took after her mother, their smiles almost identical. Another showed a much younger Saskia with pigtails standing beside an older girl, the set of her eyes vaguely familiar — maybe her sister — outside a circular stone building, and another of a teenage Saskia with her arms around the waist of a sturdy, grey-haired woman in a shapeless dress I guessed was her gran. My eye was caught by a picture further back, larger than the others. I barely recognised Saskia at first. Her hair was a golden sheet, flowing around tanned shoulders, her eyes clear and sparkling — unhindered by glasses — her expression flirtatious, couples in the background holding champagne glasses. She was wearing a dress that moulded to her body, the silver-grey shade perfectly matching her eyes.

'I barely recognised you.' I turned as Saskia came through, white-faced, her eyes bleary. 'Your hair's so different.'

She put up a hand self-consciously. 'I fancied a change, so I dyed it brown,' she said dully. 'I wanted people to take me seriously.'

Seeing her wobble slightly, I replaced the photo. 'Sit down.' I hurried over. 'I'll get you some water.'

As she collapsed onto the sofa, I shrugged off my jacket and dropped it on the armchair under the window. The temperature was set too high for my liking — almost tropical — but Saskia was visibly trembling. 'Here,' I said, after finding a glass in one of the kitchen cupboards and letting the water run icy cold.

She grasped the glass with a trembling hand and took several sips. 'Thanks.'

'Shall I call Alex for you?' Her appearance was starting to worry me. 'If you give me his number . . .' I reached for my jacket, intending to take my phone from the pocket, but stopped when I saw she was crying, great big sobs that made her shoulders heave, a hand pressed over her mouth.

'Saskia! What is it?'

'He's left me.'

'What?' It took a moment for her stifled words to sink in. 'Alex has *left* you?' I sank beside her on the sofa. 'But I thought you were getting married.' I glanced at her finger, realising only then that the ring had gone. 'The baby—'

'When I told him last night I was pregnant, he said he wasn't ready to be a father.'

'Oh my God, Saskia.' I shuffled closer and put an arm around her, but let it fall when she stiffened and shifted away. 'I'm so sorry. Is there anyone else I can call? Your sister?' I glanced at the photo I'd spotted earlier.

She shook her head, her hair falling from its tortoiseshell slide. 'She's busy. I don't want to burden her.' She wept, removing her glasses and dropping them in her lap. Her trousers were crumpled, and there was a small stain on her blouse. She seemed to be unravelling. 'Don't worry, I'll be fine.'

I'd left my bag in the car and couldn't find a tissue, so fetched some toilet paper from the spotlessly clean bathroom. I watched, feeling helpless as she sniffed, her sobs subsiding as she scrubbed her eyes. 'I really want to go home,

Nell.' Her voice was raw, her usual composure in shreds. 'To Norfolk, I mean.'

'Right.' With a burst of pity, I thought how desperately she must need her parents right now, must wish they were still alive. Trying to think of a solution, I jumped when she grabbed my hand.

'Will you take me, Nell?' Her ashen face contorted. 'I can't face getting the train, and I'll need to take a taxi to the windmill from the station, it's too far to walk.'

'Windmill?' I glanced once more at the photos on the shelf, at the two girls in front of a circular building 'Is that where you grew up?'

She nodded, dabbing her eyes again, and I felt a flash of shame that I hadn't known — hadn't asked her much about her life. The fact I'd had other things on my mind was a poor excuse. *Why had I let my relationship with Oliver take precedence when I didn't even feature on his list of priorities?*

'I'll take you,' I said, without thinking. 'I've never been to Norfolk.'

CHAPTER 25

Ruby

Ruby closed the wooden gate at the rear of Sharma's Sandwiches, and made her way across the cobbled area towards Benita, who was loading the van with trays of sandwiches.

She had lain awake for most of the night, staring into the liquid-black of the early hours, worried sick about Poppy, unsure if she'd made the right decision not to call the police. But her father's insistence that her sister would turn up — that it was the sort of thing Poppy did — had stopped her following her instincts.

She'd tried to call her father again when she got up, and later texted him asking if she could come over and discuss Poppy. He'd finally replied: *OK*. She'd called her mum too. 'I'm going to the police, once I've spoken to Dad,' she'd said.

And for the first time there'd been real concern in Fiona's voice. 'I'll come to the police station with you. Call me later. I'll meet you there.'

'You're early,' Benita said, glancing over her shoulder as she manoeuvred the final tray of sandwiches onto the rack. 'You look awful, Ruby, like you haven't slept for a month. Are you OK?'

'Thanks for that.' Ruby half-smiled. She didn't want to get into why she was so early, or that she was about to take a detour to see her dad before her deliveries. 'I'm not too great, if I'm honest.'

'Should you even be here?' Benita stepped towards her, touched her arm. 'If you need to take some time off, I can do your round. Mum will always step in to look after the shop.'

Ruby looked into Benita's concerned brown eyes. Should she confide in her that Poppy was missing? 'I'm fine,' she said, deciding against it. 'Just a rough night, is all.'

Benita narrowed her eyes, as though she could see inside Ruby's head. It was clear she knew there was more to it, but she didn't pry. Instead she turned and slammed the van door before dropping the keys into Ruby's palm. 'Well, you know where I am if you need a friend.'

'Thanks, I appreciate it.'

Benita made her way inside, and Ruby climbed into the driving seat and started the engine. Gripping the steering wheel, she sucked in a deep breath. She hadn't got many friends. Not anymore. She'd lost her school and university mates when she stopped seeing them while dating Sean, and the amazing acting crowd she hung out with while on the circuit dissipated when she moved back home after her dad left. Perhaps she should confide in Benita, allow her closer, or maybe Saskia, who'd been so supportive. After all they were around the same age. But for now her priority was finding Poppy — her first stop Marlow.

She pulled up outside The Coach House, killed the engine, and picked up her phone from the passenger seat. She'd heard the text come in as she was driving, prayed it wasn't her father making excuses. She looked at the screen, and wanted to cry:

Sorry, love. Something urgent came up. Can we meet later? Dad x

She attempted to bat down a surge of anger she didn't want to feel. The revelation of who her father really was wasn't pretty. She closed her eyes, tears bubbling through her lashes. 'Bastard,' she whispered.

She opened her eyes, glanced up at the grey sky, before moving her gaze to the house where he lived with Nell, trying to push down negative emotions. He was busy, she told herself. He couldn't ignore urgent clients. Ruby was simply tired, worried about Poppy — but why wasn't he?

She narrowed her eyes, blinked. Someone was peering at her from the downstairs window of the house. *Nell?* Whoever it was darted away.

Ruby climbed from the car, and hurried up the path, her eyes sweeping the area, taking in the river opposite, the neat garden, the empty drive, before ringing the doorbell. After some moments of pressing the bell, she bent down and peered through the letterbox.

'Hello! Nell? It's Ruby.' Her eyes travelled the dim hallway, glancing at the doors standing ajar that led to the kitchen and lounge, her gaze moving across the black and white floor tiles towards the staircase leading to the bedrooms. 'Hello.'

She was about to rise when one of the doors moved a fraction, opening further. A chill ran down her spine, and she jumped to her feet. Something wasn't right. Someone was in the house acting oddly.

She took several deep breaths and crouched down once more. Opened the letterbox. 'I'm going to call the police,' she called through. 'Whoever you are, I know you shouldn't be here.' It was as she rose, about to press the first nine on the phone screen, when it hit her. *Poppy?*

She bent down again, opened the letterbox once more to see her sister standing in the hallways, arms limp by her sides. *Thank God.*

'Leave me alone, Ruby,' she cried. 'I don't need you. I don't need anyone.'

'Poppy! Open the door.'

'No!'

'Poppy, please.'

She watched as her sister took small footsteps along the hall towards her. The door opened a few inches, and Ruby rose and dived forward, pushed it open. 'Have you any idea how worried I've been?' she cried, taking her sister in her arms.

Poppy didn't react, her arms still limp, her face deathly pale.

'What the hell are you doing here?' Ruby went on, releasing her sister.

Poppy turned and made her way down the hallway.

Ruby followed, closing the door behind her. 'You scared us all half to death. Does Dad know you're here?'

'Of course not.'

'Have you been here all the time?'

'I was in the loft.' She stepped into the kitchen. 'I come down when they're out. Get some water, pinch some food.' Her voice was a monotone. 'Not that I'm hungry.'

'We found your phone at Classics.'

She turned dull, lifeless eyes on Ruby. 'I went there. Was going to go in, head up to *her* office, but Sean and Janice were in the car park, deep in confab, so I legged it, dropped my bloody phone.'

'What did you intend to do, Poppy?'

She shrugged. 'Wreck the place.'

'Wreck the place?' A bubble of anger rose in Ruby's chest. 'Christ's sake, Poppy, this is getting way out of hand. You could get in so much trouble.'

Tears filled her eyes. 'Well, nobody gives a toss what happens to me, anyway.'

'Don't be silly.' Ruby pressed a hand against her sister's arm. 'I care.'

'Do you? The person who's in cahoots with Nell.'

'What?'

'I overheard you and her talking last night. All very cosy together.'

'That's not what it was at all. I just—'

She tilted her head. 'Just what, Ruby?'

'For God's sake, if you were listening you must have known how worried I was.'

Poppy glared at Ruby for a moment, before moving towards the kitchen worktop. 'From where I was, you sounded as though you were getting pretty friendly.'

'No, you're wrong. I was worried sick, and asking if Nell could help.' Ruby looked about her. 'And why here of all places? Why Dad and Nell's house?'

Her sister shot round. 'I was doing what you should be doing. Making sure Dad comes back to Mum.'

'How? How can you make him come back? Their marriage is over.' Ruby's voice cracked. Had she really accepted the inevitable? 'You have to see that.'

'No! No, it will never be over. Dad keeps coming round doing little jobs for her. Why would he do that, if he didn't still love her?'

'I don't know.' She shook her head, but then it occurred to her. He'd said Fiona could live in the house until Poppy was eighteen, and then she would have to sell it and split the money. Was his motive simply that he wanted the house in order to put it on the market? Was he about to tell Fiona and Poppy they had to move out?

Ruby's eyes moved to the counter, as Poppy grabbed a small bottle, and shoved it in her pocket.

'What's that?'

'Nothing. Listen, we should go. I've been caught out. Game over.' Poppy raised her hands as if she'd been arrested. 'Take me home. Please.' She went to head past, but Ruby grabbed her arm.

'What did you put in your pocket?'

'Nothing.' Poppy tried to shrug free, but Ruby was stronger. She pulled the bottle from her sister's pocket, eyes widening as she studied the label. 'Rat killer?'

'I wasn't going to use it. I changed my mind.'

'Use it?' *Oh God.* The shock hit her like a punch. 'On Nell?'

'OK. Yes, I thought about it. I really did.' Poppy suddenly crumpled to the floor, crossed her legs, and buried her head in her hands. 'But I wouldn't have. I promise. I wouldn't have. And if I did, it would only have been a tiny bit.'

Ruby continued to study the bottle, her hand shaking. 'You thought about poisoning Nell?'

'I ordered it online. Planned to put it in her drink somehow. Not to kill her. Just to punish her. Make her sick.' She looked up, eyes wide. 'She needed to be punished, Ruby. You know that.' She shook her head. 'But when it came to it, I just couldn't do it.'

Ruby crouched down next to her sister, took hold of her hands, her body crying out in despair. 'We need to get you home, Pops,' she said gently, her voice quiet, despite the turmoil swirling inside her. *We need to get you help.*

'I don't want to go home,' Poppy whispered. 'I just want to curl up here and die.'

'Oh, Poppy.' Tears filled Ruby's eyes. *How had it come to this?*

'I'm lonely,' Poppy whispered, moving her body slowly to lie on her side, a tear rolling down her pale cheek. 'I'm so, so lonely.'

Ruby lay down next to her, cradling her sister in her arms. 'I'm here for you,' she said, meaning it. 'Always.'

* * *

'Ruby? Poppy?' Oliver stood in the kitchen doorway, smart in a navy suit, his white shirt open at the neck.

Both girls shot up to a sitting position. They'd been lying on the floor for some time, and Ruby's head throbbed. 'Dad, I . . .' she said.

'Thank God you're OK, Poppy.' He moved across the kitchen towards them. 'I've been so worried about you.'

Have you? Ruby thought, but didn't say. She rose to her feet, helping Poppy up. Her eyes were swollen, her cheeks blotchy.

Oliver reached them, took Poppy in his arms. He didn't ask why they'd been lying on the kitchen floor. Where Poppy had been. Why they were here in his house. Ruby narrowed her eyes. *He didn't want to know. In fact, did he even care?* But Ruby would make him listen. Tell her father that Poppy desperately needed help. That she'd been in the loft all along — intending to poison Nell. But not right now. Poppy needed help of a more professional kind, there was no doubting that, and Ruby would make sure she got it. Her father would have to wait.

'Let's go.' Ruby said once he'd released her sister. She took Poppy by the hand, squeezed it. 'I'll take you home now.'

They headed across the kitchen hand in hand, their father saying nothing, doing nothing. And the painful realisation that Oliver Cosgrove, who Ruby had adored for so long, was a self-centred, selfish man almost took her breath away, and she wondered if she'd ever really known him at all.

'You can drop me off at the underground,' Poppy climbed into the van.

'Not a chance in hell.'

'But you need to do your deliveries.'

'They can wait. People can survive without a sandwich.' Ruby climbed into the driving seat, and clicked on her seatbelt. She glanced at the house, noticing the silhouette of her father in the window. 'I need to get you home.'

She was about to start the engine, when she noticed in the rear-view mirror a car pulling up behind them at speed. She shot a look over her shoulder. 'Mum?'

Poppy looked back too, as Fiona climbed out of the car, and rushed, face flushed, to the driver's side of the van.

Ruby buzzed down the window, and Fiona's worried eyes met Poppy's. 'Oh, love,' she cried, and raced around to the other side of the van. She opened the passenger door. 'Thank God.' She flung her arms around her daughter. 'Where have you been? Are you OK?'

'She's a long way from being OK, Mum,' Ruby said. 'We need to do something.'

'Of course — yes.' Fiona released her daughter. 'Where were you, Poppy?'

Poppy looked at the house, her body shaking. 'In their loft.'

'Their loft? But why, darling?'

'She had plans to poison Nell,' Ruby said, the horror of it hitting her all over again.

Fiona seemed to freeze for a moment. 'This is my fault. This is all my fault.'

Ruby wasn't about to argue. Fiona had to be partly to blame. She'd spent so long wallowing in self-pity, had made their childhood home an unbearable place to live. Ruby understood that her mother was broken, and she'd felt for her at first, but Fiona should have seen how her behaviour was affecting Poppy — an already volatile teenager.

'Let me take you home.' Fiona had a calmness in her voice that Ruby hadn't heard in a long time. 'We can work things out.'

'We can,' Ruby said, watching her mother ease Poppy from the van, and cradle her daughter's shoulders. 'And we will.'

* * *

Once Ruby had delivered her final sandwiches to an office block next to Classic's, she pulled into a parking space to eat her lunch.

She glanced up at the windows. Would her dad let Nell know Poppy was safe? Perhaps she should tell Nell herself? After all, she had seemed concerned. Ruby pulled out her phone, and dialled Nell's number, but it went straight to voicemail. Maybe she could go up to her office and let her know. But the thought of it didn't feel right — they weren't exactly friends.

She was about to bite into her cheese and pickle sandwich, when a sharp knock on the window startled her. 'Janine.' Ruby buzzed down the window.

'I wanted a word.' Janine's eyes darted around her as though she was worried about being caught. 'It's about Sean.'

Ruby flopped her head back against her seat. This was all she needed.

'You know my Vikki is dating him—'

'Yes. I saw them together. I hope they'll be happy.' She realised she sounded a bit sarcastic. But honestly, the chances of Sean making anyone happy were zero.

Janine looked over her shoulder, then back at Ruby. 'But that's just it. I think it's quite serious between them.'

'Well, that's nice, I'm pleased for her.'

Janine's forehead cracked as she stared at Ruby. 'Are you?'

'Of course.' She moved her gaze from Janine's anxious face, and turned her attention back to her sandwich.

'Well, I must admit I was too, at first,' Janine went on. 'Vikki's never had many boyfriends. But he seems a bit—'

'Controlling?' The word was out before she'd thought it through.

Janine nodded slowly. 'Yes, and I'm all of a dither. She's seems so smitten, bless her. I just hope he doesn't hurt her.'

'If you want my opinion, Janine—'

'I do. I do.'

'He's no good. You know what a hard time I had getting rid of him.'

Janine nodded once more. 'Yes, but I thought — well hoped really — that you might have overreacted a bit at the time.'

'Really?' Ruby wanted to say so much more, but after the day she'd had so far, she hadn't got the energy.

'Thank you for being honest with me, Ruby.' She paused for a moment, her eyes darting about her. 'Can you believe I thought you wanted him back?'

'Well, you couldn't have been more wrong.'

'Yes. I see that now. Well, I'd better leave you in peace, and get on with some work.'

'Is Nell in her office?' Ruby called after her as she walked away.

She glanced back, and shook her head. 'Saskia was taken ill. I think Nell took her home.'

Ruby closed the lid of her lunchbox, hoping Saskia was OK, her mind drifting to how supportive and understanding she'd been. Perhaps she should go round to her apartment — check she was OK, maybe even get her take on Poppy. She would be someone neutral, someone with no agenda, who would give unbiased advice on her sister.

* * *

Drainpipe tartan trousers and a red polo-neck sweater hugged Stefan's slim frame.

'Ruby, sweetie.' His smile was wide, as he beckoned her into Saskia's apartment with effervescent charm. 'I was going to call you later about rehearsals. Come in. Though Sassy isn't here, I'm afraid, in fact I haven't been able to get hold of her. I'm just picking up my laptop. Left it here last night. Thankfully I know where she hides her spare key — she always put it under a plant pot when we were at university.'

Ruby followed him through to a small, minimalist lounge, decorated in black and white, with a two-seater sofa and chair, Saskia's glasses perched on the arm.

'Sassy bought the place with her inheritance when her parents died,' Stefan volunteered.

A group of framed photographs on a shelving unit caught her eye: two little girls posing near a windmill, another, more dated, of a couple on their wedding day. Ruby picked up a study of a beautiful woman. 'Is this Saskia?'

'Saskia?' He laughed. 'God, I haven't heard her called that in a while.'

'Sorry?'

He didn't reply, instead moving over to the photos. 'She's quite the stunner when she makes the effort, isn't she?'

Ruby stared down at the picture in her hands. 'I barely recognised her.'

'I know. To be honest, I was taken aback when I saw her with you at the coffee shop. I hadn't seen her in a while. Thought she'd let herself go a bit, though I guess that's understandable. She never fully got over her parents' death, for one thing.' He moved closer to Ruby, and gestured towards the photo of the children next to the windmill. 'That's her and her sister's place in Norfolk. She lived there as a child.' He pointed at another photograph. 'And that's gorgeous Sassy and me, taken way back. I feel bad that I haven't seen enough of her through the years.'

She put down the picture. 'So you have no idea where she is.' Ruby looked about her. 'I was told she'd come home sick.'

'Really? Gosh, she seemed fine last night. Though if I'm honest she wasn't herself. Seemed agitated somehow. But then she can be a bit . . .' He pressed his lips together, as though he'd said too much.

'A bit?'

He shrugged. 'She can be a little up and down at times. I've known her for years, and love her to bits, but I still feel as though there are parts of her I don't know. Parts I've never quite been able to reach.' Stefan's phone buzzed in his hand, and he looked at the screen. 'Listen, I would love to stay and chat all day, but I've got a lot on.'

'Of course, sorry.'

'No need for a sorry — we'll catch up real soon, sweetie. Get those rehearsals rolling. I'm so excited.'

'Me too.' Ruby followed him towards the door, giving the room one last sweep, her eyes falling on a familiar jacket on the back of the armchair.

'Problem?' Stefan asked, turning, framed in the doorway.

'I think that's Nell's jacket,' she said. 'She dropped Saskia off, and must have left it behind.' She picked it up, intending to take it round to her. As she threw it over her arm a phone clattered to the floor.

Trying to ignore Stefan's impatience, she picked up the phone, and slipped it into her pocket.

Finally outside, Stefan locked the door and looped his laptop bag strap over his shoulder. It was as he air kissed each side of Ruby's cheek, that someone she vaguely recognised approached.

'Have you seen my sister?' the woman said, pushing a tendril of blonde hair from her face, her voice tense. 'She's not picking up her phone.'

CHAPTER 26

Nell

We arrived in Norfolk almost three hours later, torrential rain hammering on the car roof for the last few miles.

Saskia had slept fitfully during the journey, her coat folded against the window as a makeshift pillow. I'd turned the radio on low for company, thinking about Alex letting her down when she needed him most. Perhaps some men weren't cut out for fatherhood. *Like Oliver.* I thought of the net of love and respect that had held my family together and how it seemed to be missing in the Cosgrove family — wishing I'd noticed it much sooner.

The satnav directed me through a soggy landscape of low-lying marshland and vast skies, past fields, hedgerows, and villages, before bringing me to a standstill in a woodland clearing circled by trees where the windmill stood — a six-storey, pale-stone structure rising towards the clouds. Instead of the sails I associated with windmills, the building was topped by a boat-shaped cap with a wraparound viewing balcony.

'We're here,' I murmured.

Saskia woke with a start, blinking and rubbing her eyes as she tumbled out of the car.

She let us in listlessly, using an old-fashioned brass key in the wooden door, but seemed to brighten once inside her childhood home, showing me round the circular rooms — kitchen on the ground floor, living room on the first, bedrooms and bathroom above, all reached by a winding wooden staircase — and a loft area with a ladder, leading to the viewing area at the top.

Compared to her flat it was cold, as though centuries of winter had seeped through the stone, but Saskia didn't seem to mind. I shivered slightly, realising with a jolt that I'd left my jacket and phone behind on her sofa in our hurry to leave.

'It was converted by an architect in the seventies,' Saskia told me, pulling a wine bottle from a rack before seeming to remember she shouldn't be drinking and filling the kettle instead. 'He got itchy feet after a few years and my parents — who grew up in the area — put in an offer. My dad had always wanted to live here.' Her tone was suffused with regret, and I imagined how much more she would feel her parents' loss with a baby on the way.

'How come you didn't stay here after . . . ?' My question tapered off.

'Too many memories at first, and there's not much happening jobwise around here. My sister thought we should sell it, but I couldn't bear to, and it's not as if we needed the money.' She slid me a tired smile as the kettle came to the boil, then took a carton of longlife milk from an old-fashioned pantry next to the fridge. 'I'd planned to live here permanently, one day.' My heart ached for her, guessing she'd intended to move in with Alex and raise their child in the place where she'd spent her happy childhood.

'You still could,' I said. 'Maybe your sister can help.'

She shook her head but didn't comment. 'Thank you for bringing me home.' Her smile brightened. 'Hey, why don't you stay overnight?'

'Oh . . . I don't know.' But, suddenly, the thought of returning to work and confronting Mark, or going home to Oliver, or an empty house, didn't appeal. It was peaceful at the windmill, apart from the rain tapping on the narrow windows, and although Saskia had regained her colour, I wasn't comfortable leaving her alone yet.

'It'll serve Mark right to manage without us,' she coaxed, passing me a mug of steaming tea. 'There's food in the freezer. I could rustle us up something to eat.'

I found myself nodding. 'OK, but I'll need to borrow your phone and let Oliver know where I am.'

'I'm afraid there's no mobile phone network out here, and the landline isn't working at the moment. I meant to get it fixed.'

'That's not good.' My mood dipped as I realised how isolated we were. 'What if you needed help?'

'Look, you can try.' She gave a shrug and handed over her mobile. 'It might pick something up.'

There were no signal bars, but I pressed in Oliver's number anyway. Nothing happened, and I handed the phone back. Maybe it wouldn't hurt for him to worry about me for a change. *Would he worry about me?*

Saskia had turned pale again. After a few swallows of tea, she wrinkled her nose. 'I've got a pounding headache.' Her voice was small and tired. 'Do you mind if I go to bed?'

'Of course not. Don't worry about me.' Despite my soothing words, I felt out of my depth. Should I insist she ate something? 'Can you take painkillers? For the headache, I mean.'

'Better not.' She patted her stomach, eyebrows raised, and I flushed with embarrassment. 'Help yourself to anything you need, and pick whichever room you want to sleep in. Mine's on the second floor.'

'OK, thanks.'

'You won't leave, will you?'

'I'll be here,' I promised, touched.

Once she'd gone, a door closing above my head, the place felt a little eerie. No television to distract me as the darkness outside deepened, or anything I fancied reading on the bookshelf — mostly old children's books, some Regency romances that might have belonged to Saskia's mother, or grandmother, and a well-thumbed crossword dictionary.

I shivered, deciding not to linger in the chilly space, which was gloomy even with the floor lamp on. The pool of light didn't extend to the corners, giving the impression something might be lurking in the shadows.

After a meal of frozen lasagne, cooked in the microwave and eaten perched on a leather sofa that had seen better days, I headed to bed after using the old-fashioned bathroom, choosing a shabby room on the third floor. The décor was tired, and the whole place felt unlived in — expect perhaps by ghosts.

Shivering, I tried to ignore the mustiness of the bedding and the unfamiliar creaks and groans of the windmill, tensing when I thought I heard a female voice below.

As sleep dragged me under, I wondered what Oliver was doing, and whether he was missing me at all.

* * *

Waking abruptly from a nightmare of sitting in an empty room, unable to move and hearing footsteps behind me, I jerked upright. Weak sunlight poured through a long, narrow window and across the dark-wood floorboards. I sank back in the bed, remembering I'd stayed the night at Saskia's. Not at her flat, but a windmill in the Norfolk countryside.

Hearing movement a couple of floors down and the sound of Saskia humming, I let myself relax beneath the duvet. Despite the circumstances, it was nice to not have to think about getting up right away, like being on a much-needed holiday.

Then I flashed back to Saskia breaking the news that she and Alex had broken up and revealing her wish to go home to where she had always felt safe.

Oliver didn't know where I was. Galvanised, I swung my legs out of bed and reached for the jeans I'd discarded the night before. Once I'd determined Saskia was OK and taken her sister's phone number so I could call her, I would head home.

The bathroom was chilly, a cool draught blowing through the window frame. I made do with splashing cold water on my face and rubbing some toothpaste around my teeth with my finger. I could hardly blame Saskia for not offering to lend me nightwear or toiletries in the state she'd been in but I would be glad to get back to The Coach House and have a hot shower.

Heading downstairs, I heard the whir of a food blender, overlaid by a pulsing night-club beat. I froze on the bottom step, greeted by the sight of Saskia in the kitchen, swaying her hips to the music — her phone linked to a speaker on the worktop — arms waving above her head as she gyrated. By the phone was a bag of frozen blueberries, and a carton of soya milk.

'Just making a smoothie,' she said, catching sight of me as she twirled. 'Would you like one?' Her cheeks were flushed, her eyes sparkling with an almost manic energy that worried me more than her lethargy the day before. 'Hang on!' Darting forward, she switched off the blender then jabbed at her phone. The building was plunged into silence, apart from the sound of a dripping tap at the sink. 'Sorry.' She panted through a grin. 'I love that tune.'

I couldn't stop staring. She was wearing a slouchy top with brightly patterned leggings that clung to long, strong-looking legs. 'I feel so much better this morning,' she said, stretching her arms high. 'I had the best night's sleep.'

'That's . . . great.' I approached slowly, with the sense she was a fragile animal that might easily frighten. 'I'll have some toast if you've got any bread, and then I'll make a move.'

'There's a loaf in the freezer' — she pointed with a dramatic flourish of her hand — 'and strawberry jam in the cupboard. No butter, I'm afraid.'

'That's fine.'

She watched as I crossed the tiled floor, the soles of my trainers sticking slightly.

'Are you sure you're OK?' I asked.

'Honestly, I feel brilliant.' Despite the full-watt beam, I didn't believe her. Maybe she was putting on an act so I wouldn't feel I needed to hang around.

'I'm worried about Oliver not knowing where I am.'

She shook her head, her high ponytail swinging. 'Do you think he'll care?'

Her question took me by surprise. 'I hope so. I can't remember the last time I spent the night away from home.'

'I'm sorry.' Saskia looked contrite and reached for my hand. 'Listen, Nell, before you go, you must take a look at the view. It's really something.'

I nodded, relieved she seemed to have calmed down. 'I'd love to.' I pushed Oliver to a crowded corner of my mind. 'It must have been amazing growing up here.'

She nodded. 'Tourists used to want to look around, as if we were a visitor attraction,' she rolled her eyes, which were remarkably clear compared to yesterday. 'I suggested we charge a fee, but Mum was too nice. She liked showing the place off.' As if she'd forgotten about breakfast, Saskia tugged me towards the staircase.

'Now?'

'Why not?'

'OK.' Half-laughing, I trailed her up the winding stairs. She seemed to have discovered a boundless energy, whereas I was out of breath by the time we reached the wooden ladder in the attic room — a space filled with cardboard boxes and suitcases that hadn't been touched for years judging by the net of cobwebs and layers of dust. I sneezed a couple of times, wishing I had a tissue.

'I'll go first.' Saskia gripped the sides of the ladder and took the rungs two at a time, while I hesitated at the bottom. I wasn't keen on heights. 'Come on,' she called down cheerfully. 'What are you waiting for?'

'Give me a minute.' I took a deep breath and, with a feeling of trepidation, gripped the sides of the ladder and began to climb.

CHAPTER 27

Nell

We emerged into an area criss-crossed with old wooden beams, light flooding through a single window, highlighting the old, ironwork cogs that must have once powered the windmill.

'This is amazing.' I cast my gaze around, but Saskia was already moving away, pushing open a low wooden door that let in more daylight as well as a biting wind.

I hugged my arms around my waist as I stepped gingerly after her, regretting not wearing something warmer than the shirt I'd slept in. Saskia didn't seem to notice the cold as she looked over the balcony, hands curled over the waist-high wooden railings.

'Isn't it beautiful?' Her gaze was nostalgic as I joined her. 'My dad loved to bird-watch from here. He always had a pair of binoculars around his neck.'

'It's lovely,' I agreed, sweeping my eyes across the tree-tops swaying in the wind. In truth, there wasn't much to see apart from trees. The earlier sun had dipped behind a cloud, leaching colour from the leaves and muting the landscape.

'If you look through the branches, you can see the sea on a clear day.'

She came closer, her elbow touching mine as I strained my eyes, but all I could see were more trees. A chill of unease swept through me. I wouldn't want to live here alone. I preferred the bustle and life of a town or city.

'You're like a princess in an ivory tower,' Saskia smiled. 'Waiting to be rescued.'

Turning, I suppressed another shiver and answered lightly, 'I don't need rescuing.'

'We all need rescuing, sometimes.'

I could hardly argue with that, after leaping into the car and driving several hours to bring her here. 'I suppose so,' I said, but I was recalling how she hadn't seemed anywhere near as heartbroken down in the kitchen, dancing and making smoothies, as she had the day before. Unless she was putting on a front.

I felt a birdlike flutter in my chest. 'I'd like to go back inside. It's freezing up here.'

Saskia rested her forearms on the lip of the balcony and angled her catlike gaze at me. 'It's such a shame you decided to come here and confront me about trying to take your job at Classic Props.'

For a moment, I thought I'd misheard. 'Sorry . . . what?'

Her lips formed a pitying smile. 'It's tragic that you've been having so many problems lately,' she said softly. 'Not coping at work, dealing with a secret boyfriend because your husband doesn't pay you enough attention. And then accusing *me* of having an affair with Oliver.'

My heart gave a hard kick. 'What are you talking about, Saskia?'

'I'm going over the story I'll tell the police when they find your broken body.' Her eyes moved pointedly to the concreted area below, where a couple of faded, candy-striped sun-loungers had been pushed to one side. 'You were beside yourself, screaming obscenities, unhinged by the fact that your husband doesn't want you, your secret boyfriend has dumped you, and Oliver's daughters hate you. Being fired from your job was the final straw. You blamed me, accused me of trying to steal your life.' She moved suddenly, arms swooping up as if to protect herself. 'We had a scuffle and . . . whoops!' She peered over the balcony. 'You went over, right where the railings are rotten, see?' I shrank back as she touched the wood nearest my elbow. Sure enough, it was rotting away, the struts shifting in their moorings. 'I tried to grab you but,' — she looked me up and down — 'you're quite a bit heavier than me and I couldn't hold on.'

The cut of meanness in her words was a shock. 'I don't . . .' But understanding flooded in as my brain finally caught up. 'You *planned* all this?'

'Well done, Nell.' When she gave a sad smile, I suddenly saw it: the straight white teeth, the hint of gold at her crown, a touch of silver in her irises. The real Saskia was breaking through the version she'd been playing, like a blurry picture zooming into focus.

'You're not wearing glasses,' I said stupidly, remembering she'd left them at the apartment. 'Who *are* you?'

'Someone who thinks you don't deserve to be Oliver Cosgrove's wife.' Her smile was silky smooth, but her eyes hooked into me like a bird of prey. 'You're not his type, Nell.'

I was frozen, as if at the centre of a blizzard. 'This is about Oliver?'

'He doesn't love you.' She shrugged. 'Hasn't done for a while.'

I battled to absorb her words as I edged back towards the door. 'Is that why you applied for the job at Classics, to get close to him?'

'More to undermine you whenever I could,' she said lightly. 'It was too good an opportunity, so I took it.' Another easy shrug. 'It was easy enough to post about you on Twitter, especially after looking you up online and finding that wedding company you used to work for. I also memorised your computer password, after watching you type it in, and changed a few dates in the diary to confuse you, made sure things weren't delivered when they were supposed to be. Oh, and cutting up that costume and soaking it with paint was actually fun!'

I felt the shock as though from a distance, my feelings numbed by Saskia's revelation about Oliver. *They were having an affair?* And yet . . . somewhere deep inside, I wasn't surprised. It explained so much about his recent behaviour. I couldn't believe I hadn't even considered the possibility. 'But . . . what about Alex?' My mind tried to grab a foothold. 'Does he know what's happening? Is that why he broke off your engagement?' I shook my head. 'I thought you were in love with him.'

'I don't want to talk about Alex,' she snapped, eyes flashing a warning.

Maybe there *was* no Alex, he'd been a smokescreen to distract me.

I fought to catch up, snippets falling into place. 'I suppose you rearranged that interview time with the newspaper too,' I managed. 'And deliberately invited Poppy and Ruby, hoping things would kick off.' When she smirked, anger sparked. 'How *could* you?'

'Anything to get you away from Oliver,' she crowed. 'Soon, he'll be selling the house in Marlow and moving on.' Scorn laced her tone. 'He hates ambitious women, you know. Can't stand you being successful, just like he couldn't stand Fiona's business doing well.'

The sound of her name on Saskia's lips was a shock. 'Why not ask me for a divorce?' I practically choked on the words. 'Why all this . . . *acting*?'

'He can't go through another divorce.' Saskia tutted. 'The last one nearly wiped him out, and he still can't shake her off. The ex-wife, who hates you as much as everyone else does.'

'You gave me her number to cause trouble.' Realisation dawned. 'She didn't call the office at all, did she?'

Saskia gave a slight shrug, her head cocked. 'Another bit of fun, to stir things up. It was easy enough to get her number off that pathetic interior design website and pretend she'd called you.' Her smile fell away. 'Oliver suggested leaving you, but this way is better. He'll get all the sympathy as well as a lovely new wife in the long run. He hates to be seen in a bad light, you must know that. He likes to keep his hands clean, be the good guy.'

My breath caught as a thought struck. 'The baby . . .' *Was it Oliver's?*

She lifted her top and patted her flat stomach. 'There is no baby.' As she said it, her lips formed a tight line. 'No baby for me, Nell. Not yet.'

'But . . . Alex . . .' I struggled for words. 'Was he ever real?'

'Of course he's real, you moron, but he's in the past.'

I tried to make sense of her words. Was Oliver a rebound affair? How had they met? Scared to ask as her eyes burned into me, I felt behind me for the door handle. 'So, you said you were pregnant to what . . . make me trust you, feel sorry for you?'

For a split second, there was a flash of vulnerability in her eyes. 'I'm a pretty good actress, don't you think? Better even than Ruby. I've been in a couple of plays but didn't really like it. There's no money in acting unless you get famous.'

'You've used Ruby too.'

'I like her, actually.' Her smile was bright and innocent. 'The Cosgroves will be a happier family without you in it.'

My breathing was shallow. 'You can't seriously be planning to hurt me.'

'Hard to take in, I know.' Her eyes widened. 'Maybe I should see a *counsellor.*'

The way she emphasised the word made me stiffen. 'I suppose you think it's a joke, that I've been having marriage counselling.' And Oliver must have been laughing behind my back.

'Carla's lovely, isn't she?' Saskia sighed. 'She's all I have left in the world.'

Fresh shock reeled through me. 'Carla's your *sister*?' But I could see it now, a similarity around the eyes, the shape of her jaw. 'But . . . does she know?' I looked around, wondering whether I could make a run for it, barely able to absorb what Saskia was saying. 'About what you're doing?'

'Not yet, no.'

She came closer, as if sensing my impulse to flee, her presence pinning me like a steel trap. 'Poor Oliver, doing his best to "save"' — she made air quotes — 'his marriage, even though he knows it's doomed.'

'Oh my God, it was you who sent me those texts, and the flowers and card, and tore up my wedding photo, put the idea into Oliver's head that I was having an affair. That I was trying to insure him in case he *died*.' Everything felt unstable, the sky above me wavering. 'I thought someone had been in the house. Things missing or being moved around.' I remembered my sweater, the beers I'd found under the sink, the milk carton on the worktop I was sure I hadn't left out. 'I even thought I saw someone outside the house the night you returned my phone.'

'I had your house key copied.' She said it calmly, with a hint of pride. 'It was easy enough in my lunch break. You didn't even notice the key missing from your bag. Or your phone, come to that.' She tutted and wagged a finger. 'Maybe you shouldn't leave your bag in the office while you're in the warehouse with Janine.'

Her words bounced around my head. 'You sent my sweater to Ruby?'

'I knew she would wear it if she thought it was from her dad.' The way her mouth twisted with amusement made me shudder. It was all a game to her — a twisted piece of theatre.

'Does Oliver know you're here?' I said.

'Of course not.'

I felt a brief, dizzying sense of relief that he wasn't party to her crazy plan.

'He doesn't love you though, Nell. He'll be glad when you're gone.'

Relief gave way to fury because Saskia was right. Oliver didn't love me, that much was crystal clear. But Saskia wasn't getting rid of me without a fight.

'You won't get away with it,' I said. 'And when it comes out, how do you think Oliver's daughters are going to feel?'

Why hadn't Oliver considered them before starting his affair? How long exactly had it been going on? 'Just let me go, Saskia.' I tried to contain a tremor in my voice. 'I'll walk away. I don't want a penny of Oliver's money, I'm capable of making my own.'

'As if I can let you go after everything I've told you.' Her face was incredulous. 'You must be dumber than I thought.'

'I won't go to the police.' I inched further towards the door behind me. 'There won't be anything to tell if I go home and you stay here.' I couldn't disguise a telltale tremble. 'I won't say anything.'

Saskia was looking at something in the distance, but when she turned her eyes were a glassy void. 'That's not how it's going to play out, Nell.'

She lunged at me without warning, her lips pulled back in a snarl.

I ducked to one side, but her nails scraped the side of my face. When I touched my cheek, my fingertips came away bloody. 'What would your parents think if they could see you now?' My words emerged as a desperate cry.

'Don't you bring my parents into this.' I recoiled from her balled-up rage. 'My parents were *everything* to me. I would do *anything* for my family.' Her chest heaved and a look of intent stole over her face. 'You're heavier than me, Nell.' Her hand shot out and grabbed my wrist. 'But I'm a lot stronger than I look.'

I yanked my arm in an attempt to pull away, but she was right. She was tougher than I was, and my mind flashed back to the gym equipment in her bedroom. 'Let me go!' I pulled again, my skin burning in her grip.

She grinned, baring her teeth. 'OK.' She released me.

I staggered backwards, slamming into the balcony behind. The railings snapped with a terrible cracking sound, and then there was nothing but a rush of ice-cold air.

CHAPTER 28

Ruby

Ruby stared across at Carla in the driving seat. The woman looked pale, her face set in a worried frown, her blonde hair held back with a slide in a low bun, revealing a glimpse of expensive gold earrings. A necklace — an owl with green, glinting gems for eyes — rested against her fine knit turtleneck jumper.

How had Ruby ended up racing along narrow, winding country roads towards Norfolk with a stranger?

Seeing Carla on Saskia's doorstep the day before had been a shock. She'd recognised her from when she and Poppy had watched Nell from her van window, the first time Nell had gone for marriage counselling.

'She came home from work sick,' Ruby had told Carla, as they all stood on the small landing outside Saskia's apartment.

'But she isn't here,' Stefan had added, glancing over his shoulder at the closed door.

Carla had paced back and forth. 'I received a voicemail from her. She confessed she'd been working for Nell Cosgrove, and . . .' She stopped pacing, tears in her eyes. 'I just need to know she's OK.' Carla had taken off then, leaving Ruby with unanswered questions. And Ruby had tried to push the chance encounter from her thoughts, tried to forget that Nell had left her phone and jacket in Saskia's flat, that Saskia had left her glasses behind.

She'd spent the evening with Poppy and her mum, and they'd talked for hours, working out how to build a new foundation that would support her sister. It wasn't going to be an easy journey, but her mum had shown signs of realisation, *'My girl must come first'*, *'I've been a bloody fool'*, *'It's as though I've been wearing blinkers'*, and with the two of them now fully supporting Poppy, Ruby knew they were heading in the right direction.

Once darkness fell, and Ruby was alone in her flat, only the screen of the muted TV for light, her mind had spun for what felt like hours. Thoughts of Poppy, then Nell, and Saskia's connection to Carla — *they were sisters* — that couldn't be a coincidence, surely. The fact Nell and her dad were going to Carla for counselling just when Saskia started at Classics as Nell's assistant. Something wasn't right.

'Dad, how's Nell?' she'd asked him down the phone first thing that morning.

'She didn't come home last night. I've no idea where she is,' Oliver had said. 'I admit it isn't like her, but she's a grown woman, has every right to stay out.'

'She didn't text or call you?'

'No, but I'm sure she's fine.'

Ruby told him about finding her jacket and phone. 'It's a bit odd that she would leave them behind, don't you think?'

'She probably went out with friends, Ruby.' He sounded tense. 'I'm sure she's OK, love, and if I'm honest, things have been rocky between us.'

They were words she and Poppy had wanted to hear for so long, and yet now they barely had an impact. Her dream to have her parents back together had been a selfish one. If they were together she could get on with her life. Stop worrying about her mum and sister.

'Nell probably needs some space,' Oliver continued. 'I really have more important things to worry about than what game she's playing.'

'You think she's playing a game?'

'You don't know the half of it.' He was silent for a moment, and it occurred to Ruby how few proper conversations she'd ever had with her father. She waited, the phone pressed to her ear. Maybe he was finally going to open up to her. 'Why the sudden interest in Nell, anyway? I thought you hated her.'

Ruby felt a stab of disappointment. 'I don't hate her, Dad. I hated what happened to our family.'

She'd ended the call before he could question her further, and tried calling Saskia. It went straight to voicemail. 'Hey, this is Ruby. Can you give me a call when you get this, please?'

She raked her fingers through her hair, convinced then that something wasn't right. She tried Stefan's number, left a voicemail asking him to get back to her too. Should she call the police? But it seemed like an overreaction. There was only one other person to turn to.

'She'll be at the windmill,' Carla had said, when Ruby barged into her office, explaining she thought Nell could be with her sister. 'I haven't slept at all, have left endless messages. I knew something was wrong.'

'You sound really worried.'

Carla turned, her eyes wide. 'If I'm honest, Ruby, I am. This isn't the first time . . .'

'I don't understand. Is Nell in danger? Should we call the police?'

Carla had grabbed her coat and bag. 'God, no, everything will be OK,' she'd said, heading for the door, but the worry in her eyes told Ruby otherwise. 'I need to go to Norfolk. Make sure my sister is OK.'

Ruby had watched as the woman pulled her phone from her bag. She understood that bond between sisters, that sixth sense when you know something's wrong. 'I've only got two appointments today, I'll cancel them on the way to the car.'

'I'll come with you.' Ruby had followed her from the office and down the stairs, wasting no time calling Benita — telling her she was unwell.

And now they'd been on the road for almost three hours, infrequently speaking to each other, Radio 2 barely audible on the radio.

'Only another five minutes.' Carla's voice was croaky, her face pale. From side on, her resemblance to her sister was obvious. They both had the same shape nose, slim neck. Carla glanced into the rear-view mirror. 'I'll be glad to shake this idiot behind us, they've been following us for miles.'

Ruby glanced over her shoulder, but couldn't see anyone as they rounded a bend in the road. 'So what's the connection?' she said — the words that had been playing around in her head the whole journey, finally out there.

Carla snapped her head round. 'What do you mean, connection?'

'Well, it can't be a coincidence that you are Nell's and my dad's marriage counsellor, and Saskia recently started work at Classic Props.'

'Saskia.' Carla shook her head, returning her eyes to the road. 'I can't believe she's calling herself that.'

'Saskia's not her real name?' Ruby stared at Carla. Her hair had slipped from its slide, hiding part of her face, like a curtain.

'Her name's Emily — Emily Harris,' Carla said, almost in a whisper.

Ruby's stomach churned. Things were worse than she'd thought. 'Why would she lie?'

'It's what she does.' Carla's hands tightened on the steering wheel. 'We'll sort this out, Ruby. Everything will be OK. Only a few more miles to go.'

Ruby turned away, gazed out at the rural landscape, as rain hit the glass, trickling sideways across the window.

'They're still following.' Carla was looking in her rear-view mirror. She picked up speed, the car jolting Ruby as they took another bend. 'Do you know what it's like to lose your parents?' she said, her voice calm and even.

'Not if you're talking about them passing away,' Ruby said. But she knew about losing what she'd thought was a perfect family.

'Is there any other kind of loss?'

Ruby shrugged. It seemed wrong to compare her father leaving and her parents' marriage dying with Carla and Saskia's heartbreak, however painful it had felt.

Carla pushed her foot down further on the throttle, making Ruby uneasy.

'Slow down a bit.'

'We need to get there.' She threw Ruby a look. 'Before it's too late.'

'Too late?' Ruby felt a flash of alarm. 'What are you talking about? You said we didn't need the police.'

Carla sucked in a deep breath. 'As I said before, this isn't the first time my sister has done something like this.' She took another bend at speed. A car coming the other way swerved hard to miss them, horn blaring.

'Slow down,' Ruby yelled, gripping the overhead handle.

'Emily becomes obsessed.' Carla bit her bottom lip, her hands tense on the steering wheel.

'Obsessed?'

'Thankfully, she was found before, but—'

'Who was found, Carla?' Her heart banged against her ribs. 'Please! You're not making any sense.'

'The wife.' She sucked in a breath. 'She'd taken her to the windmill.' Carla shook her head. Spun round a corner, tears in her eyes. 'It was a long time ago. But if I hadn't got there, who knows?'

Tyres skidded and a tree loomed as if from nowhere. The sound of crunching metal battered Ruby's eardrums. She lunged forward, felt a sharp pain in her leg, and let out a scream as darkness swallowed her.

* * *

'Ruby! Can you hear me?'

Ruby peeled open her eyes to see a deflated airbag. 'Carla?'

'Are you OK?' Carla was outside the car crouched by the open passenger door, rain hammering the hood of her jacket.

Ruby moved from her slumped position, rested her head back against the car seat, her head pounding. Smoke billowed from the engine. The front of the car was a mass of scrunched up metal entangled in a tree.

'Are you OK?' Carla repeated, rubbing her own neck.

'I think so. It's just my leg.' Ruby reached down, feeling a rip in her jeans, cold blood on her fingers. It seemed to be a gash rather than a break, but still painful.

'I need to go on alone.' Carla rose, and stepped backwards. 'The windmill isn't far from here.' She looked about her. 'Call an ambulance if you need one. Best you stay here.' She turned and raced towards a clump of trees.

'No wait! Please. You can't leave me.' Ruby pulled herself round, her body jarred and aching as she tried to get out of the car, almost falling into the mud. She hauled herself to her feet, seeing Carla disappear into the nearby trees.

Ruby pulled her bag from the footwell and rummaged for her phone, fumbled with the screen. No signal. She threw the phone and bag onto the passenger seat, unsure what to do. The gash on her leg oozed blood, soaking her jeans. She winced. It hurt like hell, but she had to follow Carla — had to find the windmill.

As she stumbled in the direction Carla had retreated, she heard a car approaching. She turned, cold rain splattering her face, stinging her cheeks. She covered her eyes, the beam of the headlights blinding as it pulled into a layby further up the country lane, engine whirring. Shivering, she turned, and limped onwards, hair clinging to her face, the rain getting heavier. She glanced back again at the car, now shrouded in shadows and silent, before heading through a gap in the trees.

The sight of the windmill on the other side of a field made her heart leap. She could just make out Carla disappearing through a line of trees that surrounded the building. Was Nell inside the windmill? Was she in danger? She stepped onwards, knowing she had to find out.

CHAPTER 29

Nell

As I fell, I curled my arms around my head, a scream flying from my throat. Braced for impact, I bounced off something, onto the concrete below.

I opened my eyes and lay still, waiting for the pain to hit. Rain dripped down my face. I couldn't move, could barely breathe, on the verge of blacking out.

A groan escaped. Was Saskia watching, checking for signs of life?

I slowly twisted my head, the white sky above almost blinding me, rain stinging my eyeballs. *Nobody there.* Inching further around, I saw one of the sun-loungers tipped on its side. It had broken my fall, its cushioned seat no doubt saving my life.

Sucking in shallow sips of air I tried to sit up, dropping back as a grinding agony shot up my arm. It was twisted, probably broken. Sickness rose as I shuffled upright, whimpering with pain and fear. My whole body felt shaken and bruised, my vision blurred at the edges. A knifelike pain in my right side told me I'd broken at least one rib.

I was alive, but for how much longer? Saskia would be on her way to check I was dead. *How could this be happening?*

She tried to kill me. Fear bolted through my brain, clearing the fog. I had to get away.

I clumsily shifted onto my knees, keeping my injured arm clamped to my side, and pushed myself up to standing with my other hand. Shivers wracked my body. Every breath made me clench with pain.

I stumbled, weak and disoriented, my clothes soaking wet, nausea rising once more. My arm throbbed, agony radiating up to my shoulder. I longed to sink down but knew I mustn't. With a jagged sob, I wobbled forward, the view ahead zooming in and out of focus. *The trees.* If I reached the woods, I could hide.

I set off with painful, lurching steps, gaining speed, imagining Saskia emerging to find me gone. I toppled a couple of times, gasping as the movement jolted my arm, before propelling myself at the dense perimeter of trees. The breath tore in and out of my lungs, and my face burned. I didn't stop or try to look back until I'd crashed between a pair of solid trunks into sudden gloom.

Above, the wind blustered through branches, but the only other sounds were my ragged breath, and the blood roaring in my ears. With a choked sob, I darted my eyes around, seeking a path, but the trees were tightly packed, a carpet of mulch and mud underfoot from the rain. I doubted anyone came through here, or where I would end up if I carried on. Saskia had mentioned being able to see the sea, so maybe if I went in a straight line I would reach a road. Except, there was no straight line that I could see.

My arm felt on fire and the stabbing in my ribs had intensified. *What if I had internal injuries?* The thought of bleeding to death out here, with no one knowing where I was, Mum hearing her only daughter had died alone in the middle of nowhere spurred me to keep moving.

My trainers sank into muddy puddles. I stumbled over tangled roots, yelping as I imagined movements, glancing up at the dark, swaying canopy shrouding the sky.

Hearing a sound behind me, I froze.

'Ne-ell!'

Saskia. My breath erupted in short sharp bursts as I started moving again.

'Are you forgetting I grew up here, Nell?' Her voice was light, amused. 'I know these woods like the back of my hand.'

Panic ripped through me as my gaze flicked from side to side. There must be somewhere to hide. Saskia couldn't know every inch of the place — not anymore.

My mind flew to Oliver, probably going about his day with the smile he kept ready for everyone he met, and a spurt of anger lent me strength. I darted off to the side and swung my leg over a tangle of fallen branches, pushing deeper between the trees.

Ahead, a patch of daylight glimmered through the leaves, spotlighting an oak that looked centuries old, its ancient limbs creaking in the wind. I shuffled towards it, keeping low, grateful my shirt was patterned with dark colours, helping me to blend in.

The tree trunk should be wide enough to conceal me.

'You can't hide forever, Nell!'

Her voice was closer, reminding me of the Stone Angels in *Dr Who*. If I looked round, would she be right behind me?

Recalling the absent expression in Saskia's eyes brought a shiver of revulsion. How had I not realised how damaged she was? *I'm a very good actor.* Everything about her had been a lie, yet she'd been so convincing, I'd given her a job. Did Carla have any idea what Saskia was up to, how far she was prepared to go, to get what she wanted — that she actually seemed to be enjoying herself? I still couldn't wrap my head around Carla — my counsellor — being Saskia's sister. Had they cooked up the counselling sessions between them with the intention of persuading me to leave Oliver, in case he didn't believe I was having an affair? But I'd found Carla by chance, on the internet, so it didn't make sense. She couldn't have known who I was when I emailed her, and Saskia had been at the company for a week before I even saw Carla. I thought how uncomfortable she'd looked at our last session, almost as if she was worried about me, but surely that was natural in her position, after listening to the things I'd told her. I couldn't work out where she fitted, but the thought of Saskia getting away with it made me want to be sick. Alex — if he existed — had clearly dodged a bullet by leaving her.

'I'm coming to get you!' Her voice coiled through the air, taunting and somehow seductive, as though relishing this perverted game of hide-and-seek. What was she planning to do? Throttle me with her bare hands? Or maybe she'd taken a knife from the kitchen. *What then*? Bury my body in the woods? If she did, it was unlikely I'd ever be found.

'I'm impressed you survived that fall, Nell.' Her voice was a taunt. 'Maybe you wish you hadn't. You must have broken something, apart from the sun lounger.'

She was close, judging by the squashy tread of her feet. Feeling the scrape of rough bark against my back, I edged further round the tree, stifling a scream as I dropped backwards, knocking my damaged arm. On the verge of fainting, I realised I'd fallen into a deep, mossy hollow inside the trunk.

Fighting the pain, I shuffled back, tucking my knees up, ignoring the throbbing in my ribcage as I lowered my head to my knees, so my face wasn't visible. With any luck, Saskia would walk by, and I could run back to the windmill and call for help — then I remembered. There was no working phone. *I would have to drive away.*

The wind had dropped. In the sudden silence, I heard a burst of birdsong. Tears spilled over. I should be at work, chatting to Janine — even Sean — taking a trip to a local antique fair to source new stock, pitching to new clients; all the things I loved. I wished I'd never set eyes on Saskia French. *I wish I hadn't married Oliver. When I get out of here, I'm going to—*

'There you are.'

My head jerked up, eyes meeting Saskia's arctic gaze. She was crouching, head tilted. 'I used to come here with a book sometimes.' Her tone was almost wistful. 'You know, a cavity like this in an oak means it's been starved of water and nutrients.' Her expression brightened. 'Maybe I should try that with you next.' I was breathless with pain and shock. 'Lock you up and starve you.'

'You might as well leave me here.' I shrank back as she held out her hands to pull me out. 'It's not like I can go far.'

'You can't stay there,' she dragged me to my knees by one arm while I yelped with pain. 'It would be bad luck for a bunch of ramblers to get lost and find you.'

'Please let me go, Saskia.'

She pretended to think, screwing up her face. 'Sorry, no can do.' She smiled, an arch of neat, white teeth. 'You don't have much of a future anyway, so what's the point?'

'Neither will you, once you're a murderer.'

'Ah, but no one will know that.'

'Your sister?'

She pulled her chin back. 'Did you listen to me at all, Nell? Your death will be a terrible, tragic accident, nothing more.'

'It's going to be harder to explain with this . . .' I tried to move my injured arm, wincing as red-hot pain seared down to my wrist. 'And I've broken some ribs.'

'Natural, after a terrible fall from a great height.' A nerve twitched beneath her eye.

'Look, I don't even want Oliver, not after this. I promise I'll walk away.' I gave a strangled sob. 'You're welcome to him.'

'Oh my God!' She squatted again, filling the space in front of me. 'You think Oliver and me . . . that we're. . . ?' She laughed, throwing her head back. 'That's hilarious.'

'What?' Confusion ran through me like cold water. 'Isn't that what this is about? You moved on to my husband when Alex decided he didn't want you anymore.'

'Don't talk about Alex like that.' Her eyes were furious slits, all humour gone. 'He would have married me, I know he would, if I hadn't . . .'

'Hadn't what?' I said as she lost the thread. 'How did you even meet Oliver?'

Her gaze refocused. 'He's too old for me, and not my type at all.' She shook her head, a fresh smile hovering. 'I'm not doing this for *me*.'

'I don't understand.' Numbness took hold and my teeth began to chatter. 'Who *are* you doing it for?'

'Carla.' She spoke as though it was obvious. 'I'm doing it for my sister, so she and Oliver can be together, be a family. She's crazy in love with him and one of us deserves to be happy, after everything we've been through.' Saskia's voice grew cold once more. 'You're the only thing standing in their way.'

I couldn't make sense of it all as I slipped towards unconsciousness. 'Please don't do this, Saskia.'

'Actually, that's not my real name. I became Saskia French for a while when I joined the drama group at university, where I met Stefan and starred in a couple of plays he put on. I actually prefer being Saskia, or Sassy as he still calls me. I don't think Stef even remembers that I was born Emily Harris.' *Carla's surname.* Her voice came closer. 'I couldn't risk you telling Oliver my real name in case he mentioned it to Carla and she put two and two together. She would have freaked out and spoiled everything, especially after . . .' She paused, looming at me, her face losing detail. 'Enough small talk.' She pushed a strand of hair off her face. 'I'm afraid this is going to hurt, Nell.' As she hooked her hands under my armpits, a voice cut through the air.

'Emily!' A woman's voice; familiar. 'Emily, where are you?' *Carla.*

'Let me help you,' I breathed, my pulse feverish. 'It's not too late.'

Saskia's grip had loosened, and she backed away, muttering under her breath.

I tried to cry out, to move, but my voice wouldn't work, and my body felt weak and broken.

'Emily, I know you're out there!' Carla was closing in. Twigs cracked and leaves rustled, branches moving around us. 'Please, talk to me!'

Through my lashes I watched Saskia spin around. She was doubled over, hands tearing at her hair. It sounded as if she was chanting, '*No, no, no, no, no,*' but darkness was descending, and I couldn't be sure of anything anymore.

CHAPTER 30

Ruby

The sound of a car door slamming made Ruby's heart thud. Was the driver following her? Was it the same car Carla thought was tailing them?

Maybe she was overreacting. Perhaps it was someone who had seen the accident. Seen her limping away, and was simply concerned. Wanted to check she was OK.

Then why did she feel so uneasy?

She took a deep breath and attempted to pick up speed. The rain was easing off as she made her way across the field towards the windmill, which looked menacing, eerie against the swirling dark clouds.

She could no longer see Carla, and the pain in her leg seared as she stumbled onwards, the ground slipping and sliding under her feet. Why was she here? What did she owe Nell? Carla?

Ruby reached the tall trees that surrounded the windmill, and flashed a look over her shoulder. A figure, hunched in a dark hoodie, stood near the tress by the road. Was it the driver of the car? It was as though they didn't want to get too close, preferring to observe her from a distance. She shuddered, and, heart thudding, dived through brambles, her trainers squelching as she made her way into dense trees.

Voices came from deeper in the wooded area. 'This is for you, Carla. I'm doing this for you.' *Saskia?*

Ruby opened her mouth to call out, but something told her to stay quiet. She moved closer to the voices, soggy twigs breaking under her feet.

'I don't want this, Emily. You're not doing this for me.' Carla's voice radiated calm, smooth, like the counsellor she was. 'Please, let's go home. We can work things out.'

'I am home. This is our sanctuary. The windmill where we grew up, remember?' There are angry tears in Saskia's voice. 'Where we were so happy.'

Ruby moved through the trees and froze behind a gnarled trunk. She peered round, seeing Nell on the ground, soaked through, her face milky pale. Saskia was clutching a tree branch, pacing across the sodden earth, dragging her fingers through her soaked hair.

'Of course I remember, Emily. We had good times here as children.' Carla's voice was still controlled, level, she wasn't moving.

'They were. And I'm going to make everything right for you and Oliver, so we can be a proper family again.' Saskia came to a halt, staring into her sister's eyes. 'You can live here at the windmill. And I'll live here with you. Everything will be perfect. You'll see.'

'Just give me that.' Carla tilted her head, and reached out her hand towards the tree branch. 'We can sort this out, lovely. But Oliver isn't right for me. I know that now.'

Nell's eyes flicked from one sister to the other, her hand clutching her ribs, her face contorted in pain.

'What are you talking about?' Saskia's eyes flashed, her fingers clenched around the branch, her knuckles white. 'Of course Oliver is right for you. He has to be. Everything's going to be perfect this time, Carla, you'll see.'

'I made a mistake.' She looked across at Nell. 'Oliver's not the man I thought he was.'

Ruby covered her mouth, holding in a gasp. Unable to believe they were talking about her father as though his wife wasn't lying injured on the ground.

'But you said you loved him,' Saskia continued, her voice cracking. 'You said so, Carla. And I know you love him. I could see it in your eyes. You've never felt like that about anyone.'

'I was wrong, Em—'

'No, no—'

'And we need to get you some help.'

'Help? What sort of help?'

'Someone who will talk you through this.'

'I don't need anyone to talk me, Carla. I've got you.'

'Yes, of course you've got me.' Carla stepped closer to her sister, touched her arm gently. 'Everything's going to be just fine.' She turned and reached out her hand towards Nell. 'Let's get—'

'What the hell are you doing?' Saskia screamed. 'Nell is the only thing standing in the way of your happiness — our happiness. Can't you see that?'

Nell let out a cry of pain as Carla hauled her to her feet.

Saskia's face morphed, witchlike. 'No, Carla! Stop! Stop!'

'We have to get Nell to a hospital. She's badly hurt,' Carla continued, her calm tone of earlier sounding increasingly panic-stricken. 'I'll call an ambulance from the windmill.' Nell let out a groan as Carla looped her arm around her shoulders, and they turned as one towards the building.

'Don't you dare turn your back on me, after all I've done for you.' Spittle flew from Saskia's mouth as she spoke, tears filling her eyes. 'Don't you dare leave.'

'We need to use the phone, call for help.'

'No, no, no.' Saskia lurched forward, and raced in front of them, stepping backwards. 'Stop! I won't let you take her away.' As she raised the branch, Carla jumped in front of Nell who dropped to her knees. Saskia brought the branch down, cracking it against her sister's skull, and Carla fell hard against the muddy earth.

'Oh God, no!' Nell cried, grabbing her ribs, crying out in pain, her hair wet against her scalp. She looked up at Saskia with frightened, tear-filled eyes. 'What the hell have you done?'

Ruby couldn't move for fear and shock, her eyes fixed on Saskia — the blooded branch dangling against her side like an axe.

'Carla?' Saskia said after a few moments. 'Carla?' Her eyes moved to Nell, and in a cold, harsh tone she said, 'That was meant to be you.'

'We need to get your sister help, Saskia, please.' Nell was crying now, attempting to take Carla's pulse. 'She's unconscious. We need to call an ambulance.'

'This is your fault, Nell Cosgrove.' Saskia yanked a clump of Nell's hair, and hauled her to her feet. 'And now it's time to pay.'

Ruby watched as Saskia dragged Nell through the trees in the direction of the windmill. She desperately wanted to follow, to help Nell, but Saskia was fuelled with so much anger, and still holding the branch. Truth was, Ruby was afraid.

Was Saskia intending to kill Nell?

Was Carla dead?

She had to do something.

She looked about her, spotting a large misshapen stone. If she was to creep up behind Saskia, she might be able to knock her out. She picked it up and began following. If she could disarm Saskia, she could maybe get to the windmill, call for help.

She was inches away, creeping through the trees, when Saskia spun round. Saskia was strong, and within moments, she dropped Nell to the ground and lunged at Ruby with a roar, tossing her across the muddy ground, against a tree trunk.

'Do you really think a skinny thing like you can beat me?' Saskia wiped the back of her hand across her mouth. Rain dripped from her hair. 'What the hell are you doing here, Ruby? Surely you don't owe Nell anything. She stole your father, didn't she? Leaving you to cope with an alcoholic mother and a disturbed sister. She deserves what's coming to her.'

It was those words, and the small, cold laugh that followed, that triggered it. All the built-up anger at everything that had happened since her father left came rushing to the surface. Ruby grabbed the stone she'd dropped when she fell, leapt towards Saskia, and whacked her across the temple. The shriek of Saskia's scream was bloodcurdling as she fell sideways to the floor.

'We need to go,' Ruby said to Nell in a rush, not daring to look back, as she reached her hand down towards her. But Nell was in agony. 'Please try,' Ruby pleaded, her heart thudding. 'We don't have much time.'

And then, somehow, Nell was on her feet and they were stumbling together towards the windmill, towards safety.

CHAPTER 31

Nell

Blackness danced at the edge of my vision as we lurched away from Saskia, who was crumpled like a rag doll in the dirt, not moving.

My brain wasn't firing properly, struggling to put things in order: Carla turning up, then Ruby appearing like a vision, apparently to save me from whatever deranged new plan Saskia had hatched. Saskia, who was really Emily.

Carla and Oliver were together.

'Come *on,* Nell!'

Carla and Oliver. Oliver and Carla. I couldn't get my head around it.

'Nell, *quick!'* Ruby's cold fingers wrapped around mine, her eyes too big for her face, which was unnaturally pale. 'We have to go.'

'Hurts,' I managed, sweat breaking out on my forehead.

'I know, but we have to get back to the windmill and call for help.'

'No phone,' I managed, but Ruby didn't slow down, practically dragging me after her, more sure-footed — despite a limp — than I was, tripping and stumbling, the pain in my arm and ribs threatening to bring me down.

By the time we emerged from the woods, I was on the verge of collapse. I gasped at the sight of the windmill etched against the grey-shrouded sky. Disoriented after the gloom of the tree-clustered woodland, we faltered. Ruby was breathing heavily, casting her eyes around, while my vision blurred with tears.

'I think we were followed here.' Her voice was low, the words laced with tension. 'Carla and me.'

I tried to catch my breath. 'What?'

'There were headlights behind us, and someone pulled their car over when we crashed.'

'You crashed?' Feeling slow and stupid, I glanced down. Blood seeped through a rip in her jeans. 'You're hurt.'

'It's a long story.'

'Was it your dad?' Mentioning Oliver brought a surge of panic and nausea. 'Following you?'

Ruby shook her head. 'No.' But something in her tone suggested she was no longer sure about her dad. 'I've been followed before, but I don't think it's him.' She was moving again, making a beeline for the door I'd innocently walked through with Saskia the day before. 'When I spoke to Dad earlier he seemed to think you were fine, even though you didn't go home last night.'

Had he been glad when I didn't turn up for dinner, going straight to Carla's? Perhaps he invited her over. Had he even tried to get hold of me, knowing it was unusual for me to not put in an appearance? How had Carla known where we were?

My brain spun with confusion, everything around me tilting.

'I don't think Dad knows what's going on,' Ruby said, as though reading my thoughts. 'Carla told me this isn't the first time Saskia, or whatever her name is, tried to hurt someone linked to one of her sister's boyfriends.'

Boyfriends. Oliver was my husband. I struggled to keep up with Ruby's hurried pacing, the solid ground jarring my body.

'She should have been arrested back then,' Ruby said. 'Carla got her out of it somehow.'

I couldn't see Ruby's face, only the swish of her long hair as she yanked open the door into the windmill, turning to grab my hand and haul me inside. She closed the door and looked around the kitchen. 'Where's the landline?'

'I tried to tell you, it's not working.'

Her head jerked round. 'I left my phone in the car,' she said, moving her hands into her hair. 'I'll have to go back and get it.'

'No mobile network.' I leaned against the wall. 'I tried using Saskia's phone, but there was no signal.'

'Shit.'

The room seemed to sway as we briefly eyed each other.

'You look half-dead,' Ruby murmured. 'What the hell happened?'

'She pushed me off the balcony at the top of the windmill.'

'Jesus.' Ruby's eyes widened. 'You're being serious?'

'She was going to make it look like suicide, leaving Oliver free to marry her sister.'

'Oh my God.' Ruby's laugh was one of disbelief. 'She seemed so . . . normal.'

'I would be dead if I hadn't landed on a sun lounger.' Ruby's colour drained even further. 'She's dangerous.'

'I got that.' Ruby gave a panicked look towards the door. 'She could be on her way back.'

'We'll leave in my car.' It was an effort to speak. 'Are you OK to drive?'

She nodded. 'We'll call for help once we're away from here.' She limped towards the door. 'Where are your keys? I'll go and—'

She stopped, angling her head at the ceiling. 'Did you hear that?'

I nodded as a floorboard creaked. 'There's someone upstairs.' Numbness descended again. I felt as if I was shutting down, my brain and body no longer able to communicate.

The sound came again. Someone was walking around.

'They might not realise we're here.' I whispered. 'Let's hide.'

Ruby spun around. 'Hide where?'

'Pantry.'

'What?'

'There's a pantry.' I pointed behind her at the door by the fridge, where Saskia had taken out a carton of long life milk the night before. 'In there.' For a second, I wondered whether Saskia might have made it back before us and was lying in wait to finish what she'd started. 'Or we could make a run for the car.'

'You're not fit for running, and I'm not leaving you here,' Ruby hissed.

Barely breathing, I let her half-carry me across the kitchen, wincing when the pantry door opened with a loud squeak. The sudden silence upstairs was somehow more terrifying than the movements had been.

'I think they heard,' Ruby whispered.

The pantry was dank and dark, but I welcomed the icy coldness that seeped into my bones like an anaesthetic.

Ruby pulled the door shut and fastened both hands around the handle while I backed against the shelves lining the stone walls. There was a sour smell as though milk had been soaking into the floor tiles for years, and a faint, scratching sound that I didn't want to think about.

'Maybe they'll leave if they think we've gone,' Ruby whispered. I could see the whites of her eyes as she turned her head and her breath misting the air.

'Or they saw us come back and won't leave until they've found us,' I whispered back. 'My car's still out there, remember?'

'Who do you think it is?'

'I've no idea.'

There was a pause, the sound of our frightened breaths filling the air.

'I'm sorry this has happened to you, Nell.'

Tears filled my eyes. 'How come you're here?'

'I went to Saskia's to find you,' Ruby whispered. 'I saw Stefan—'

'Stefan?'

'That theatre friend of hers.'

Something occurred to me. 'Dark hair, tall, good looking?'

'That's him.'

'I thought he was her fiancé, that they were having a baby.' My teeth started to chatter. 'I trusted her, but she's lied about everything.'

'My dad's lied too.' Ruby's whisper couldn't disguise the hurt and disgust in her voice. 'I've been an idiot. He had affairs before — or at least one that I know of — when he was with Mum, but I didn't realise at the time. Or rather, I didn't want to know because he was . . . well, my dad, I suppose. And Mum loved him so much. We all did.'

'It's not your fault.' I tried to breathe through a wave of pain, then froze. 'What was that?'

'Someone's coming.'

I sensed Ruby bracing herself, planting her feet wide apart as she gripped the door handle tighter.

Inhaling a sharp breath, I turned to run a hand across the shelf behind me, looking for something I could use as a weapon. Not that I'd be any use, the state I was in. Despair crashed through me.

'Is someone here?'

We stiffened, recognising the voice on the other side of the door.

'It's Sean,' Ruby said. 'What the hell is he doing here?'

My heart was going berserk. 'Do you think he's in on it with Saskia? Maybe he's come to help her finish me off.'

Ruby jerked forward as Sean tugged at the door.

'I know you're in there,' he said. 'Ruby?'

'*Shit*,' she muttered. 'He was the one following us.'

In a sudden movement, she pulled back and kicked violently at the door. As it flew open there was a cry of outrage. I peered past Ruby to see Sean reeling back, clutching his face. Blood oozed through his fingers.

'What did you do that for?' He snatched up a tea towel and pressed it to his nose, glaring at her from under a lowered brow. 'That really hurt.'

'Why are you here, Sean?'

'I could ask you the same thing.'

'Yes, why are you here, Sean?' said a familiar voice.

Saskia. My stomach plunged. Wrapping one arm around my frozen body, I joined Ruby in the kitchen. She was circling Sean warily, hand skimming the worktop as if hoping to find something to protect herself with, but she stopped as Saskia staggered into view, looking as bad as I felt. There was a bloody gash at her temple and her hair was a sodden, tangled mess, her clothes wet and patched with dirt. The dazed look in her eyes was probably due to the injury Ruby had inflicted — or a sign that her grasp on reality had slipped further.

'Are you two in on this together?' My voice was weak. I couldn't stand up straight and grasped for the edge of the counter, head spinning. 'You won't get away with it.'

'She's nothing to do with me.' Sean sounded stunned, eyes darting from Saskia to Ruby as though I wasn't there.

'This is all your fault.' Though slurred, Saskia's words were loaded with spite and the look she gave me sent a shudder of fear down my spine. 'My sister's hurt because of you.'

'I think you'll find that was your fault.' Ruby crossed the floor to stand in front of me. Her boots were encrusted with mud, a clump falling onto the tiles. 'Whacking someone over the head will do that to them. Poor Stefan. Does he know what you're really like?'

'Leave him out of this.'

'Who's Stefan?' Sean had inched closer to Ruby. Even as the room started to whirl, I realised I still didn't trust him.

'Probably the only friend she has, am I right, Saskia? Or should I call you *Emily*?'

I wished Ruby wouldn't goad Saskia, who was edging further into the kitchen. She was breathing hard, sweat glazing her face.

'Listen, you don't have to worry,' Sean's gaze briefly flickered to where I was slowly sliding to the ground. 'When I came in and looked around and realised you weren't here, I called the police.'

'That's a lie.' I pushed the words through clenched teeth. 'There's no network.'

'I used the landline in one of the bedrooms.' He sounded genuine. 'They're on their way.'

'The phone doesn't work . . .' my words trailed off. It had been another of Saskia's lies. The voice I thought I'd heard as I drifted to sleep last night — had she been happily chatting to her friend Stefan, all the while knowing she was going to kill me?

For a second, nobody spoke or moved. Not that I could have, if I'd tried. The pain in my arm intensified. I thought I might throw up.

Then: 'Why aren't the police here yet?' Ruby said at the same as Saskia dived towards me and yelled, 'Give me your car keys, Nell.' When I didn't move, she swung away, staggering out of the kitchen.

Sean sprang into action, leaping after her, while Ruby made a sprint for the door.

As the sound of sirens filled the air, I slid further down on the floor, the tiles cool beneath my cheek. I closed my eyes, mind drifting.

There was a distant scuffle and a muffled scream, then a hand on my back, and Ruby saying urgently, 'Hang in there, Nell.'

'I came to help you not hurt you, Ruby.' Sean's voice was a mix of hurt and tenderness. 'I love you.'

It was the last thing I heard before blackness fell.

CHAPTER 32

Ruby

Saskia, Carla and Nell had been taken to hospital by ambulance, Saskia with a police escort. Ruby had been assured they would be OK, that they would survive their ordeal, physically at least.

The paramedics had patched up Ruby's leg, and wanted to take her too, but she'd insisted she was fine, that Sean was going to take her to her mum's house. She couldn't face being alone, needed her family around her. She needed a good night's sleep too, though she doubted she would get that with her head jumping and buzzing with everything that had happened over the last few hours.

Now, she looked across at Sean from where she was slumped, sleepy, in the passenger seat of his car, having never imagined she would share a journey with him again. His eyes were focused on the wet road ahead, his face a silhouette in the darkness. The wipers strummed the windscreen rhythmically, causing her to drift in and out of light sleep.

A sudden surge of guilt rose that she'd pushed Sean out of her life, accusing him of stalking her. She'd even set her father onto him. And yet Sean had come to her rescue today, maybe even saved her life. 'Thanks,' she whispered for the third time.

'You don't have to keep saying it, Ruby.' He turned and smiled. He had a nice smile, a dimple always forming in his cheek when he was happy. She realised she hadn't seen him smile in a long time. Even dating Vikki hadn't made him smile, at least, not that she knew of. 'Anything for you, Ruby, you know that.'

She opened her bag — she'd picked it up from the wreckage of Carla's car, before getting into Sean's 4 x 4 twenty minutes ago — and pulled out her phone, turned it over and over in her hands. She wanted to call her father. Ask him why he cheated on Nell. Why, after sending her mother spiralling into alcoholism and depression because of his desire for Nell, and God only knows how many women before her, had he moved on to Carla? But she knew why. He might be her father, but he was no good. Never had been. Tears stung her eyes. She so wanted to feel the unconditional love she'd felt for him growing up. She so wanted to believe in him again — her father — but there was no going back. She saw him differently now. Saw exactly who he was.

It was dark now, the gloomy grey sky of earlier pushed back, replaced by a starless night — and the journey stretched on, long and silent.

'Do you mind if we stop for a bit?' Sean said, indicating to pull off the main road.

'Why?'

'My legs ache, just need to stretch them.'

'Oh. OK.'

He drove along a country lane. 'And I'd like to talk for a bit, if that's OK.'

'I'm not really in the mood for chatting, Sean. I want to get home. I feel like crap.'

He pulled the car onto a grass verge, dragged on the handbrake, and killed the engine.

Ruby looked about her, seeing nothing but blackness, a sense of unease washing through her. Had she been wrong to trust him? 'Can we make it quick? I really want to get back.'

He flicked on the overhead light, illuminating the car, and stared at her for some moments, his eyes shining, pupils contracting by the sudden burst of light. 'You know I've always loved you, Ruby.'

'Sean. Please. You did good today, don't spoil things.'

'Spoil things?'

'You saved me, Nell and Carla, and I'm grateful for that. Maybe we can even be friends, but—'

'But I love you, Ruby.' He grabbed hold of her hands, squeezed too tightly, and her heart started thudding. She wrestled free, pulled away from him. 'I would do anything for you,' he said.

Doubt flashed through her mind. Why had Sean followed them to the windmill? He couldn't have known she was in danger. What was he even doing there in the first place?

'Take me home.' The assertiveness in Ruby's voice belied the panic surging inside her. She could run, but how far would she get with the pain in her leg? How dangerous was Sean? 'I'll call the police,' she said, when he made no move to start the car, but continued to stare at her. 'Have you arrested for stalking.'

'Really?' He tilted his head. 'I tell you I love you, and you come back accusing me of stalking you?'

Oh God, had she got it wrong? Was she overreacting? After all, she was tired, had been through a terrible ordeal.

'You'd call the police on me, after I saved you?'

'I'm sorry. I—'

He raked his fingers through his hair. 'This is your father's fault.' There were tears in his words, as he banged his palms against the steering wheel. 'He turned you against me. We would still be together if it wasn't for him.'

'No, you're wrong. My father is guilty of a lot of things, but he didn't turn me against you.' *You did that yourself.* 'We're just not right for each other. I'm sorry. I never meant to hurt you. We can still be friends.' But she knew that could never be. She needed to get as far away from him as she could.

'Your father wrecked everything.' He started the engine, rubbed a hand across his chin, and pulled away from the grass verge. 'I'll take you to your mother's, Ruby. You might not love me now, but you will one day. I know you will. You have to, because I can't live without you.'

'What about Vikki, Sean? She thinks you're in love with her.'

Sean's eyes stayed on the road his voice cold as he said, 'Vikki means nothing to me.'

* * *

Fiona and Poppy were in bed when Ruby let herself into her mother's house. She didn't climb the stairs to the spare room, too tired to take those extra steps, instead crashing on the sofa, and pulling a throw over her. But despite her exhausted body, her mind wouldn't settle, going over and over everything that had happened. Saskia's wild eyes; Sean's biting anger; Nell weak and helpless as they stumbled towards the windmill, all flashing through her mind over and over.

She tried to call her father in the early hours, left a jumbled voicemail asking him what gave him the right to mess with women's emotions, wondering how he would charm his way out of this one. She blurted down the phone that Saskia tried to kill Nell. That Nell and his *girlfriend* Carla were in hospital. That he needed to take some responsibility for that. She'd hung up without saying goodbye.

She finally dozed off at 4 a.m. facing vivid dreams, a windmill spinning out of control, a blooded stone in the palm of her hand, Sean hovering in the shadows.

'Darling?' It was Fiona, making her way across the lounge in her dressing gown. 'What are you doing here?'

Ruby shuffled herself to a sitting position. 'It's a long story,' she said, her throat parched. 'I need some coffee first.'

By the time Ruby had drunk her first coffee, she'd filled her mum in on everything that had happened. There was a small moment, as Ruby told her Oliver had cheated on Nell, when her mother's eyes lit up, but that spark vanished as Ruby explained what Nell had gone through. Even Fiona wasn't that vengeful.

'I'm guessing the police will want to talk to Dad,' Ruby said, as they sat in the lounge together. She touched her mum's arm. 'I know he's my dad, but you're better off without him, Mum, always have been.'

'You girls could never see any wrong in him.' Fiona's eyes flooded with tears. 'Thought he was the best thing ever. So did I for a long time.'

'We were kids. He was charming, and we thought he was amazing. But we're not kids anymore.' Ruby paused for a moment. 'Why did you stay with him for so long, if you knew what he was like? Why did you even want him back?'

'We were so happy once, and I suppose I wanted to recapture that.' She shook her head, her eyes watery. 'I loved him, Ruby. Still do, I suppose. And I thought he'd get tired of chasing after younger women eventually, and we'd grow old together.'

Poppy appeared in the doorway, stretching and yawning as she entered the lounge. 'Ruby? What are you doing here?'

Ruby was grateful when Fiona took the baton, and filled Poppy in on the whole story. Both seemed stronger than Ruby had seen them for a long time. She knew it would be a bumpy ride, Poppy still had a long way to go, but it suddenly seemed possible that they would get there.

'Does Dad know what happened at the windmill?' Poppy asked, now perched on the arm of the sofa, pale with shock. Ruby knew how hard it was for her to hear about their father's spectacular fall from grace.

Poppy rose, and picked her phone up from the dresser where it was charging. 'I'll call him. Tell him what I think of him.'

'No, don't do that.' Ruby rose too, the throw she'd covered herself with falling to the floor.

'What happened to you?' Fiona had spotted Ruby's bandaged leg.

'It's fine, honestly.'

'I can't get hold of him,' Poppy said, and Ruby and Fiona looked towards her. 'It keeps going to voicemail.'

It was then that Ruby's phone rang. She looked down at the screen, answered the call, pressing the phone to her ear. 'Nell, how are you feeling?'

'I'm good, Ruby. Getting better.' Her voice sounded weak, broken. 'But there's something I have to tell you. It's not good news. I've had a visit from the police. Have you got anyone with you?'

Ruby looked at her mother and sister, both listening. 'Yes, my mum and Poppy are here.'

'Good.' A pause. 'I'm so sorry to be the one to tell you this, Ruby. It's your dad—'

'My dad?' A sense of foreboding filled her senses, panic bubbling in her chest. 'What is it, Nell? What about Dad?'

'Your dad . . . your dad is dead, Ruby.' She was crying. 'I'm so sorry.'

CHAPTER 33

Nell

I said goodbye to the last of the mourners outside the church with a feeling of unreality.

Oliver was dead. I'd sat through the service — his mother had insisted on a traditional funeral — and watched as his coffin was lowered into the ground, but the fact he'd gone was only now beginning to sink in.

He'd apparently been on his way to see Ruby after receiving a message from her, though no one knew for sure — only that the message was the last thing on his phone after repeated texts he'd sent to Carla, asking why she wasn't picking up. That and the fact he'd been heading towards Ruby's flat.

There had been no obvious reason for the crash. No signs Oliver had been speeding, or drinking, or was on his phone at the time of impact. The stretch of road he was on wasn't dangerous, and — as far as I knew — he wasn't suicidal. The police had impounded his car and were still investigating.

He hadn't survived the accident, a bright-eyed officer told me, had died instantly. In spite of everything Oliver had done, I hoped that was the case.

'I'm so, so sorry,' Carla had wept when I agreed she could visit me in hospital. I was numb with shock, dazed by painkillers, my broken arm set in plaster, the rest of me miraculously unscathed apart from a fractured rib, but I desperately needed answers. 'It should never have gone that far. I'd already decided to end things with Oliver after getting to know you and hearing how he'd treated you and his family.'

'But you knew he was married when you started seeing him.'

'Not to you,' she told me, wringing her hands as she sat on the chair at the side of the bed, a gaunt and hollow-eyed version of the calm and controlled counsellor I'd confided in. 'When you both turned up that first day, I was genuinely shocked,' she continued after blowing her nose, and haltingly explained how Oliver told her later he'd looked her up after I booked our counselling appointment and engineered 'bumping' into her, sending her crashing into a shop window. He'd insisted on buying her coffee to make up for his clumsiness, turning on every ounce of the smiling charm that had once enchanted me. 'We talked for ages, and he ended up telling me his marriage was all but over, how his wife was work-obsessed,' — I'd taken a sharp, painful breath when I heard that — 'and he was ready to walk away but was concerned about her mental health.' *Like he'd professed to be about Fiona's.* Carla had paused to blow her nose again, tears leaking from the corners of her swollen eyes. 'I hadn't been in a relationship for a while, by choice, but really fell for him.'

The horrible thing was, I'd understood, had felt almost sorry for her.

'We met again a couple of times and he was . . . he was everything I'd been looking for. He didn't talk about his marriage after that first time, or tell me much about his first wife or daughters, only that he'd married too young and the break-up had been amicable, then he'd rushed into a second marriage he now regretted.'

In that moment, I'd hated Oliver with every fibre of my being.

'When you turned up for counselling, he did an excellent job of being shocked to see that the therapist you had booked was me and I truly believed he *was* shocked, until he confessed later to knowing all along who I was, and even then he made it sound as though he'd been powerless to stop himself finding me, that he'd fallen in love the moment he saw me.' Red patches of embarrassment scoured her cheeks. 'I can't believe I was taken in by him, but Emily will tell you . . .' she stopped, as if remembering what her sister had done, and I had to remind myself she was talking about Saskia. 'I'm great at giving advice, but terrible at choosing partners for myself. I should have ended it right away and I'd give anything now to turn back the clock.'

'So, Saskia . . . your sister knew from the start?'

'I told her I'd met someone.' Carla briefly closed her eyes. 'I know now that it was a mistake to let her know after what she did last time, but I thought she'd changed, moved on. She seemed happy, got herself together after she met Alex. He was good for her, but I hadn't realised how desperate she was for them to have children, to be a family. It was too much, and she tricked him into thinking she was on the Pill and fell pregnant. He couldn't forgive her and called off the wedding and she lost the baby soon after.' Seeing my face she said quickly, 'Not that I'm making excuses or expect you to feel sorry for her, but . . .' She paused, shoulders sagging. 'Anyway, I'd mentioned Oliver was married and that his . . .' She hesitated again. 'That his wife was refusing to accept their marriage was over and he'd said he was going through counselling to keep her from doing something silly, like hurting herself. When I mentioned his wife was a workaholic, and that she was advertising for an assistant to help her out, Emily must have decided to apply for the job behind my back, using a different name. I didn't know, I promise.' She stopped to dab her eyes. 'I had no idea Emily's demons were back and that she was determined to get you away from Oliver, no matter what.'

'She set out to destroy me the moment she started that job.'

Carla gave a twisted laugh. 'The thing is, she unwittingly made me see Oliver in a different light. When you started describing how things really were, how he was working longer hours, changing his mind about having a baby, acting as though he believed you were having an affair and not looking out for his daughters. . .' She shook her head. 'She unintentionally made me realise what I'd got myself into.'

'Well, she'll be going to prison anyway.'

Although Saskia — I couldn't think of her as Emily — had insisted she'd only planned to scare me, the evidence, combined with her history, which Carla had relayed in a statement to the police, meant she would undoubtedly be locked up this time.

Carla swallowed and patted her eyes once more with the crumpled tissue. 'She never got over our parents' death.'

'Other peoples' parents die, and they don't turn into murderers.' One emotion after another tumbled through me. 'I would be dead if Ruby hadn't decided to go to the flat and then to see you.'

'I'm so glad she did.' Carla sniffed. 'I love my sister, but she's damaged. It's one of the reasons I became a counsellor, but even I couldn't help her. Alex leaving, and our grandmother's death pushed her over the edge.'

I recalled Saskia's reluctance to provide her bank details. No wonder. It would have been game over, but then again, she hadn't intended to be working for me by payday.

'She'll never recover from this,' Carla had concluded.

Sometimes, I wasn't sure I would either. When I closed my eyes, I flashed back to Saskia at the top of the windmill, the look in her eyes before I fell. The knowledge that she'd meant me to die sat like a ball of barbed wire in my chest but talking to Ruby had helped, knowing she'd been there, had put herself in danger to help me, and I was going to talk to a therapist soon — someone my mother had found who specialised in PTSD.

I'd only been back to the house in Marlow once since being discharged from hospital, to collect my things with Mum. It had never felt like a home, I'd realised, glancing around the well-proportioned rooms, furnished as though staged for a play, my wedding photo a mockery of what a marriage should be. I had never been able to imagine it ringing with children's laughter, just as I'd never been able to see myself growing older there with Oliver.

'Maybe you always knew you wouldn't stay together,' Mum had said, holding me when I wept.

'I didn't want him dead, though.'

'Of course you didn't.'

But even as I cried, I knew part of my grief came from knowing I could never confront him with everything I'd discovered; couldn't tell him how deeply his betrayal had hurt me, and everyone who loved him. I would never have the satisfaction of walking away, and he would never suffer for the way he'd treated us.

'He wouldn't have suffered anyway.' Ruby's face had darkened when I told her how I felt, the night before Oliver's funeral. I hadn't wanted to attend but I needed to support Ruby after what she had done for me. He was her father, and she'd loved him longer than I had. 'He never felt any guilt about anything,' she continued, pulling a pair of black trousers from the wardrobe at her flat. 'I looked it up. I reckon he had psychopathic traits.'

'Saskia definitely did.'

We both shuddered, my broken arm and Ruby's scarred leg outward reminders of the lengths she'd gone to, not to mention the memories of that day we would carry forever.

'He would never have divorced you,' Ruby went on. 'I overheard him telling Mum once that he would never go through that again and risk losing half of everything he'd worked so hard for, no matter what happened — as though it was her fault, and he wasn't the one who started it. He would have got bored with Carla and moved on to someone else, no matter what he told her. He liked the thrill of the beginning, being the hero of his own story, seeing himself through someone else's eyes.' She gave me an apologetic smile. 'Sorry if that hurts.'

But everything Ruby had said made sense. I was only sorry I'd fallen for him in the first place, that I'd been so keen for the structure of marriage after losing dad, and then my job, I hadn't seen that Oliver preferred things new and shiny, that the day-to-day reality of marriage held no appeal — though I liked to believe he'd meant his wedding vows at the time. Surely no one — not even Oliver — could have faked the love I knew I'd seen in his eyes. 'I would have walked away with nothing.'

Ruby nodded. 'I know.'

'I'm glad Sean turned out to be a good guy. Thank God he called the police.'

'Yeah.' Ruby looked as if she was going to say something else, but Poppy came in at that moment, wanting to know when Ruby was going back to the family home with her. She didn't speak to me, but I felt no hostility. It was obvious from her red-rimmed eyes that she was grieving for her father and would be for a long time, though, according to Ruby, their mother seemed stronger now. Without the shadow of her ex-husband lurking, and the final confirmation that he wasn't a good person — when the story played out in the media, she'd quoted an American author, Tucker Max, saying *The devil doesn't come with horns, he comes disguised as everything you've ever wanted* — maybe she could move on and be strong for her daughters.

I watched her now, leaving the grounds of the church with Poppy, both dressed in black, arms tightly linked. Fiona paused and gave me a faint smile that didn't touch her eyes, while Poppy kept her head down.

'Will you come back to the house?' Fiona asked Ruby, warmer now as she laid a hand on her daughter's arm.

Ruby nodded, her dark hair, scraped into a neat twist, shining under the sunlight. 'I'll make my own way there.'

Fiona and Poppy were followed by a handful of people I didn't recognise, perhaps there because of the court case rather than to mourn Oliver, a man that Anita, who had interviewed me for the local paper, had labelled a *greedy love cheat.* Even his oldest friend hadn't put in an appearance. Mark had come to the hospital to see me when he heard the news, white-faced with shock and disbelief.

'I knew what he was like,' he shook his head; eyes glazed with tears, seeming to have aged ten years. 'I turned a blind eye, and I shouldn't have.'

'It's not your fault.'

'I should have trusted you.'

Oliver's mother Sylvia was the last to leave, resplendent in an old-fashioned, veiled hat that covered most of her face. She didn't glance at Ruby or me as she passed on the arm of a younger man who helped her into a black Mercedes that pulled silently away.

'She was never much of a grandma,' Ruby watched the car disappear. 'She approved of Mum but didn't seem to like children. I dreaded visiting, and Poppy was scared of her. She never took us out for treats or babysat, was more interested in helping my grandfather with the wine business, always away on trips. It made me wonder what she was like with Dad when he was a child, but he never spoke about it.'

'He didn't talk to me about his childhood either,' I said with a pang of sadness. 'His parents have a lot to answer for.'

'So, what's next for you?' Ruby turned, concern in her dark eyes. I was touched that, despite how conflicted she must feel, she cared what happened to me.

'I could go back to Classic Props once the plaster's off my arm, but to be honest, I can't face it.' I adjusted my bag, still unused to doing things one-handed. 'I'm going to stay at my mum's for a while, and maybe start up on my own when I feel ready.'

'That's a great idea.'

It was a struggle to not feel I was taking a step backwards — that I'd failed — but Mark had promised to help, and I had contacts in the business. Once the Marlow house sold, I would have money to tide me over for a while.

'I might take a trip with Mum. She's keen for us to get away for a while.'

'You'll stay in touch?'

I studied Ruby's face for a moment and saw the same doubt in her eyes she no doubt read in mine. 'It might be too painful.' A flicker of relief crossed her face. 'Too much of a reminder of everything that's happened.'

She nodded.

'You've got my number though,' I said.

'Maybe you can catch me in a play sometime.'

'That would be good.' I knew, as she must do, that I probably wouldn't. 'I hope you make it, Ruby. You deserve everything good and thank you again for rescuing me.'

She leaned forward and caught me in an awkward hug. I breathed in her perfume, caught the glisten of emotion in her eyes. 'Take care, Nell.'

My throat tightened. 'Goodbye, Ruby.'

I watched her walk away through a haze of tears, wishing with all my heart that Oliver had been the father she deserved, yet I knew, somehow, she was strong — that she would get through the weeks, the months, the years ahead and be fine.

And I would be too.

'Ready to go, love?'

I turned to see Mum waiting patiently, her face soft with love and understanding. I nodded and squared my shoulders. 'I'm ready.'

CHAPTER 34

Ruby

Three months later

Life was different without her dad in the world. Ruby sometimes found the pain unbearable, and would collapse in floods of tears. Other times the sadness was fleeting, no more than the pang she might feel if her favourite shop closed down. Grief was a law unto itself, she'd learned. It didn't matter that her father had let her down, the good memories still flooded in, and she had to go with it. The hardest thing to bear was, at the end, he hadn't been the man she'd adored all her life. He wasn't the man she'd built him up to be. He'd been knocked off the pedestal that Poppy and she had stood him on, and now there was no chance of them holding him accountable, no opportunity for him to explain his actions. No way of making things right. But then perhaps, with his pathological egocentricity, they never would have found the answers they craved even if he'd lived.

'Ruby?' Poppy sat wide-eyed opposite her in the London café where they used to meet their father for breakfast. Ruby had thought it might evoke happy memories, but it wasn't working. It was a bad idea, and she wanted to leave and never come back.

'Sorry.' Ruby dashed the back of her hand across her cheek, feeling the moisture of a straying tear, realising she'd drifted into her own world.

'Shall we go?' Poppy sniffed, pulled out a tissue, and dabbed her eyes. 'This isn't helping much, is it?'

They rose, and, leaving their half-drunk coffee, made their way outside onto the pavement, the sunny day brightening the mood. Poppy moved in close, slipped her arm through Ruby's elbow as they walked.

'How's Mum?' Ruby asked.

'Good. She's joined a dating agency for over forties.'

'Wow, that's good, I think.'

Poppy shrugged. 'Not sure, I reckon she needs to find herself before she adds a man to the mix.'

Ruby smiled. 'You're getting more feminist every day, Poppy.'

'Yeah, well, it's not all about being with someone. It's great, yeah, if you find the right person, but you only have to look at Mum, Nell and Carla to see the crap that happens if it goes wrong. I never want to be in a relationship like that.'

'Not all relationships turn out like Mum and Dad's.'

'I know. I've met up with James a few times and he's OK.'

'The guy you met on Twitch?'

'Yep. And before you go all big sister on me, we meet in Costa and talk non-stop about gaming. I'm careful, Ruby, honestly. I've got a good role model.' She paused for a moment. 'That's you, by the way.'

Ruby smiled. Maybe she had finally got through to her sister. 'So will you see him again?'

Poppy shrugged. 'He's a geek, but yeah. He's a good laugh, you know.' Her cheeks pinked. 'So, have you seen any more of Stefan?'

Ruby laughed at her sister's seductive tone. 'Stefan is gay, Poppy. We're friends, is all.' They were. Good friends, in fact. Ruby had gone round to see him after what happened at the windmill. He'd been shocked, but said he always knew Sassy was a troubled soul. He'd wanted to go and visit her in prison, but she'd refused to see him, and he admitted feeling a bit relieved.

'So are you ready for Saturday?' Poppy asked.

Ruby nodded. 'Can't wait.' It was opening night for the show she'd been rehearsing, Agatha Christie's *The Body in the Library*. She was playing Josie Turner, a dance and bridge hostess, and cousin of the murder victim, and was so excited to be getting on the stage again. And Stefan had contacts too, had arranged for her to audition for a couple of West End roles and she had been called back. Life was moving on without her father in it, however strange that felt.

She was relieved too that she no longer had anything to do with Classic Props where Mark was now back in charge, running the place with Janine.

'We'll be OK, won't we?' Poppy said, as they made their way through the throngs of London shoppers.

'Of course.' Ruby squeezed Poppy's arm. It was hard to believe her sister, who was now seeing a counsellor, had planned to poison Nell, so desperate to get her away from their father. Ruby was glad Nell would never know. 'We've got each other.'

* * *

It felt amazing to be on stage again, Ruby's body buzzed with adrenalin for the first time in ages, and now, as the cast held hands and took excited bows, she spotted her mum and Poppy in the front row, clapping and cheering, and Benita a few rows back.

She'd thought about inviting Nell, but somehow, although they were on amicable terms, Ruby couldn't see them ever being friends. Fiona had forgiven Nell, and moved on, knowing the woman she blamed for breaking up her marriage was as much a victim as she was, but Ruby didn't think she would have wanted the woman Oliver left her for at the theatre.

Ruby and Nell had exchanged a few messages, but they were getting fewer as the weeks went by. Nell was doing OK. Like Ruby, it would take time to get over everything that had happened, but Nell was strong, capable, she would rise up and move on.

As the clapping slowed, and the curtain began to lower, Ruby's eyes flicked across the audience, settling on the back row. *Janine?* Ruby smiled, pleased to see her. She hadn't seen her since the funeral, when she'd approached, and in her motherly, caring fashion, taken Ruby into a warm hug.

Once the curtain had fallen and they were backstage, the cast and Stefan high-fived each other. Ruby couldn't stop beaming. She was doing what she loved best, and it went some way towards balancing out the tragedy of three months ago.

'Have you seen the chocolates, Ruby, love?' Stefan said, air-kissing each side of her face. 'Somebody loves you.'

They were standing on a ledge near the stage door — a hamper from Hotel Chocolat. Her heart sank. She knew they were from Sean. Since his outburst in the car on the way back from Norfolk, she hadn't heard from him. Thought he was over her, that he was making a go of it with Vikki, despite Janine's concerns.

Slowly she made her way into the shadows, towards the hamper, pulling free the blonde wig she'd worn for her performance, feeling oddly vulnerable in bright red lipstick and a floor-length halter-neck dress.

She opened the small envelope, read the card.

Dear Ruby. I will do everything it takes for us to be together — I will never stop loving you. Sean x

'Are they from Sean?'

Ruby spun round. 'Janine? What are you doing backstage?' She flashed a look over at the disappearing cast members, still jubilant, patting each other's backs.

'Love can be so cruel, don't you think?' Janine's eyes were watery.

'It can be, yes.' Ruby put down the card, but Sean's words continued to bounce around her head, a fear rising in her chest. He still loved her. He would never leave her alone.

'My Vikki still adores him, you know. She's so naïve, thought they were making a go of it.' Her eyes flicked over the chocolates. 'I knew deep down he was a wrong-un, but she was so smitten. And it seems I was right. It's still you he wants.' Her eyes met Ruby's.

'But I don't love him.'

'Oh, I know that, love. Though I admit I thought it was your fault at one point, even sent you a note telling you to stay away from him.'

A ripple of shock raced down Ruby's spine. 'That was you?'

'I'm so ashamed of that now, of course. I know now this obsession with you isn't your fault.' She sighed deeply. 'I just wanted my Vikki to be happy — was that so much to ask?'

Ruby shook her head. 'I don't love him, Janine,' she repeated. 'I'm not sure I ever did.'

'I know, love. I know.'

'We were over a long time ago. My father . . .' the words caught in her throat, and her heart thudded. 'My dad even threatened him to make him stay away.'

Janine lowered her head. 'Yes, I know. But Sean is never going to give you up.'

Ruby looked again at the chocolates, and back at Janine's flushed face, the euphoria of the wonderful evening dissipating, leaving her unsettled.

'He's determined,' Janine went on, biting down on her lower lip. 'Will do anything, and I mean anything, to get you back into his life.'

'What do you mean by anything?'

Janine touched Ruby's cheek. 'Oh come on, love. Has it never occurred to you how conveniently your father died?

The fact Sean knows his way around a vehicle. The fact he believed Oliver stood between you and him.'

'Darling!'

Ruby turned to see her mum and sister racing towards her. Within moments, Fiona had taken her in her arms. 'You were fantastic.'

'Amazing, Sis,' Poppy said. 'I've even put a photo of you on my Instagram. That's how bloody proud I am.'

There was a sudden clatter, and Ruby turned from her mum's embrace to see the hamper on the floor, chocolates scattered across the wooden boards — the tall, slim shape of Janine disappearing through the stage door.

She shook off a feeling of unease. Janine was wrong. Sean was a lot of things, but he was no murderer. Her father's death had been an accident, hadn't it?

'Is everything OK?' Poppy placed her hand on Ruby's arm.

'Yes.' She pushed the doubts from her mind. Determined she wasn't going to let Sean ruin her night — her life. He was her past, and her future was right there waiting for her. 'Let's go and get something to eat.'

EPILOGUE

Six months later

Janine

'What do you want, Janine?' Sean looks grey, his eyes bloodshot. Prison life isn't agreeing with him at all, and I'm glad about that. 'What are you doing here?'

I'm not sure how to answer. Do I want to see for myself that he is locked away, where he can do no more damage? Where he can't hurt Vikki anymore? Or am I here to gloat?

He still believes these obsessive feelings he has for Ruby are love. But they're not. He's suffering with Obsessive Love Disorder. I read about it online some time ago, when I was trying to work the man out. It's a real condition: OLD for short. Sean definitely has it. I've no doubt of that. Once I realised, I feared he would never change. That he would forever keep my Vikki dangling, whilst mooning after Ruby. That he would never stop hurting her. He had a lot in common with Oliver Cosgrove. Oliver Cosgrove who almost caused Nell's demise.

'I just wanted to see if you're OK,' I say now, using my best syrupy tone. Of course, it's not true. I don't care a bloody bit if he's OK. I hope he rots in here forever.

The sad thing is, I quite liked Sean once. Even fought his corner when Ruby warned me about him. I was so sure he loved Vikki. I can't believe I was so naïve.

I tilt my head, look into his lifeless eyes. Vikki could have made him so happy, if he'd given their relationship a chance. But no, despite moving in with my baby girl, he kept hankering after Ruby Cosgrove.

But I had an ace up my sleeve. I could get him off the streets should I need to. And that's exactly what I've done.

I suppose I hoped I wouldn't have to. Hoped he would finally realise he loved Vikki, and make her happy.

Now, he's looking everywhere but at me, and my mind drifts to the night he came home late, flustered, talking to Vikki in loud whispers. He didn't know I was there, staying overnight. That Vikki had called me — that I'd spent the whole evening comforting my daughter, because he'd taken off after Ruby.

I rose from the spare room bed when I heard Sean come home, and pressed my ear against the door. He spewed out everything that had happened at the windmill. How Oliver had been having an affair. Cheating on Nell, of all things. How bloody dare he? What an awful, awful man. And then Sean dropped the bombshell. *'I love Ruby, Vikki, and I'll do anything to make that happen.'* OK, so he dotted an *'I'm sorry'* in there somewhere, but I knew he wasn't sorry — he wasn't sorry at all.

He walked out that night, leaving Vikki in floods of tears. *'I'll be back for my stuff, tomorrow,'* he'd added, slamming the door behind him.

'What is so special about Ruby?' I say to him now, but it's a stupid question, and I wish immediately I hadn't asked it.

He moves his gaze to my face. 'Have you ever been in love, Janine?' he says. 'A love so powerful that the thought of losing that person sends your whole world spiralling. The need to protect them, to be with them, is more important than breathing.' He narrows his eyes. 'I can't imagine that you have.'

But he's wrong. I have felt that kind of love, a very long time ago. I loved Vikki's father in the painful way he describes. My world spiralled when my husband had an affair, and walked out on Vikki and me. But it was OK, all that love was absorbed into my daughter — a daughter I would never see hurt like I was. A daughter Sean would continue to destroy if I hadn't done something to stop it.

'A love as strong as that becomes obsession if it's not reciprocated,' I whisper.

'Ruby loves me, Janine.' He drags his fingers through his greasy hair. 'She just doesn't know it.'

It was me who reported Sean to the police. He got back with Vikki after that night when he walked out, and I gave him a chance to make things right, but he never did. He continued to smash her heart to smithereens. He deserved to be punished.

I'd come to realise Ruby had no feelings for Sean, but I needed to talk to her — to make sure things were over between her and Sean. I booked a ticket for her show, and when I went backstage and saw the chocolates, I knew I couldn't let him continue to hurt Vikki. It was time to report him. Not only had he devastated my daughter's life, he was never going to leave Ruby alone.

I told the police how Sean was covered in oil on the night of Oliver Cosgrove's accident, that I suspected him of sabotaging the man's car. I even handed in a pair of his jeans and a hoodie that were covered in oil from Oliver's car. I recommended that they looked at footage from a neighbour's CCTV camera. That further examination of the car might be enough to charge him.

'Ruby loves me, Janine,' Sean says, rising to his feet. 'She needs me. We're destined to be together, and once I'm out of here, we will be.'

As he walks away, his shoulders slumped, I smile. I have no guilt for setting him up. When Sean slammed the door on Vikki the night of Oliver's accident I'd fished out his jeans and hoodie, and using his tools I'd tampered with Oliver's car on his drive. It would be my back-up plan if I ever needed to frame Sean for Oliver's murder. It was my ace to play, if you like, if — *no when* — he let Vikki down again.

And as for killing Oliver Cosgrove — well, when I heard how he treated Nell I thought enough was enough. I'll never regret his death. Men like Oliver and Sean must be taken off the streets, where they can never hurt women again. Thanks to me, my Vikki, Ruby and Nell all have a fresh start.

My conscience is clear.

THE END

Thank you for reading this book.

If you enjoyed it please leave feedback on Amazon or Goodreads, and if there is anything we missed or you have a question about, then please get in touch. We appreciate you choosing our book.

Founded in 2014 in Shoreditch, London, we at Joffe Books pride ourselves on our history of innovative publishing. We were thrilled to be shortlisted for Independent Publisher of the Year at the British Book Awards.

www.joffebooks.com

We're very grateful to eagle-eyed readers who take the time to contact us. Please send any errors you find to corrections@joffebooks.com. We'll get them fixed ASAP.

Printed in Great Britain
by Amazon

24294976R00148